THE ART OF WISHING

The Art of Wishing

LINDSAY RIBAR

Dial Books

an imprint of Penguin Group

(USA) Inc.

DIAL BOOKS

An imprint of Penguin Group (USA) Inc.

Published by The Penguin Group

Penguin Group (USA) Inc., 375 Hudson Street, New York, NY 10014, U.S.A.

Penguin Group (Canada), 90 Eglinton Avenue East, Suite 700, Toronto, Ontario,
Canada M4P 2Y3 (a division of Pearson Penguin Canada Inc.)

Penguin Books Ltd, 80 Strand, London WC2R 0RL, England

Penguin Ireland, 25 St. Stephen's Green, Dublin 2, Ireland
(a division of Penguin Books Ltd)

Penguin Group (Australia), 707 Collins Street, Melbourne, Victoria 3008,
Australia (a division of Pearson Australia Group Pty Ltd)

Penguin Books India Pvt Ltd, 11 Community Centre,
Panchsheel Park, New Delhi - 110 017, India

Penguin Group (NZ), 67 Apollo Drive, Rosedale, Auckland 0632,
New Zealand (a division of Pearson New Zealand Ltd)

Penguin Books, Rosebank Office Park, 181 Jan Smuts Avenue,
Parktown North 2193, South Africa

Penguin Books China, B7 Jaiming Center, 27 East Third Ring Road North,
Chaoyang District, Beijing 100020, China

Penguin Books Ltd, Registered Offices: 80 Strand,
London WC2R 0RL, England

The publisher does not have any control over and does not assume
any responsibility for author or third-party websites or their content.

Designed by Mina Chung · Text set in Perpetua

Printed in the U.S.A.

1 3 5 7 9 10 8 6 4 2

Library of Congress Cataloging-in-Publication Data

Ribar, Lindsay.
The art of wishing / by Lindsay Ribar.   p. cm.
Summary: When eighteen-year-old Margo learns she lost the lead in her
high school musical to a sophomore because of a modern-day genie,
she falls in love with Oliver, the genie, while deciding what her own wishes
should be and trying to rescue him from an old foe.
ISBN 978-0-8037-3827-0 (hardcover)
[1. Wishes—Fiction. 2. Magic—Fiction. 3. Genies—Fiction. 4. Theater—Fiction.
5. High schools—Fiction. 6. Schools—Fiction.] I. Title.
PZ7.R3485Art 2013   [Fic]—dc23   2012013035

FOR MOM, DAD, AND MEGAN.

You guys are awesome.

Prologue

The plan was this: I'd get up on that stage, blow them away with the best damn audition they'd ever seen, and walk out knowing the part I wanted was mine.

And when I was called into the auditorium, that was exactly how it happened.

I walked over to the piano and handed my sheet music to George. "You know this one?" I asked him.

He peered quickly at the title. Nodded and said, "Yup." Of course he did. Silly question.

George flexed his fingers, and I strode up the little side staircase and onto the stage. Bright lights flooded my face, but I was used to that. I shielded my eyes so I could focus on the lone figure sitting in the first row: Miss Delisio, math teacher by day and play director by night. I smiled warmly at her. This was the woman who was going to cast me in my dream role.

"Margo McKenna," she said in greeting. "I do love a straight-A trig student with stage presence. How's calculus treating you?"

I wrinkled my nose. "Straight A minuses this year. Calc is hard. Who knew?"

Miss Delisio laughed appreciatively. "Why do you think I don't teach it?" she said. "All right, what are you singing for us today?"

"I'm doing 'Last Midnight' from *Into the Woods* by Stephen Sondheim," I recited.

"Great song," she said. "Whenever you're ready."

This was it. I took a moment to steady myself, then nodded to George. On my cue, he started playing. I molded my body into the shape of the song, and the lyrics flowed out of me like I owned them. For those few minutes, I became someone totally different from my real self. Someone worldly and manipulative. Someone with very real power.

I'd chosen "Last Midnight" because of that power. And as the song grew in intensity, and my performance grew to match, and the air in the theater seemed to dance to the rhythm of George's piano and my voice . . . I knew I'd chosen right.

When I finished, a couple of breaths passed before anyone said anything.

"That was lovely, Margo," said Miss Delisio. I couldn't see her face, but I could hear the smile in her voice. "Really, really lovely."

"Yup," said George.

"Thanks," I said breathlessly.

I heard the rustle of a notebook page being flipped. "Stick

around for a little while, okay?" said Miss Delisio. "We'll pair you up and have you read from the script."

"Sounds good," I said. "I'll be in the hallway."

Naomi Sloane, my best friend and Miss Delisio's stage manager, was manning the door that stood between me and the hallway full of nervous students outside. She gave me a thumbs-up as I approached her.

"McKenna, you just nailed that," she said. "Don't tell the masses, but you're the best audition I've seen so far."

I flashed her a coy smile. "I bet you say that to all the girls."

She laughed and held the door open for me, and I floated out into the hallway as she called the next student's name. Sure, I still had to do the reading part of the audition, but that would be a piece of cake. The hard part—the important part—was over. And Naomi was right.

I'd nailed it.

Chapter ONE

Sweeney Todd is a musical about cannibalism. More specifically, it's a musical about a barber named Benjamin Barker, alias Sweeney Todd, who kills his customers and gives the bodies to his landlady, Mrs. Lovett, so she can turn them into meat pies and serve them to people. There's a lot more to it than that—love and obsession and revenge, everything you'd expect to find in a good musical—but for most people, cannibalism is the show's biggest selling point.

For me, though, it was all about the music. Nothing in the entire universe made me happier than sinking my teeth into a really juicy song and performing it for anyone willing to listen—and of all the musicals I've ever loved, *Sweeney Todd* was the ultimate source for juicy songs. Especially if you were playing Mrs. Lovett, which was exactly what I planned to do.

A week after the auditions, Miss Delisio announced that she'd made her casting decisions and the list would be up at the end of the day. So when the last bell rang, I raced out of my last class and up to the theater. There was already a throng of drama club students milling around the door. A piece of light green paper was there, held up with Scotch tape.

I started pushing my way through the crowd, but a hand on my shoulder stopped me before I could get very far. "Congrats, girl!" said Naomi, pulling me into a quick hug. "You got a lead. Told you so, didn't I?"

Naomi had never been interested in acting, but she'd stage-managed our shows ever since freshman year. She was a natural at it, too: level-headed, loud, and popular enough that people actually listened when she told them to do things.

"Really?" I said, returning her grin. "Wait, don't tell me. I want to see for myself."

Call it superstition, but even in a case like this, where I knew beyond a doubt what part I'd gotten, I had to see it in writing before I let it become real. *Margaret McKenna—Mrs. Lovett.* Ever since Miss Delisio had announced that *Sweeney Todd* would be our spring musical, I'd pictured those words in my head, willing them to come true.

I skirted around Naomi and wove through a bunch of guys high-fiving each other, until finally I reached the cast list. It only took a few seconds for me to zero in on my name, about half-way down the green paper. I followed the line that would lead me to the name of my character.

Margaret McKenna—Tobias Ragg.

No way.

The chatter around me dissolved into white noise, and I

blinked a couple times, just to make sure I wasn't imagining things. I traced the line with my finger. No, I'd really been cast as Tobias Ragg. Toby, who only had a couple of songs. Toby, who was young and simple-minded, the exact opposite of the devious and amazing Mrs. Lovett, who I was certain I'd get to be.

Toby, who was a boy.

I mean, sure, I was short and kind of flat-chested, but come on. . . .

"I'm Toby," I said to myself, trying the idea on for size. It didn't fit.

"Yeah," came Naomi's voice from just over my shoulder. Apparently she'd followed me through the crowd. I turned to her, and her congratulatory smile faltered when she saw my face. "Listen, I know you wanted Mrs. Lovett, but Toby's still a really good part. You'll be so awesome."

But her consolation-prize words washed over me, totally devoid of meaning. "Who *is* playing Lovett?" I asked. I hadn't even thought to check. "Wait. Don't tell me."

So she didn't. She just bit her lip and waited for me to find the name. Find it I did. Recognize it, I did not.

"Who the hell is Victoria Willoughbee?"

Naomi went quiet for a moment, her face frozen in an expression that I couldn't read. "You know Vicky," she said at last. "Sophomore? Plays clarinet in the band?" Nothing rang a bell, so I just shook my head. Naomi shrugged. "Well, she's nice."

"But why—"

"Woo-hoo!" came a shout, so close it made me flinch. Just behind me was Simon Lee, looking over my head at the cast list. "I'm Sweeney Effing Todd, suckers! I am the Asian Johnny Depp! I've always said that! Haven't I? Haven't I always said that?"

He punched the air, and a few people yelled out their congratulations and gave him those back-thumping man-hugs. Nobody seemed to begrudge him the lead role, or even the bizarre victory dance he was now doing. Mostly because we all knew he was the most talented boy in the entire school. Not to mention the cutest.

Simon found me in the crowd and gave me one of those lopsided grins that made my chest feel like a tiny hot-air balloon. That was when it hit me.

I wouldn't get to be Simon's costar.

Suddenly, I was absolutely certain I was about to lose it. I had to get out of there. I couldn't let all these people see me cry over a part in a high school musical. Especially not Simon.

"Congratulations," I managed to choke out, and ran like hell toward the girls' bathroom.

I didn't even see the boy coming around the corner until I bumped right into him. My shoulder smacked into his arm with a force that nearly spun me off my feet.

"Sorry!" he said automatically, stepping gingerly out of my way as I looked up in alarm to see who it was. I didn't know him.

But his eyes widened as he looked down at me. "Margo," he said. "Oh. I'm really, *really* sorry."

I gave him a quick once-over—dark hair, light eyes, thin and wiry, cute enough in a nondescript sort of way—but no, I definitely didn't know him. "Sorry about what? Who are you?"

"Nobody," he said quickly, holding his hands up like a white flag. "I'm nobody. Never mind."

I darted past him. Out of the corner of my eye, I saw him turn to watch me go.

The bathroom smelled faintly of weed and cigarettes, and the powers that be had long since stopped scrubbing away the rude graffiti that covered the walls, but at least it was empty. Feeling about nine years old, I locked myself in a stall, drew my knees up to my chin, and shut my eyes.

Miss Delisio always gave the lead roles to seniors. That was how it worked. You paid your underclassman dues in the chorus, or maybe in small roles if you were lucky, and then you got a good part right before you graduated. So why were the rules different for that Vicky Willoughbee girl?

I only allowed myself out of the stall when I'd calmed down enough to form a new plan of action. If I couldn't be Mrs. Lovett, then I would be the sort of person who was totally okay with *not* being Mrs. Lovett. I smiled at myself in the bathroom mirror until it looked real, and then I took a deep breath and headed back toward the theater for the first rehearsal.

Miss Delisio was already sitting primly on the stage when I came in. In addition to being my tenth-grade trig teacher, she'd directed every musical I'd been in since freshman year. I liked her well enough—but sitting next to her, wearing tight jeans, clunky boots, and a black biker jacket, was the real talent: George the Music Ninja.

Even when George was just noodling around on the piano during breaks, it was like listening to some crazy musical genius at work. And that wasn't even counting his other job. When he wasn't musical-directing us, he was the front man of an indie band called Apocalypse Later. He didn't write their music, which probably explained why I wasn't totally sold on their sound, but his vocals and guitar solos were absolutely killer.

"Grab your script and have a seat," Miss Delisio announced in her usual buoyant voice. "We'll start as soon as everyone's here."

One by one, we made our way up to the stage, where there was a pile of scripts, each labeled with the name of an actor and the role they were playing. I watched Miss Delisio closely as I approached, wondering if she would say anything to me. She knew I wanted to be Mrs. Lovett. In fact, last time I spoke to her, she'd stopped just short of outright promising me the role. Would she bother to explain why she'd given it to someone else?

Apparently not. By the time I reached the stage and fished my script from the pile, she and George were engrossed in conversation. I took a deep breath. It didn't matter, I reminded myself. What's done is done. I was okay with it. No, I was more than okay; I was going to kick ass in this role.

Most of the actors with leads had settled in the front row: Callie Zumsky as Johanna, MaLinda Jones as Pirelli, Dan Quimby-Sato as Anthony, Ryan Weiss as Judge Turpin, Jill Spalding as the Beggar Woman. All seniors, of course. But I joined Naomi in the second row instead.

"You okay, McKenna?" whispered Naomi as I sat down beside her.

"Why wouldn't I be?" I whispered back. "Just because Sophomore McWhatserface got Lovett and I didn't?"

Naomi snickered. "You mean Willoughbee," she said, trying and failing to sound disapproving.

I grinned. "That's what I said. Anyway, whatever. I'm over it."

"You don't look over it."

I raised an eyebrow at her. "Perhaps your eyes deceive you."

She looked like she wanted to press the issue, but I was saved by the arrival of Simon, who slid into the empty seat on my other side. "Heya, Toby," he said, grinning.

There was something witty I could say in response to that. I was sure of it. Unfortunately, the best my brain could cough up was: "Actually, it's Margo."

He feigned shock and slapped his forehead with his palm. "Duh. I'm always doing that. Calling people Toby. When will I ever learn?"

Something witty. Something witty. I needed to think of something witty.

But his arm kept brushing against mine as he arranged his stuff on the floor, and that was enough to distract me. I was just about to give up on being witty and blurt out something inane like "Never, I guess," when Miss Delisio began to shush us.

"We've got almost everyone," she said, frowning down at the scripts beside her. "We're just missing Vicky—oh, there she is!"

Her gaze shifted to the back of the auditorium, and everyone twisted around to see who she was looking at. There, at the top of the left aisle, was a girl I was pretty sure I'd never seen before. Clutching a small pile of books to her chest, she hesitated there like she'd been caught in the act of . . . what? Walking into a room?

This was the girl who'd been cast in the role of a lifetime?

"Here you go," said Miss Delisio, holding out a script. Hugging her books closer, Vicky darted down the aisle to collect it. Miss Delisio, beaming, said something I couldn't hear, and Vicky gave her a tight smile in return. Miss Delisio gestured to the front row.

But the front row had already filled up. Vicky hesitated again, and for one relieved moment I was sure she would head toward the back, with the other underclassmen.

Then Simon waved at her. "Saved you a seat over here!" he called, much to my dismay. Vicky slid into the seat on Simon's other side as he gave her his trademark arched-eyebrow smile.

The one that made my heart beat just a little faster when he used it on me. The one that, last spring, had led to an incredibly awesome kiss at the cast party of *Bat Boy: The Musical*. The kiss had never been repeated. In fact, after that night he'd never even brought it up again. But still: awesome.

Vicky, however, seemed oblivious to his flirty look.

"Margo, right?" she whispered to me, across Simon.

"That's me."

"I saw you as Ruthie in *Bat Boy* last year. You were really good."

"Thanks," I said, and smiled at her, exactly like I'd practiced in the bathroom mirror. I was okay with this. I was not allowed to hate Vicky Willoughbee.

Once we were settled, Miss Delisio introduced George, like there was anyone here who didn't know him. He flashed us a grin and settled himself at the piano. We wouldn't be singing today, since we hadn't officially learned the songs yet, but that didn't mean he couldn't underscore us. He began to play the opening bars of the show, and a little shiver flitted up my spine.

With Naomi reading stage directions, we jumped right in. As usual, speaking the lyrics was odd since, without rhythms and melody, lyrics just sound like really weird poetry. But this was the way the first rehearsal always went: just a read-through, so we could all learn the story together. Most of us were used to it. Some people, like Simon, even managed to make it sound kind of good.

Vicky, however, was no Simon. She read all of her lyrics in

an awful monotone, like she couldn't quite figure out what the words meant. And it wasn't just the lyrics, either. The way she read the dialogue was just as bad. It was all I could do not to cover my ears and run screaming out of the theater.

When we finally reached the end of Act One, Miss Delisio called a ten-minute break. I thought about going outside, but when Vicky got up, I decided to stay right where I was. Running into her in the hallway and accidentally punching her in the face were definitely not part of my I'm-okay-with-this plan.

As I skimmed the second half of the script, I saw a student approach Miss Delisio. A student who wasn't in the cast, which was a little unusual. It took me a minute, but I recognized him as the boy from earlier. The one I'd almost mowed down on my way to the bathroom.

He spoke with Miss Delisio and George for a few moments before digging through the pockets of the hoodie he wore, then through the backpack he'd slung over one shoulder. He pulled out what looked like a camera case. I heard the word *yearbook* come out of someone's mouth, and I groaned softly as I realized what was going on. They were starting rehearsal photo shoots this early in the game? Not fair.

When the cast had settled back in their seats and quieted, Miss Delisio took a moment to confirm my fears.

"Guys, this is Oliver Parish." The boy gave a shy little wave to nobody in particular. "He just transferred here in January. He's going to be photographing our rehearsal process for the drama club's section of the yearbook. And maybe, if we're lucky, he'll get enough to put together a slide show for our cast party."

Naomi nudged me and rolled her eyes, which made me grin. I looked at Simon, to see what he thought of this turn of events, but he was busy typing out a text message on his phone. Beside him, though, Vicky was watching Oliver. And she wasn't wearing that timid, deer-in-the-headlights expression from before. She was absolutely beaming.

I looked at the photographer. He smiled back at Vicky, like there was a secret in the room, and they were the only two people who knew it.

The porch lights were already on when I got home that night, and my mom's car sat ominously in the driveway. And the house, as I'd feared, was a mess. There were coats draped over the back of the couch, shoes strewn all around the floor, and four suitcases in the hallway, one of which was open and spilling clothes everywhere. I tried not to think about how I'd cleaned this room just three days ago.

Ziggy was the first to greet me when I opened the door, jumping off her perch on the couch and rubbing herself against my legs. She purred as I bent to scritch her little tabby head. "Did Mommy and Daddy come home?" I whispered to her. "Did they remember to feed you?"

"Margo?" came Mom's voice from the kitchen. "Honey, is that you?"

I rolled my eyes. "No, it's a burglar. I've come to steal all your silverware and jewelry. And your cat," I added, giving Ziggy another scratch.

"As long as you don't steal our daughter," she replied. Emerging from the kitchen with a huge grin on her face and Dad trailing behind her, she gave me a quick hug and a peck on the forehead.

"How was the cruise?" I asked, unzipping my boots and placing them neatly on the shoe rack by the door. I'd deal with my parents' shoes later.

She sighed dramatically. "Absolute heaven. Maybe even better than the last one. I know they say you should wait for summer to visit Alaska, but what's a little cold?"

"Cold schmold," added Dad. "That's what the parkas were for. Not to mention the indoor cabin."

Mom gave him a secretive little smile. "The honeymoon suite, you mean."

"Honeymoon suite, still?" I asked, doing my best to ignore the dewy-eyed looks they were exchanging. "What is this, the third honeymoon you've been on since the wedding?"

Mom thought for a moment. "Fourth, if you count the Grand Canyon trip."

"Which I do," said Dad. "Oh, and we have pictures!" He ran over to the open suitcase and began rifling through it. "Wait till you see these, Margo. Some of the ones your mother took are just, wow."

Ever since the wedding last May, our lives had been one continuous cycle of Mom and Dad planning a trip, Mom and Dad leaving on their trip, a week or two of peace and quiet, Mom and Dad coming back from their trip, and the grand finale, Mom and Dad showing me pictures of their trip. The pictures were always the same, too: Mom pretending to fall over the railing of a cruise ship, Dad wearing another cheesy Hawaiian shirt, stuff like that. Sometimes it felt like they were the teenagers and I was the adult.

"How's school?" asked Mom. "Anything exciting happen while we were gone?"

"Nope," I said quickly. "Same old same old."

I thought about telling her about the cast list fiasco, but this wasn't the time. At best, they'd both go "Aw, that's too bad" and jump right back into honeymoon talk. At worst, they wouldn't even understand why I was so upset. As far as they were concerned, it didn't matter what role I had, as long as their daughter was onstage. These were, after all, the people who'd thrown me a party after I'd played Frightened Theatergoer Number Two in my first-grade musical about Abraham Lincoln.

"Where did I put that camera?" muttered Dad.

"Red suitcase, inside pocket, next to the toothbrushes," replied Mom almost absently, and then turned back to me. "You'll never guess what movie was playing on the plane today. *The Parent Trap*. Can you believe it?"

"Oh, I almost forgot about that!" said Dad, unzipping the red suitcase.

"It was the old Hayley Mills one," said Mom. "The good one, not the remake they did with that awful drug addict girl."

I was about to point out that Lindsay Lohan probably hadn't been a drug addict at the time, but Mom continued, "And we said, take away the twin thing and the summer camp, and that's our Margo! Making us back into one big, happy family."

"It wasn't exactly me," I said, but neither of them seemed to notice.

"Aw, Celia," said Dad. Camera finally in hand, he came back over and enveloped us in a bear hug. Mom hugged back just as hard, so I did too.

If I'd been a character in a musical, this would have been the point where the lights went down on my parents, leaving them slow-dancing in the background like living scenery, as I stepped forward into a lone spotlight for my big solo. It would be a quirky ballad, probably called "I Am Not Hayley Mills" or something like that, and people would applaud when I was done. Maybe they'd even give me a standing ovation.

Of course, people don't usually get standing ovations in their living rooms, but I still toyed with the idea of dashing upstairs, pulling out my guitar, and writing that song. It wasn't worth it, though. I'd tried a million different times to write a million different songs about a million different things, but it was never worth it. My songs always sucked.

Chapter TWO

Right from day one, Oliver Parish came to almost every single rehearsal. Whether we were learning songs, blocking scenes, or just talking things through, there he was. Always right on the fringe of the action, blinding flash at the ready. Constantly tempting me to jump off the stage and throttle him with my bare hands—which, to my credit, I did not do.

Meanwhile, my favorite part of rehearsals was watching Simon learn his songs and use them to find his way into the Sweeney character. He was totally bizarre in just the perfect way, and he attacked every song like it came from the deepest part of his soul, instead of from a script. It was, in a way, even cooler than watching him sing to a fake severed cow's head as Edgar in *Bat Boy*.

And he wasn't the only one doing well. According to Naomi, who had to go to every rehearsal, Callie Zumsky and Dan Quimby-Sato were starting to develop some serious stage chemistry as Johanna and Anthony. Not surprising, since I'd done shows with them before, and they were both seriously talented. But when I asked how Ryan Weiss was doing as Judge Turpin, Naomi just rolled her eyes. She didn't have to explain. Everyone knew Ryan only got lead roles because he could hit low notes that none of the other guys could. He was the kind of actor who missed his cues all the time, thought every line should be accompanied by a sweeping arm gesture, and always looked vaguely angry.

But as bad as Ryan was, Vicky Willoughbee was even worse. Sure, she was okay at remembering lines, but that was about it. No matter how much direction Miss Delisio gave her, she remained as expressionless and monotonous as a robot. I kept waiting for someone to call her on it, but Miss Delisio, Simon, and everyone else kept saying how great she was, and Oliver Parish kept taking pictures and smiling proudly at her.

It was the strangest thing. "Vicky's so nice" and "Vicky's so pretty" and "Vicky's so talented" swirled constantly around me, and nobody ever said anything about how the rest of us were actually singing and acting, while Vicky was just . . . saying words.

I tried talking to Naomi, but all she did was shake her head at me. "Don't get all catty about it," she said. "I know you wanted that part, but it isn't Willoughbee's fault, okay?"

That shut me right up. Maybe Naomi had a point. Maybe I was being too critical—even petty. And since petty wasn't a thing I ever wanted to be, I kept my head down and concentrated on learning my songs, figuring out my character, and staying out of everyone else's business.

Which would have worked great, had I not happened to overhear voices from the band room during rehearsal one Tuesday night.

While Simon and Danny Q went through their first scene for the bazillionth time, I sneaked out to retrieve my French workbook. As I reached my locker, I heard two people talking. This wasn't unusual, since the drama club was far from the only group that stayed at school after hours, but these voices were speaking in low, urgent tones, which smacked of secrecy. And that, of course, piqued my interest. I followed the sound to the band room door. The lights were off inside, but the door was cracked open. So I listened.

"And it's not just the play," a female voice was saying. "I mean, it *is* the play, but it's everything else, too."

Vicky. I hadn't even noticed that she wasn't upstairs in the theater. She sounded so different when she wasn't speaking in her annoying monotone.

"But that was what you wanted," said a male voice that I couldn't place.

"Yeah," she said, and I heard a hint of a sniffle. "But it's too much. I can't get away. It's like everyone wants something from me, all the time. I hear my name everywhere. A football player hit on me yesterday, for god's sake."

The male voice let out a low laugh.

"It's not funny, Oliver! Did you know there's a petition going around to vote me into the student council? As the president? Sophomores can't even run for student council, and the election was back in September!"

I pressed my ear closer to the door. First the musical, now the student council? What the hell was that about? And what did Oliver have to do with it?

"Do you want to undo it?" he asked.

"Yes!" she said, with more emotion than she'd given to the entire script of *Sweeney Todd*. "Wait a sec. Would I have to use my third to undo it?"

"Yes," Oliver replied.

"But then I'd be wasting two," she said. "I don't know. This is too much. Why didn't you just do it right in the first place?"

"Do it right?" came his affronted reply. I tensed. "I did it exactly like you wanted. Exactly. That's as right as it gets. It's not my fault you can't deal with it."

I braced myself for her to yell, or to cry, or to throw some accusation back at him. But all that followed was silence, which was even more unnerving. I waited, but after a full fifteen seconds passed, I couldn't stand it anymore. I peeked into the band room. Vicky was sitting in one of the black plastic chairs, resting her hands on a music stand and looking troubled. There was no sign of Oliver.

She jumped up when she saw me. "Margo. Did you hear . . . ?" Instead of finishing the question, she made a vague gesture at the space around herself.

"I heard you fighting," I said. Her eyes went wide behind her glasses, but she didn't say anything. "Where'd he go? Are you okay?"

She gave a weak little laugh, ignoring my first question. "Yeah, I'm fine. It's just . . . Never mind. I'm fine."

"Oh. All right." An awkward silence descended, and she made no move to fill it. So I did instead: "What was the thing about the student council?"

Vicky's gaze grew sharp. "You *were* listening. Did you follow me down here?"

"No! I just came down to get my, um, my French book," I finished lamely, painfully aware of my empty hands.

"Sure you did." She skirted around me, heading for the door. "Just leave me alone, okay? Why can't everyone just *leave me alone*?"

For nearly a week, I kept an eye on Vicky and Oliver, just in case their behavior yielded any more clues to what the band room fight had been about. But aside from acting noticeably cooler toward each other, neither of them did anything particularly noteworthy. Oliver kept taking pictures; Vicky kept not being able to act. That was all. Maybe I'd been imagining things,

I decided eventually. Maybe all I'd witnessed was a run-of-the-mill breakup fight.

So I stopped paying attention to them and went back to concentrating on the important things. Like watching George play, and listening to Simon sing.

And doing some singing of my own.

Once I started digging my claws into Toby's music, I began to get a feel for who his character was. His songs all had a brash, jaunty quality to them. A distinctly *boyish* quality. I sang them over and over again, until I could imagine the musical phrases seeping through my skin, settling deep in my bones, and becoming part of me—changing not only the way I sang his songs, but the way I spoke his lines, and even the way I moved onstage.

I started walking differently during rehearsals. I'd never thought much about the way I walked, but now that I was paying attention, I noticed I had a tendency to swing my hips from side to side, just a little bit. But when I was playing Toby, I held my hips straight, like a boy would, and it had a weird ripple effect on the rest of my body. I found myself angling my head and shoulders differently when I talked to people. I took bigger steps. I swaggered. All because of a few short, surprisingly brilliant songs.

"You're doing such a lovely job with this role," said Miss Delisio during one of our rehearsal breaks. "I knew it would be a challenge for you, but I had a feeling you'd be up for it." She paused, a frown flitting across her face. "And Margo, I want to thank you for being so mature about my casting decision. I know you wanted to play Mrs. Lovett, and I know you would've been wonderful. But I had to do what was best for the whole company. You understand, don't you?"

I didn't, especially since there was no universe in which Vicky playing a lead was best for the company. But I made myself nod. "Sure. I get it."

"And you're having fun playing Toby, aren't you?" Her eyes were hopeful as they searched mine.

"That I am," I said, just to make her feel better. But to my surprise, it was actually kind of true.

Even George the Music Ninja complimented my work—and this was a guy who never complimented anyone at all. He'd correct people when he had to, and he'd do everything he could to make the singers and the band sound their absolute best—but when everything was going smoothly, he usually just nodded to himself and went "Yup." But this time was different.

An entire Thursday evening had been set aside for us to work through my biggest song, which was called "Not While I'm Around." It was a quietly beautiful song, and my character had to sing it to Vicky's character, without anyone else onstage. Probably thinking to have a small, intimate rehearsal that reflected the small, intimate nature of the scene, Miss Delisio let Naomi off the hook that night, and even asked Oliver not to come and take pictures.

Since George and I were the first ones there, he suggested we go over my song while we waited for Miss Delisio and Vicky. With his clunky boots working the pedals of the crappy school piano, George took me through the song twice: once to listen to how I'd been singing it on my own, once more to make suggestions. They were clever, nitpicky things—the softening of a line here, or the lengthening of a note there—and I had a lot of fun taking his notes. When we were finished, he dropped his hands into his lap and gave me a calculating look.

"You're good. You know that?"

My jaw literally dropped, and a moment passed before I managed to speak. "Thanks. That's, wow, that's really nice of you to say."

"It's not nice. It's just true." He pointed a finger at me. "You are damn good. *Darn* good. You even allowed to say 'damn' here, or will those morons on the school board . . . ? Never mind. Anyway, your voice. You've got substance there. Depth. You write songs, too? You seem like the type who writes songs."

"Yeah." I paused, surprised at myself. I never told people about that. "Badly, though," I added quickly.

"You being modest? Tell me straight."

"No, I'm serious. I mean, I'm okay on the guitar, but my lyrics are terrible. I mean truly terrible. Like, 'unholy love-child of *Dance of the Vampires* and *Carrie*' levels of terrible."

"Huh."

For a second I thought he might ask me to play something

anyway, but I was saved by the arrival of Vicky and Miss Delisio, both bundled in coats and armed with scripts.

"How's the song coming?" called Miss Delisio cheerfully as she came down the aisle. "Are we ready?"

"We are darn ready," I replied. George snickered.

As soon as Vicky shed her coat, we dove right in. I was eager to show off the song that had completely changed the way George looked at me—but when you're in a scene with someone, you can't just decide how you're going to sing your song, and then do it. You have to react to the other people onstage with you. You have to connect with them, let them influence you, interact with them like real people do with each other.

Unfortunately, with Vicky being her usual monotonous self, there was nothing I could connect to. I sang at her, but she just stared at me and recited her lines like a robot, which made me feel like my own lines were being sucked into a black hole of awfulness. It was infuriating.

George didn't say anything when we finished. All Miss Delisio said was, "Lovely, ladies! Let's take it again, from the top of the song."

It was anything but lovely, but I couldn't exactly say so out loud. Silently seething, I moved back over to stage left, where I was supposed to start the scene. George began playing, and I began singing, and with every lyric I willed Vicky to connect with me, willed Miss Delisio to see how terrible she was, so she could find a way to fix it.

I plowed through the song ruthlessly, infusing "Listen to me, just listen to me" into every note. It came out harsh and cracked and sometimes even off-key—but to my surprise, it felt absolutely real that way. I didn't have to care that Vicky wasn't really listening. In the scene, Mrs. Lovett wasn't listening to Toby, either. So he, like me, had every right to be pissed off.

When the scene ended, I found my heart was racing. Slowly I fell out of Toby's posture and back into my own. George was staring hard at me, his lips pressed into a thin line. He gave me a single, firm nod, and I saw him mouth the word *yup.*

Miss Delisio looked back and forth between Vicky and me, absolutely beaming. "Vicky, Margo, that was—"

"Can I take a break?" came Vicky's small voice, before Miss Delisio could finish. She stood a few feet away from me, her shoulders hunched miserably. Guilt flared through me. Vicky was a terrible actress, but that didn't mean she was stupid. And I'd practically yelled the whole song at her. I tried to catch her eye, but she wouldn't look at me.

"Go ahead," said Miss Delisio. Vicky jumped off the stage and dashed out of the auditorium.

"Told you she couldn't handle it," said George, carefully flexing his fingers.

Miss Delisio gave him a sharp look. "We've talked about this," she said, and moved toward the piano where he sat. I would have asked what exactly they'd talked about, but their conversation quickly became too hushed for me to hear. Which left us with one absent actress, a director and a musical director who were about to either fight or make out, and me.

Without bothering to excuse myself, I hopped off the stage and went to take a bathroom break.

I half expected to find Vicky outside the auditorium, maybe making a phone call, maybe huddled in a corner and crying to herself. She wasn't there. But when I reached the girls' room and began to push the creaky door open, I heard someone turning on the sink inside, and I actually hesitated.

But there was no reason for me not to go in. If she'd wanted to be alone, she'd have gone someplace a little less obvious. I swung the door open. Vicky met my eyes in the mirror, but she quickly looked back down at the sink. As she scrubbed furiously at her hands, I slipped into a stall.

She left almost immediately, but I took my time, hoping she'd deal with whatever issue she was having before I got back to rehearsal. I even paused for a second to check myself in the mirror, though there wasn't much to check. Hair: still short, but starting to get too long for the pixie cut I'd gotten last month. Two tiny zits right by my nose: still covered with foundation. Minimal eye makeup: still not smudged. Little glint coming from the window behind me—

Well, that was new.

Curious, I turned around and peered at the sill. I had to stand on my tiptoes to do it, since all the first-floor bathroom windows were ridiculously high up, probably to keep us from using them to escape during school hours. Although, if you wanted to play hooky, it was a whole lot easier to walk out the front door.

There was a silver ring there, shiny enough that it caught even the dim fluorescent bathroom light. The band was thick, and deeply engraved with a wavy pattern that looked like one of those Celtic knots.

I couldn't remember seeing anyone at school with a ring like this, but this was a public bathroom in a big school, and I was hardly the most observant person when it came to jewelry. It could have belonged to anyone.

I picked it up, rolling it between my thumb and index finger so I could get a better look at the design. It was a really pretty ring, actually, and for a second I was tempted to keep it for myself. But even if I could justify keeping it, I would have no reason to. I had a small collection of jewelry, mostly given to me by my mom, but I never really wore any of it.

Lost and found, then. I tossed the ring in the air and caught it, the way I thought Toby Ragg might do if he'd found it instead of me. Grinning at the thought, I pocketed the ring and headed for the door. But the door opened before I could get there. Into the bathroom, wearing jeans and a gray hoodie, walked Oliver Parish.

"What is it?" he asked—and his eyes locked with mine. He snapped his mouth shut with a frown. Drawing his head back warily, he said, "Margo. You're not Vicky."

"Very observant," I said, rolling my eyes. "Here's another observation: This is the girls' room, and you are a boy."

"But it came from in here," he said. Squatting down, he peered under the stall doors. "Where is she?"

"Probably back at rehearsal," I said. "Which is not in the girls' bathroom. What the hell are you doing in here?"

Oliver straightened suddenly, his shoulders tensing like he'd just gotten a chill. He pressed one hand to his temple, then looked at me with eyes grown just a little bit too wide. If we hadn't been in a bathroom in a high school, I'd have said that he looked almost scared. I crossed my arms, waiting.

When he finally spoke, his voice quavered. "I'm looking for a ring. You, um . . . you didn't happen to pick up a ring, did you?"

"A ring?" I repeated.

"Yeah. A silver one." He made a small circle with his fingers, like maybe I didn't know what a ring was.

I nearly reached into my pocket to retrieve it, but then stopped. Something didn't make sense here. "Why would your ring be in the girls' room?"

"Vicky must have left it," he said. "I should give it back to her."

"Wait, okay, time out for a second," I said, making a little T sign with my hands. "If Vicky sent you in here to get her ring, then why'd you think I was her?"

His expression remained carefully neutral. "Because she was the last person who had it. Please, Margo, do you have it or not?"

"Yeah, I do." Oliver took an eager step toward me, and for the first time I was aware of the height difference between us. He wasn't unusually tall—about average for a guy—but he still had more than six inches on me. I took a step back, putting up a defensive hand. "But if you want it back, you'd better tell me why you're here. Especially since you weren't at rehearsal tonight. Why are you even in the school?"

"If you'd just," he began, and then stopped abruptly, wincing. Rubbing at his forehead like he'd just gotten a migraine, he muttered, "Ohhh, this is awkward."

"What is?" I asked, thoroughly confused.

"This," he said through clenched teeth, looking at me with painfully squinted eyes. "All right, all right. I'm here because the ring called me here, okay?" And then he let out a whoosh of breath, dropped his hands, and let his face relax—like his migraine had disappeared as fast as it showed up.

"Did you just say it called you?" I said, one hand wandering downward to linger protectively over the pocket of my jeans.

"Yes, I did," he said, the sharp look in his eyes daring me to contradict him.

"Are you gonna tell me what that's supposed to mean?"

"No," he said. "Don't you have to get back to rehearsal?"

He had a point. I'd been gone way longer than I should have, and they were probably wondering where I was. But still . . .

"Come on," I said. "What's the short version?"

Oliver's expression grew pained. "The ring is tied to me.

31

When someone touches it with their thumb and forefinger, it calls me. And here I am. Ta-dah," he said, making the most unenthusiastic jazz hands I'd ever seen.

I burst out laughing.

Oliver didn't.

He looked down at his shoes, his hair falling forward and into his eyes. My laughter faded into an awkward "Heh." Biting my bottom lip to shut myself up, I looked for some crack in his serious veneer. There wasn't one. "So . . . you're trying to tell me that this is a magic ring."

Annoyance darkening his expression, he looked up at me again through unruly bangs. "No, I'm trying to tell you that it's *my* magic ring, and I want it back."

I narrowed my eyes. "I thought you said it was Vicky's."

"No, I didn't. I said Vicky must have left it." He frowned, looking around like he was lost. "And that's worrying enough as it is. But the point is, I need it back."

"Uh-huh," I said. "Look, you and Vicky can play *Lord of the Rings* all you want. I'm just here for rehearsal. But I think it's incredibly weird, and maybe a little bit creepy, that you followed me into the girls' bathroom for this thing, so if you don't mind, I'll just go give it back to her myself, okay?"

Oliver looked like he was about to protest, but after a moment's thought, he gave me a curt nod. "That'll work."

I blinked at him, slightly thrown. Why did that seem too easy? "Um, okay," I said slowly. "Then I'll just . . ."

A knock sounded on the door, making me jump. "Margo, are you in there?" came a voice from outside. Miss Delisio. The door began to creak open.

Oliver tensed, a panicked expression crossing his face. I didn't blame him. Eli Simpson had been caught in the girls' room last fall, and on top of the detention he got, Coach Kendall had actually kicked him off the baseball team. I raised my eyebrows at Oliver, waiting for him to hide in a stall or behind the door or something. But he did neither.

Instead, he disappeared.

Chapter THREE

I t was as simple as that: One second he was there, and the next second he wasn't. And there I was, gaping like a complete moron, as Miss Delisio poked her head inside and peered at me, clearly worried. "Is everything okay?"

"I, uh," I faltered, as my eyes darted around, looking in vain for signs of Oliver. "Yeah. Sorry, I was just . . . um . . . Is Vicky ready?" I hoped she wasn't. There was no way I could force myself to concentrate through the rest of our rehearsal.

Miss Delisio smiled wanly. "She asked to go home early, actually."

There was a pause.

"So you can go home, too, if you want," she said, raising an eyebrow. Right. I hadn't moved.

"Yes," I said. "Good. I mean, not good, but . . . okay."

Giving me a bemused smile as I headed for the door, she said, "I'll see you tomorrow. Get some sleep."

I would indeed get some sleep, but not until I found out what

was going on. I'd spent the better part of eighteen years thinking magic just meant card tricks and Harry Potter books and
questionable vampire movies—and here was what seemed very
much like the real thing, right in front of me. Even though I
knew it was impossible.

After a quick stop back at the theater to pick up my stuff, I
headed for my car, thinking about what Oliver had said. Just a
touch of my thumb and forefinger.

Oakvale, the little town where I'd lived my entire life, was
right in the middle of northern New Jersey. Drive too far
east, you got those towns squished so close together that you
couldn't tell where one ended and the next began. Too far west,
you got towns that looked like permanent campsites between
vast swathes of woods. To the south, you had tangled messes
of factories and highways and all the pollution New York City
didn't want. And to the north, a mere ten minutes away, you
had New York State. Oakvale managed to be a happy medium
among all these things—which meant it had very little personality of its own.

What it did have was the centerpiece of every self-respecting
New Jersey town: Tom's 24-Hour Diner, festooned with neon
lights and proudly situated across the street from a gas station.
Not to be confused with the Tom's Diner of song and legend
(which was supposedly somewhere in New York City), our
Tom's was the favored weekend hangout of elderly couples,

families with small children, bored high-schoolers, and even the occasional group of surly college students who were too young to drink at the Sand Bar down the street. During the week, though, it was usually just as empty as every other place in town.

When I left rehearsal, Tom's was the first place I thought of: a big, bright space full of shiny tabletops and vinyl seats. There were two giant jukeboxes, neither of which actually worked, and the walls were lined with framed prints of smiling cartoon food. If ever there was a competition for Place Least Likely to Contain Magic, then Tom's was a surefire winner.

I parked my car in the lot out front, got myself a back-corner booth under an unnaturally happy fajita, and told the waiter I was expecting a friend. Then I reached into my pocket and touched the silver ring with my thumb and forefinger, just like Oliver had said. My breath falling shallow in my lungs, I watched the front door with eagle eyes. The sooner he showed up, the sooner I could find out what the hell was really going on. Once I'd set my mind at ease, I could eat some dinner, then go home and finish tomorrow's homework.

It only took him five seconds. As I watched, Oliver appeared just inside the door, still not wearing anything heavier than that gray hoodie. Even though it was freezing outside.

It occurred to me that I hadn't actually seen him come *through* the door.

He stood there for a second, scanning the diner for me. His

hands were tucked casually into his pockets, and his shoulders were set back, like an actor. His stance radiated confidence, and even his shaggy hair now seemed less like a shield and more like a fashion choice. The whole picture was a far cry from the jumpy, pissed-off Oliver of only twenty minutes ago. A bright smile lit up his face as he spotted me, and he came over and slid into the seat opposite mine.

"Good choice," he said, picking up one of the old, cracked menus. "I'm starving. Do they have nachos here? I could really go for some nachos."

"Nachos?" I repeated vaguely. Disappearing, reappearing, then nachos. I could feel my brain about to short-circuit.

"Or a milkshake, maybe," he mused, skimming the menu. "Or waffles. Ooh."

"Waffles, sure," I said, staring at him in disbelief. "Did you follow me here?"

"Nope." He grinned up at me. "You called me and I came. I thought you might. And I'm glad you did."

Our waiter appeared, clad in a wrinkled Tom's T-shirt and bravely wielding a notepad and pen, and I managed to mumble something about a cheeseburger deluxe with extra bacon. Oliver very enthusiastically ordered a Belgian waffle with three kinds of berries, vanilla ice cream, and sprinkles. And then he asked for a cherry on top. The waiter, who didn't seem to notice anything odd about Oliver's aggressive cheerfulness, took our menus and slipped away.

"So!" said Oliver, folding his hands on the table and leaning eagerly toward me. "Where do you want to start?"

I narrowed my eyes at him. Without bothering to ease into it, I lowered my voice and said, "You disappeared."

"Yes," he said proudly. "Yes, I did."

"And then you reappeared," I continued. "And suddenly you were all happy and 'Let's have nachos' about everything."

"Waffles," he corrected smoothly.

"And that, I might add, was after you materialized out of thin air, instead of walking through the door like a normal person who, I dunno, wears coats and stuff."

A slight frown creased his forehead. "A coat," he said, looking down at his hoodie. "I knew I forgot something."

"You materialized," I said, spreading my hands to emphasize that this was far more important than coats. "Out of *thin air*."

"It's just like I said: You called me. I came. That's how my magic works."

"Magic," I repeated flatly. "You're still trying to tell me this is magic?"

"Indeed I am," he said, with a grin that made the skin around his eyes scrunch up. Bright green eyes, I noticed, framed by dark lashes. "And you're still trying to tell me you don't believe me?"

"Obviously," I said. "Magic isn't real."

"Says the girl who just saw me materialize out of thin air."

He had me there.

"The ring holds the same magic that I do," he explained. "It's part of me. Or, I guess what I mean is, it has part of me inside it. That's why you can call me with it: Because it's me, more or less. It's called a spirit vessel. Does that make sense to you?"

"A spirit vessel," I repeated, nodding. This whole conversation might be making my head spin, but at least I could handle the terminology. Good for me. Twisting my paper napkin around one finger, I asked, "So what does the spirit vessel do?"

"It binds me to whoever holds it, and lets that person use my magic for themselves."

Oliver was watching me closely now. His fingers were pressed together so forcefully that the tips had gone white.

"You don't mean . . . do you mean me? This is magic I can use?"

"Yes," he said easily, but his eyes still searched mine for a reaction.

I licked my lips. "Why me?"

"Because you found my ring," he replied patiently, like it was perfectly obvious.

I frowned at him. "Well, sure. But I found it by accident."

"Most people do," he said.

"Oh." I shifted in my seat, all too aware of the ring's presence in the pocket of my jeans. I'd been wrong. Tom's definitely wasn't the appropriate place to talk about things like this. "So, what now? What do I do?"

"Well," he said, holding my gaze steadily with those intense green eyes, "you could give the ring back to me, and forget any of this ever happened. Or you could tell me what you want me to do for you."

I paused. He hadn't offered me this choice back in the girls' bathroom. What had changed between then and now? Why was this supposed magic suddenly at my disposal?

"Okay," I said, pressing my flimsy napkin between my hands. "Let's say I kept the ring. Theoretically. And let's say all this magic stuff is for real. Again, theoretically. What could you do? If I asked?"

"Well, there are limits," he said, almost apologetically. "Like, I can't change the past, and I can't see the future. But other than that, you can ask me for any three things you want. And if I have enough power for them, I'll give them to you."

Something slid into place in my head. "Wait. Did you just say three things?"

He nodded slowly, watching me begin to understand.

"Are you . . . ?" But I couldn't quite bring myself to say the word. It was too impossible—and I would feel too stupid if he told me I was wrong.

"I'm a genie." Oliver's face shone with pride. "Which means I have the power to grant you three wishes. Now, where are my waffles?"

As if on cue, our waiter returned with our food. Oliver used the side of his fork to cut his waffle, and I watched as he carefully assembled each forkful, making sure to have at least one taste of each topping on every bite. He set the cherry aside. I wondered if he was going to save it for last.

So we were still going to eat a meal, like normal people. Okay, I could do that. But when I picked up my burger, I realized my hands were unsteady. So I went for the French fries instead, dipping them in ketchup, chewing them slowly, and watching Oliver the whole time.

"Good fries?" asked Oliver, about halfway through his waffle. He was a hell of a fast eater.

"Uh-huh," I managed.

"Can I steal one?"

That was it. Claiming to have mystical, supernatural powers was one thing, but doing so while eating my food was quite another.

"Okay, you said you're a *what*?"

"A genie," he said, lowering his fork to his plate.

"Right," I murmured. "So, genies are real. You are a genie. I get three wishes. Okay. What else? Do you live in a bottle?"

"No," he said, sounding almost offended. "I live in an apartment."

"Oh. Sorry."

There was a pause.

"Are you seriously telling me the truth about all this?" I asked.

"I seriously am," he replied. "I was also serious about stealing a fry."

"Oh, for heaven's sake, take the fries. Have as many as you want. But, I mean, you don't look like a genie."

He raised an eyebrow. "You mean I'm not blue and I don't sound like Robin Williams?"

"That's not what I meant," I said.

He grinned at me.

"Okay, fine, that's what I meant. But I mean, look at that movie. Aladdin rubs the lamp, right, and it's all fireworks and explosions, and out pops this genie, and you look at him and you go, 'Oh, hey, look, it's a genie.' But you? You look . . . normal."

"Except for when I disappear."

"Well, yeah, except for that. But how do I know——"

"How do you know I'm not going to wait for you to make a wish, and then point and laugh and tell everyone at school that you fell for it?"

I stared at him. Yes, it was exactly that. In fact, the thought was so true that it could have come out of my own mouth, if only I'd known how to phrase it accurately.

"Try it," he said, waggling his eyebrows conspiratorially. "Make a wish. I won't tell anyone, I promise."

I suddenly felt very small. "What, you mean right now?"

"Why not?" He popped a fry into his mouth. "I'm a genie, and you're a person who wants a whole bunch of stuff. Let's do this."

A trillion dollars. A mansion. A pony. What was I supposed to wish for, anyway? And how disappointed would I be if it didn't work?

"Ponies are hard to take care of," said Oliver, taking a few more fries. "Really messy, too. You'd be surprised how many people don't think of that."

"Wait, what?" I said, my heart suddenly racing as I sat up straight in my seat. "How did you . . . Do you read people's minds, too?"

"Not everyone's," he said, and a hint of pride flitted across his face again. "But yours, yes. When you picked up my ring, it opened a link between your mind and my magic. I can't see all your thoughts, but I can see the ones about wanting. The ones that might turn into wishes. That way, when you make your wishes, I can see the shape of the desire behind them. None of that stuff about wording things exactly right so your genie doesn't screw you over. You make a wish, I give you what you want. Easy as that."

Too easy, I thought, for the second time that night—but even as I thought it, I could feel curiosity stirring. There was something perversely fascinating about the idea of someone else being in my head. My ego stood at full attention, wondering what other thoughts Oliver could see.

"I could tell you, if you want," he said, which startled me. As cool as it might be to have him in my head, the one-sided conversation was definitely weird.

"Why not?" I said, throwing my hands up. "Go ahead."

He leaned forward in his seat, folding his hands neatly and cocking his head just so. The entire pose looked staged, right down to the thoughtful expression on his face, like this was a show he'd performed a thousand times before.

"Let's see. Well, first off, you want this conversation to be happening somewhere classier than a diner."

Oliver was absolutely right, but before I could tell him so, he gave a casual wave of his hand—and suddenly we weren't in the diner anymore. Where the tacky food cartoons had been, there were now panels of light wood, tastefully decorated with simple, bright paintings of flowers and trees. Soft light shone from candles in sconces, illuminating our food, which now rested on delicate china instead of cracked diner plates. Savory, mouthwatering smells emanated from the kitchen.

I put my hand against the seat to steady myself, but pulled it away again when my fingertips touched velvet instead of vinyl.

"What the," I breathed, half enthralled and half terrified. "What did you do?"

"I gave you what you wanted," he said smoothly. "Well, one of the things you wanted. I can also see that you want me to be lying, so you can finish your dinner and go home with everything back to normal."

He paused to let me reply, but I didn't. Nothing was going back to normal any time soon, whether I wanted it to or not.

"Next," he continued, "you want your family back to the way it was."

"Ha!" I said, pointing at him. "You're a year too late for that one. My family's already back to how it was."

He regarded me steadily for a moment, like he was trying to piece something together. After a moment he gave a huff of laughter and shook his head. "Oh, I see. My mistake. Well, you want Vicky's part in the musical, but everyone knows that. You also want everyone to think you're perfectly fine with the part you got instead."

I narrowed my eyes. "I *am* perfectly fine with it."

"If you say so," he said with a shrug. "You want to be closer to your mother than you are. You want to get accepted to a good college, so you can move away. You want to write your own music, so you aren't stuck putting your own spin on songs that have been sung by hundreds of other people before you—"

"Okay, okay, stop it," I said, forcing a laugh. "I believe you, all right? But can we get back to the part where this is not Tom's Diner? We were just in Tom's, and now we are in a fancy café."

"Yes we are," he agreed, smiling like it was the most natural thing in the world. "And I'm glad you believe me."

"I believe *something,* anyway," I murmured, pushing myself to my feet. An elegant older woman was smoking a cigarette, *Breakfast at Tiffany's* style, near the door, and I was struck with the sudden urge to go over there and become her best friend so we could sip coffee together and talk about our endless *ennui*. I wondered if the Eiffel Tower would be across the street, instead of the Exxon station.

But before I could figure out how to move my feet, our waiter appeared beside me. Except he was definitely not the same waiter as before. Standing as straight as a soldier, he wore an expensive-looking vest over a crisp button-down shirt, and regarded me with the benevolent patience of someone who knew exactly how to get a good tip.

"May I interest either of you in a glass of wine?" he asked.

"Wine?" I said. I'd had wine with my mom a couple of times, and I didn't like it much. But the cozy, elegant atmosphere of this place somehow made the idea of wine very appealing. "Wine . . . yeah . . . I mean no! No wine. Thanks, but we're fine."

The waiter nodded, and I watched him move toward the woman with the cigarette. He said something to her, and she laughed: the tinkling laugh of a black-and-white movie star.

"Go ahead," came Oliver's voice, cutting into my thoughts. "Pick any three things you want, and wish for them."

Finally I forced myself to look back at him. He was lounging in his seat like he owned the place—like a salesman trying to impress a customer. Except there was a nervous edge to his posture, and a sharpness in his eyes, that gave me pause. There was way more happening here than just a sales pitch from him and a yes-or-no answer from me.

I narrowed my eyes a little. "What's in it for you?"

"What?" he said, clearly taken aback.

"If I make three wishes, what's in it for you?" Reaching into my pocket, I pulled out the ring. I put it on the table in front of me, and it glinted in the candlelight. "Before, you wanted me to give this back. You weren't even going to tell me about the wishes, and now you're all, 'Make wishes and solve all your problems, and by the way, let's go to a fancy café!' Why? What do you get out of it?"

"A job well done," he said.

I laughed. "Please. I want a real answer, Oliver. I'm serious. Why did you do all this? Why do you want me to make three wishes?"

He raised his eyebrows. "Real answer, huh?" he said. I nodded, and he shifted anxiously. "All right, then. I like your wishes, Margo. The ones I can see in your head. I want you to make three wishes because after I leave this place, I won't be able to grant wishes again for a very long time. Maybe forever. And if that's the case, then, well, I want the last wishes I grant to be good ones."

Now it was my turn to be startled. "Good ones? Wait. Why do you need to leave? Didn't you just transfer to Jackson High a couple months ago?"

"I did. And I need to leave because there's someone looking for me, and I . . ." He paused for a breath, then said carefully, "I'd rather he didn't find me."

"Who is it?"

Oliver shifted in his seat. "He was my master once. And a friend, at least for a while. I granted two wishes for him, but he returned my ring without making a third. He said it wasn't time yet."

I peered at him. "But it's time now?"

"Yes."

"And I'm guessing his third wish won't be of the happy, spar-kly, cupcakes-for-everyone variety."

"You could say that."

"So why wait?" I asked, exasperated at how little sense he was making. "Why are you sitting here with me, instead of hiding?"

"For the reason I told you," he said with a soft smile. "Well, that and the logistical stuff."

"Logistical stuff?"

"Sure. The moment you picked up my ring, it bound me to you. So until you make three wishes or give the ring back to me, my magic and I are yours to command. I can't leave until then. Like I said: logistics."

His tone was light, but that serious edge still lingered around his eyes. He was here because he was trapped here, that was what he was saying. Suddenly, the candlelight and fancy décor were terribly distracting.

"Take me back," I said immediately. "The diner. I want the diner again. Take me back, okay?"

Alarmed, Oliver waved his hand again. The French café thing vanished, and I was surrounded once again by vinyl seats, cartoon food, and useless jukeboxes. I made myself breathe. Oliver watched me uneasily.

"Are you serious about wanting to grant wishes for me?" I asked. "Instead of, you know, running away?"

He nodded, relaxing again. "I was. Still am. I mean, the sooner the better, obviously, but . . . yes."

"How soon?"

He lifted his wrist, like he was checking an invisible watch. "Five minutes ago?" he said, with a little laugh that I didn't quite believe.

I bit my lip, more torn than I could say. Make three wishes now, when my brain was full to bursting and I could barely think, or lose my chance to make wishes at all.

"Vicky had your ring before me, didn't she," I said. It wasn't a question, but he nodded anyway. "So why not just let her wishes be the last ones you grant?"

"Why not indeed," he said, an edge of bitterness in his tone. "Well, she made a wish that . . . let's just say she wasn't happy with the result. But instead of letting me fix it, she abandoned my ring. That's when you found it," he added hopefully.

So she'd made crappy wishes, and he wanted me to do better. No pressure at all. I shook my head. "Listen, Oliver, thanks for all this—the mind-reading, the teleporting-me-to-a-café thing, the wishes—but I can't do it. Not this fast. If you want me to keep the ring and make wishes, then I will, but I have to make a plan first."

"A plan?" he said, raising his eyebrows.

"Yes," I said firmly. "I can't just pull wishes out of thin air, you know? I need time to think about them."

"How much time?"

"I don't know! Just . . . time. A day or two, maybe." I paused, taking in his troubled expression. "And you obviously don't have a day or two. Look, you said you can leave if I give the ring back to you. So here's me, giving it back."

I pushed the ring a few inches toward him. He looked at it with suspicion, but didn't move to take it back.

"Go ahead," I said. "It's your choice."

He was silent for a moment as he studied me with a gaze so keen that I found myself fighting the urge to sink down in my seat. "A day or two won't kill me," he mused thoughtfully. Then he smiled—a small, hopeful smile that spread slowly until it reached his eyes and made them shine.

"I think you should keep it."

Chapter FOUR

"If you had three wishes," I asked Naomi, after we'd finished our in-class assignments in French the next day, "what would you wish for?"

"Random," she said, resting her chin in her palm. "Probably the usual stuff. Winning the lottery, finding true love, world peace. What about you?"

"I don't really know," I replied, which wasn't exactly the truth. I had some ideas, most vague, one very specific. But world peace—I hadn't even thought of that. Should I wish for world peace? That's what any decent person would do, right?

"Then why'd you ask?"

Because if I'm going to be the sort of person who believes in magic, I want to do it right. But obviously I didn't say that. What I did say was, "Just curious. I watched *Aladdin* last night."

That part was true. I'd dug out my DVD last night after dinner, which had thrilled Mom. She and Dad had raised me on a steady diet of all the Disney classics, and she was quick to turn my hour and a half of genie research into a full-blown popcorn-fueled family night, just like when I was a kid. Not that any of the research paid off, of course. Aside from a few interesting wish ideas—I mean, who wouldn't want their own pet monkey?—all I'd ended up with was a weird dream about Oliver Parish piling baklava on top of me, then vanishing in a puff of blue smoke.

She grinned. "Aw, I love that movie. Hey, remember my Princess Jasmine costume? Second grade, right? I won the costume contest that year."

The memory of Naomi in a blue tiara and poofy pants made me laugh. Which, of course, brought Mlle Bernstein slinking suspiciously over to our desks. She gave extra credit assignments to Naomi and me, mostly to keep us quiet until everyone else finished. That was fine by me. I was counting down the minutes until the bell rang and I could find Oliver in the hallway, and the extra work kept me from watching the clock.

World peace. Huh.

When French finally ended, I darted into the hallway—and there was Oliver, waiting for me just outside the door, wearing a backpack and the same gray hoodie.

"Hey!" I said, a little bit taken aback. "I was just about to come find you."

"I know," he replied. My confusion must have shown on my face, because he grinned down at me. "You want to make a wish."

I narrowed my eyes. "You can read my mind from three classrooms away?"

He laughed. "Hey, don't look at me like that, okay? I wasn't eavesdropping or anything. I just sort of . . . overheard you. So what'll it be? I have a few minutes before Brit Lit if you want to wish right now."

"Whoa, whoa." I held a defensive hand up. "Calm down, okay? I thought you said you'd give me time."

A frown creased his forehead. "But you want—"

"I know what I want," I interrupted, letting out an exasperated laugh. "And for the record, I still think it's weird that you know it, too." I paused. "You do know how weird it is, right?"

"It's pretty weird," he said seriously, though there was a hint of a smirk around his eyes.

I smiled. "As long as we're on the same page. Anyway, yes, I do have a wish. Three, in fact," I said, lowering my voice as some girl I didn't know passed close enough to brush my shoulder. "And I want to run them by you first, so I don't screw them up. But preferably somewhere not in the middle of school."

"Hey McKenna, you coming?"

Naomi was already halfway down the hallway, and she looked impatient. She and I always walked to chemistry together after French, but I hadn't thought to ask her to wait for me today. "Oh! Sure, right, um. Naomi, you know Oliver, right?"

"Sure," she said briskly, walking back to us. "How's the yearbook coming along? Got enough pictures yet?"

"Mm-hmm," he said, shoving his hands into his pockets and letting his hair fall into his face. "But, you know. Always room for more. I mean, not in the yearbook. There's only a four-page spread there. But for the slide show, and for me. I'm, um, kind of a perfectionist, I guess?"

I frowned as I watched him. Naomi nodded and asked him something else, and he mumbled his reply without quite looking her in the eye. Granted, a lot of guys had that reaction to Naomi, but this was different. It was like watching Superman turn into Clark Kent. What was his deal?

"So, call me after school?" said Oliver. "We can talk before tonight's rehearsal."

"Hmm?" I said, refocusing my thoughts as I sensed words directed at me. "Oh. Yeah, sounds good."

"Cool," he said. Shooting me a secretive grin from under his unruly bangs, he darted into the hallway traffic. As I watched him go, a stray thought meandered into my head. It went like this: *Wow, his eyes are really pretty when he smiles.*

"What was that?" said Naomi, her shrewd gaze locked on to Oliver's retreating figure.

"What?" I said innocently, even though I already knew the answer.

"You and Parish, obviously," she said, rolling her eyes at me. "I know flirting when I see it, McKenna. Never thought you'd go for a sophomore, but I'm not one to judge. Younger guys are so deliciously *malleable*."

"It's nothing like that," I told her. "There's no flirting. We're just friends." But for some reason, even though that was the truth, knowing Oliver's secret made it feel like a lie.

"Too bad," she said, and looked back down the hall, where Oliver had disappeared into the crowd. "I thought maybe you were finally moving past your mooning-over-Simon phase."

I winced. "Am I that obvious about Simon?"

"Oh, sweetheart," she said, slinging an arm around me and propelling me toward our next class. "Don't make me answer that."

Chapter FIVE

As soon as school was over, I called Oliver from the park. Bundled in my coat and gloves, I touched the ring and leaned against my car to wait for him. In about four seconds, he appeared a few feet away from me, wearing snow boots and a puffy jacket, just like mine—only mine was bright blue, like my car, and his was gray, like his hoodie.

For a moment I wondered if the hoodie had magically turned into a jacket. But that was just dumb.

"Want to walk for a bit?" he asked smoothly, without any of the awkwardness from earlier. But when he saw me staring at him, he grew shifty again. "What?"

"Nothing," I said quickly. "Actually, that's not true. It's just . . . you're different, somehow, depending on who's around. You went all flaily and awkward around Naomi this afternoon, but now that it's just me, you're . . . and at the diner last night, you were all suave and debonair and 'Look at me, I'm a genie and

I'm so awesome,' and . . ." I trailed off with a shrug. "You know what I mean."

"Did you just call me debonair?" he said, blinking in astonishment.

"Never mind," I said, feeling my cheeks go hot. "Yeah, let's walk."

Hamilton Park was popular for picnics in the summer and sledding in the winter, but right now it was empty, probably because of the unappetizing expanse of slush covering the ground. But it was nothing my Doc Martens and Oliver's snow boots couldn't handle.

"So," said Oliver, after we'd taken a few minutes to let the wintry quiet sink in. "You have a plan for your wishes?"

"That I do," I said, kicking at a little mound of snow. "I was thinking, if I have three wishes, at least one of them should be something for someone else, right?"

He looked at me curiously. "If you want."

"I do want," I said. "I mean, it seems to be the done thing. So, how about this: I keep one for myself, wish for world peace with the second—"

"Whoa, wait a second," he said, holding up a finger. "You want me to give you world peace?"

"Um . . . yes?"

Closing his eyes, Oliver turned his face to the sky and let out a laugh. "If I had a dollar for every time I heard that one."

"Really?" I said, suddenly feeling very wrong-footed.

He looked back at me again, eyes shining with mirth. "Really. Don't get me wrong, I'd grant that wish in a heartbeat if I could. But I don't have enough magic for that. Not nearly. Even if I lived to be a hundred thousand years old, I wouldn't have enough."

"Oh. I didn't know. Sorry."

"Don't worry about it," he said, and started walking again. I followed. "What about the third?"

"Well," I began hesitantly. I'd been so sure of this, ever since Naomi had given me the world peace idea in French class. But now that he'd shot it down, the whole plan felt unstable. Still, I went ahead and told him:

"I figured I'd use the third one to wish you free."

When I'd planned this conversation with Oliver, I'd assumed he'd be happy about the idea. Maybe even elated. But as I watched, his face drained of color. "Don't," he said. "It doesn't work like that. Just . . . please don't."

"What? Why?"

One of his hands drifted up toward his collarbone, and his face was pale and terrified. Haunted. I actually turned around to see if there was something scary behind me. There wasn't.

"Oliver," I said, alarmed. "What is it?"

Oliver didn't answer. But then he winced, his whole body going tense. "If you wish me free," he said shakily, "you'll unbind me from my ring. It would kill me."

"Kill you?" I whispered, struck dumb by the simple finality of his answer. "But . . ."

"But nothing," he said evenly, relaxing again. "You didn't know. Don't worry about it."

"Are you okay?" I asked warily.

He raised an eyebrow at me. "Of course. Why wouldn't I be?"

"Whenever I ask you stuff, you go all . . ." I mimicked the motion as best I could, squinting and squinching my shoulders up. "You keep doing that."

"Ah," he said.

I waited for him to elaborate, but when he didn't, I said, "What is it? Is something wrong?"

"Nothing's wrong. It's just a matter of questions and answers." I shook my head in confusion, and he went on. "When you ask me a question, I have to reply as honestly as I can. And as quickly. My magic usually gives me a second or two, depending, but not much longer." He trailed off with a shrug.

I frowned. "Not much longer before what?"

"Before it starts to hurt," he said shortly. "A lot. Come on, let's keep walking. It sounds like there's running water nearby."

"There's a stream over there," I said quickly, pointing. "I'm sorry. I didn't know it would kill you. I just assumed—"

He reached over to nudge my arm, smiling again. "Hey. I'm serious, Margo. Don't worry about it. So . . . stream?"

Right. He was trying to change the subject, which was downright generous of him, considering. "Stream," I said, walking toward the far side of the field. "I used to wade there in the summer, but I got so many cuts on my feet, my mom stopped letting me go in. But I did anyway, whenever she wasn't around."

The little stream was swollen with melted snow, which filled the quiet air with a gentle rushing sound. I sat on one of the wooden benches a few feet away from the water. The seat of my jeans felt damp almost right away, but I didn't care. Oliver sat gingerly beside me, and we watched the water swirling around the rocks in the streambed.

"So, aside from the obvious, what did Vicky wish for?" I said—and then realized I'd asked yet another question. "Crap, I'm sorry. You don't have to answer if you don't want to."

Oliver blinked owlishly at me, and for a moment I couldn't read his expression. "No, it's fine," he said finally. "It's not like . . . I didn't mean you should stop asking me things. Where'd that one come from?"

I shrugged. "All my wish ideas sucked, and I don't have a backup plan yet. I need inspiration."

Oliver gave me a sidelong look. "Well, she used her first wish on her dad. He was injured in a car accident last year, and his physical therapy wasn't going well. So she helped it along with a wish."

"Seriously?" I said, amazed. I hadn't known about Vicky's father, but the idea of a miraculous recovery was pretty awesome.

"Seriously."

"And then she wished for the lead in the play," I said flatly, looking at the ground.

"Actually, no, she didn't," he said. I looked up, confused. "Her second wish was for more people to like her. And believe me, that was a logistical nightmare to grant. See, she didn't want *everyone* to like her. She said that would be too weird. Just more people than before. I actually saw her thinking *seventy percent* when she made that wish. So at first, I thought about taking seventy percent of the world's population at random, and tweaking them just the tiniest bit, so they'd be inclined to like Vicky if they ever met her. But that's huge magic. Way beyond my power.

"So I changed Vicky instead. Not her personality, because that's not what she wanted, but the reaction she inspires in people. I changed her so that seven out of every ten people she meets has a positive reaction to her. Wish number two? Granted." And with that, he leaned back on his hands, looking prouder than a cat.

"That's like magical math," I mused. "I didn't know it took that much work. Pretty damn cool. Although it would've been cooler if I were in that lucky seventy percent. Or if Miss Delisio weren't."

His grin faded, and I immediately felt bad for saying anything.

"Yeah, I know," he said. "You wanted that part. Everyone thought you would get it, too, including Vicky. I'm really, really sorry. I didn't realize it would work out that way."

I'm really, really sorry. Something about the cadence of that phrase brought a memory to mind. Oliver, on the day the cast list went up, looking at me with pity, saying how sorry he was. Me, wondering what the hell he was apologizing for.

Who are you?

Nobody.

He hadn't been anyone important to me, nor did he have any intention of ever being so, but he'd still wanted to apologize for what he'd done. Even if he hadn't meant to do it. There was something incongruously kind about that.

Oliver got up, looking away from me and stretching his arms over his head. It was a casual gesture, but the timing of it made me wonder what he'd seen in my mind just now.

"What about her third wish?" I asked quickly.

"She didn't use it. That's why I thought you were her, when you called me yesterday." He shot me a dark look. "She'd promised to use her third wish within a week, and instead of following through, she just abandoned me. Left my ring in the *bathroom,* of all places, without even telling me first."

"Why?" I asked, alarmed at his tone.

"I don't know!" he said, his hands curling into fists as he began to pace in front of the bench. "I tried asking her in school today, but she wouldn't answer. She just kept avoiding me." He stopped abruptly, turning a hard expression on me. "You have to understand, Margo, I'm good at what I do. I'm very, very good at it. But she . . ."

"She wasn't happy with her second wish," I supplied, remembering the band room fight.

"She's miserable," he said bluntly. "And of course she blames me for it. But she's the one who didn't set boundaries, so all I had to work with was the wording of her wish, and the images in her head of people smiling and being friendly and including her in things. And unless she learns how to deal with the effect she has on people, or uses her third wish to undo it, she's going to keep being miserable for the rest of her life." Then he sighed, letting his features soften again as he shook his head. "I'm sorry. I shouldn't complain about her to you."

"Why the hell not?" I said automatically. He looked sharply at me, his expression unreadable—and before I knew it, we were both laughing.

The tension broken, he extended a hand to help me up. I took it and stood, wriggling uncomfortably in my wet jeans. Maybe sitting down hadn't been the best idea.

"You know," he said softly, his eyes slightly downcast, "if anyone new had to find my ring, I'm glad it was you."

I felt myself blush.

"Uh-oh," said Oliver.

"I'm not blushing," I shot back, just a fraction of a second before realizing that he hadn't said anything about blushing. In fact, he wasn't even looking at me. Standing and turning around, he shaded his eyes with his hands and scanned the park. It was just as deserted as before.

"What-oh?" I asked, hoping he hadn't noticed my previous comment. Or that he'd be gentlemanly enough to ignore it.

"That felt like . . ." Trailing off with a sharp shake of his head, he took a couple of steps toward the middle of the field. I hung back, watching as he peered around the empty field. Splaying his fingers, he began to move his hands through the air, carefully, like someone feeling his way through a room in the dark. Or like a mime. Only less stupid-looking.

I watched him, fascinated, wondering what he was feeling for. I slipped my gloves off and pushed at the air, hoping I might be able to feel it, too. But all I felt was the cold, nipping at my fingertips.

Apparently I wasn't the only one. When Oliver turned back to me, he looked bewildered, and more than a little relieved. "I guess I imagined it."

"Imagined what?" I asked.

"A call. You know how you can call me with my ring? It felt like . . ." He crooked one of his fingers, and mimed using it to hook me through the chest and pull. "God, I'm getting paranoid."

"You mean a call for another genie?" I frowned. "I never even asked. There are other genies, aren't there?"

His face darkened, just for a moment. "Yes. And yes. But let's talk about that first wish of yours! The selfish one. What'll it be?"

"Ah, right," I said, thrown by the sudden change of topic, even if my wish was why we were here in the first place. I twisted my hands together, feeling very uncertain. It was one thing to think about what I wanted, what the result of the wish would be, what it would feel like once I had it—but it was another thing to say it out loud. I wondered if it would sound stupid. But I went ahead and said it: "I want to write music. *Good* music."

Oliver nodded thoughtfully. "I had a feeling you'd go for that one." He gave me a conspiratorial smile. "And don't worry, it doesn't sound stupid."

I waved away his comment with one hand, like that had never even been a concern. "So what now? Is there a ceremony or something?"

He pursed his lips, looking very serious. "Well, there's a special hat you have to wear, made of ferns and cat food cans and glitter. And then—" He stopped abruptly, wincing, and looked accusingly at the sky. "For heaven's sake, I was *kidding*. No, there's no ceremony."

"Good thing, too," I said quickly, before the light mood could disappear again. "The cat food cans are no problem, but I was wondering where we'd get ferns in March."

Oliver paused, narrowing his eyes like he was plotting something. "Wait here," he said, and vanished. A handful of seconds passed. A handful more. Then, right before I could start to worry, Oliver was there again, a couple of feet in front of me. In one hand, he clutched the thin stem of a many-fronded plant.

"Is that . . . ?"

He nodded, holding it out so I could take it. "There's a great little greenhouse, just south of San Diego. Not very busy at this time of day."

I blinked at him. "And you went there? In like fifteen seconds?"

"Yeah," he said, with a dismissive wave of his hand. "Just a little trick I can do."

I shook my head mutely, turning the fern over in my hand. It was a perfectly ordinary fern, but . . .

"Just a little trick, huh?" I said faintly.

"Yup." He raised a sly eyebrow at me. "What, was that too debonair for you?"

With a laugh, I reached up and placed the fern on my head. "No such thing as too debonair. So, my good man, where do we begin?"

Oliver grinned in approval. "You need my ring, dear lady." I dutifully pulled it out of my pocket and presented it to him. "Now, it'll work as long as you're holding the ring, like you do when you call me—but it'll be more powerful if there's contact between us. If I'm touching you, I'll be able to dig deeper into your intentions when you make the wish, so I can make it as close as possible to what you really want. Can I . . . ?"

He tentatively reached his hands out, the question reflected on his face. I blinked in surprise. We both went to a school where everyone hugged and backslapped and high-fived each other without a second thought, and here he was, actually asking permission to touch me. Oddly charmed, I nodded and held my hand out to him.

He touched me slowly, his forefinger against mine—and when his skin made contact, I realized why he was being so cautious. With a yelp, I jerked away.

"What was that?" I asked, looking uneasily at the offending finger. "That was like—like static or something." Except it wasn't. I'd experienced plenty of static shocks, and this was different somehow. Warmer. More fluid.

"It's magic," he explained, running his thumb over each of his fingertips in turn. "I know it feels a little weird, but . . . is it still okay? I don't have to touch you, if you don't want me to. It's just better if I do." He held his hand out again, more tentatively this time.

"No, it's fine," I said quickly. "Just . . . warn me next time I'm in for something like that, okay?"

He nodded firmly. "Consider this your warning, then."

I held out my hands, and he eased them into a cozy, rounded shape that cradled the ring at its center. He held them steady with the pressure of his own palms, and warmth flowed from his skin into mine—far more than just body heat. More like the heat you feel on your tongue after eating something spicy. It almost tingled.

When I'd asked, half jokingly, about a ceremony, I'd been

thinking vaguely of candles and incense and Persian rugs. But this secret warmth that we held, while the March air hung still and cold around us—this felt like a ritual too. Like the whole world was bending toward us, listening, waiting to see what we'd do next.

When I looked up at him, his green eyes were dark, solemn, and every bit as warm as the magic that flowed from his hands. "Go ahead," he told me.

I swallowed. This was it. "I wish," I said, and paused to clear my throat when my voice faltered. "I wish to be a talented song-writer."

And just like that, my part was over. Oliver closed his eyes and breathed deeply. He was silent, and for a moment I wondered if I'd done it right. Should I have been more specific? Should I have defined what I thought of as talented, or mentioned lyrics in particular? Was there a script for this?

But then the ring started to heat up. Oliver stood solemn and still, but every time he breathed in, the ring grew a little bit warmer. His fingertips kept tingling, and the ring became uncomfortably hot. It began to burn. I wanted to drop it, but I knew I shouldn't. So I concentrated on my wish. On how it might feel to shape my thoughts into meaningful melodies and honest lyrical phrases. To play them for other people. To sing my life out loud.

Just when I thought the ring would become too painful to

hold, Oliver opened his eyes. He pressed my hands together with his, and when he did, the air shimmered around us. Just for a split second. Then everything went back to normal. The ring had become cool again.

He let his hands fall away from mine. He looked tired. Tired, but sated. "Now *that's* the kind of wish I'm talking about," he said, eyeing me appreciatively. "Thank you for that."

"For what?" I said as that strange warmth seeped out of my hands, leaving them open to the cold air. I shivered and tucked them into my pockets.

"For letting me grant your wish, of course," he said, rubbing his hands together.

I looked down at myself, like maybe the results of the wish would be visible somehow. They weren't. "Is it done?" I asked.

"The ceremony is complete," he intoned. His eyes flicked upward. "So you can probably take that fern off your head."

I'd forgotten all about that. With a little laugh, I shook my head backward, letting the fern fall to the ground. Then I thought better of it and picked it up. It felt like something I should keep.

"Sun's going down," I said, clasping my hands together around the plant's stem. "What time is it? I have to be at rehearsal by seven."

"You've got time. I can leave you alone, if you want to go home and try out your wish." He paused. "Unless . . ."

"Unless what?" I asked, ready to remind him that since he'd turned down my world peace idea, I didn't have a second wish yet.

But it wasn't that at all. "Unless you want to get something to eat. With me, I mean."

I looked sharply up at him, fully expecting to see the confident smile that seemed to be his default around me. But there was a little crease between his brows, and a hint of uncertainty hovered in his eyes. He seemed genuinely anxious about my answer. I wondered what that meant.

"Something to eat," I said, rushing to fill the silence that had begun to stretch between us. "Sure. I don't have any plans, so . . . diner? I can get hot chocolate. Day in the snow equals hot chocolate. That's how I roll. The more marshmallows, the better."

"And I can get those waffles again," he said. The confident smile returned, this time with a distinct edge of relief. "My lady, may I escort you to your carriage?"

"You may," I said with a laugh. I turned to head back toward my car, but Oliver's hand stopped me in my tracks. Oliver's bare hand, which was now extended toward me, palm up, silently offering to hold mine.

The strange shock of his touch was still fresh in my mind, but that wasn't why I hesitated. Unlike before, this wasn't about a genie sharing his magic with me. This was about a boy wanting to hold my hand. Such a simple thing. So why did it feel so huge?

Oliver's skin was still warm, even though there wasn't a wish waiting to be granted. That strange, spicy-tingly heat spread through my fingers again, and I squeezed his hand a little as we walked. Maybe it was just a reaction to him being inside my head, or to feeling him use his magic, but I suddenly found myself thinking about his pretty eyes, and wondering what it would be like to kiss him. I wondered if his lips felt like magic, too.

He glanced curiously at me, and I remembered: He could hear what I wanted. Our eyes locked, and my heart leaped into my throat. What *did* I want? Did he know, when I wasn't sure? Was that even possible?

But then he drew his head back a little, blinking rapidly. And just like that, the moment was gone. He smiled at me again as he belatedly returned the hand-squeeze, but it was a friendly smile, nothing more.

Chapter SIX

When Oliver and I arrived at the theater, nearly the entire cast was already there, filling the room with the low hum of chatter. Naomi and Miss Delisio sat on the stage, writing in identical binders. Simon gestured wildly at MaLinda Jones, who was laughing appreciatively at him. And over in the corner, Vicky hovered near the piano, singing something as George accompanied her.

As we walked down toward the stage, Vicky looked up and caught my eye. Her gaze shifted to Oliver, then back to me. Something hardened in her expression. She stumbled over a lyric. For a moment, I was certain she'd march up to me and demand that I return the ring. I fought the urge to halt in my tracks or, worse, to turn and run.

But Vicky just pressed her lips together, adjusted her glasses, and turned back to the piano. Bewildered, I turned to Oliver, just in time to catch frustration flitting across his face. He composed himself quickly, but that tiny look had already given him away. She didn't want her third wish, and that offended him—which made sense, considering how proud he was of his magic. But who in her right mind wouldn't want a third wish, even if only to set the second one straight? Had something happened between them?

As I put my things down, I kept my eye on Vicky, waiting until George was finished with her before I pounced. "Hey, can I talk to you?"

She didn't look at all surprised that I'd approached her. Giving me a wan smile, she said, "Hey. Sorry I had to leave rehearsal yesterday. I felt sick."

"Oh," I said. With everything else going on, I'd totally forgotten about her leaving early. "Right. Well, I'm glad you're feeling better, but that's not actually—"

"I don't want to talk about it," she said, brushing past me and plopping herself in an empty seat.

I blinked, taken aback by the firmness of her tone. I tried again: "But the ring—"

"I'm serious. I don't want to talk about it. Leave me alone." She paused, her shoulders hunching almost imperceptibly. "Okay?" she added, looking meekly up at me.

I started to say something else, but Vicky had spoken loudly enough that a few people were now looking at us, waiting to see what would happen next. Simon was among them. Knowing that anything else I did would just make me look needlessly aggressive, I threw my hands up and walked away.

Oliver shot me a questioning look, but I just shook my head.

Almost as soon as I reached my seat, Miss Delisio quieted us and started the rehearsal. I climbed onto the stage, took a deep breath, and tried to get into character—into Toby mode—the way I'd been practicing. Steady my hips. Bring my shoulders forward a little bit. Hold my chin up. Try to ignore how Vicky was avoiding my eyes.

But as Miss Delisio walked us through the song that opened Act Two, and we wrote down our blocking in our scripts, a camera flash distracted me. Just two days ago, that flash had been nothing but a nuisance, but now it meant something entirely different. Oliver was watching me. I wondered what he was seeing. The camera flashed again and again, sometimes in my peripheral vision, sometimes in my eyes.

Once, it came from right above my head.

Nobody else seemed to notice it, but I looked up just in time to see Oliver perched on the catwalk, just below the ceiling. He grinned, gave me a little wave, and then vanished. Two seconds later, he strolled out of the wings and into the audience, like nothing unusual had happened.

A little while later, Miss Delisio announced a ten-minute break, and I headed immediately for the water fountain. "What were you giggling about back there?" came a voice from beside me, just as I reached the theater door.

I grinned, expecting to see Oliver falling in step with me—but no, it was Simon, all shiny hair and baggy clothes and confidence.

For the first time in recorded history, I was actually disappointed to see him.

"What do you mean, giggling?"

Simon jerked a thumb over his shoulder at the theater. "Back there, dude. You were giggling at the ceiling like a stoner."

"Oh," I said, thinking happily of Oliver on the catwalk. "Nothing. Just having a moment."

"Right on," he said. I turned down the hall, fully expecting him to leave it at that, but to my surprise he followed me. "Ladies first," he said when we reached the water fountain, making a sweeping gesture toward the dinky little spout.

Suppressing a grin, I bent to take a quick drink, then stepped aside so he could do the same. But he just looked at me, like he was trying to figure out how to say something. For one crazy moment, I found myself hoping it would be something along the lines of: "You know how it's almost the one-year anniversary of that time we made out? Let's do it again to celebrate."

Instead he asked, "What do you think of Vicky?"

I blinked at him. "Oh."

"What?"

"Nothing."

"Well?"

I hesitated, weighing honesty against diplomacy. Diplomacy won. "She's getting better."

Simon let out a bark of laughter. "I guess so. Hey, you think she's going out with that Oliver kid?"

I laughed before I could stop myself. "No. No, she's definitely not."

He frowned. "Really? You sure?"

"Very sure. But I can see why you thought she was. I thought that, too, at first." Simon looked pensive, and suddenly I realized what he was getting at. My shoulders slumped, and I sighed in annoyance. "Look," I said, keeping my voice as even as I could, "if you want to ask her out, then do it, but leave me out of it. I'm not gonna be your wingman."

"My wingman?" he echoed blankly. "Oh, no way, I wasn't gonna ask her out. She's way hot, sure, but so not my type."

I raised an eyebrow. "Then what do you care who she's dating?"

"I don't, not really." He shoved his hands into the pockets of his jeans. "I dunno. I just thought they were a weird couple."

"Because of him, or because of her?" I asked.

"Both," he said with a grin. "But mostly him. I mean, say what you want about Vicky, but at least she, like, talks to other people."

As opposed to Oliver, who didn't?

"Hm," I said.

"I mean, seriously," said Simon, rolling his eyes. "Does that kid have any friends at all?"

He's got me, I thought protectively, but kept it to myself. Ever since the wish this afternoon, my brand-new friendship with Oliver had begun to feel like something private. Something for my eyes only. So I shrugged and said, "No idea."

I kept an eye on Oliver for the rest of rehearsal, and from

what I could see, Simon was right. He kept to himself, took pictures now and then, and didn't talk to anyone. But then again, he seemed perfectly content that way, so what was the big deal?

When Miss Delisio finally dismissed us, Oliver asked if he should come along while I tested the results of the wish I'd just made, and for a moment I honestly didn't know how to answer. But the thought of Oliver watching and listening as I fumbled my way through brand-new lyrics and half-formed musical phrases, even if they turned out to be brilliant, was nothing short of terrifying.

Before I could figure out a polite way to tell him no, he nodded. "Don't worry about it," he said. "Just think about that second wish, okay?"

Slinging my backpack over one shoulder, I smiled at him. "I had a feeling you'd say that. I promise I'll think about it, and I promise I'll call you as soon as I have a new plan, okay?"

"Sounds good." A wistful smile shaded his face, and he said, "Have fun writing."

"Thanks," I said. We looked at each other for a moment. "I'm sorry about, you know, not wanting you around while I write. It's not you. It's just—"

"You want to make sure your songs are perfect before you show them to anyone," he finished smoothly. And accurately. "Like I said, don't worry about it. I really do understand." With one last smile, he put his camera into his coat pocket and slipped out of the theater.

Much to my lack of surprise, I was the first one home, even though it was nearly ten o'clock at night. I vaguely remembered Mom telling me about some fancy benefit dinner for one of the women who owned her company, which probably meant she and Dad would come home around two in the morning, dressed in fancy clothes and giggling too loudly. This was not uncommon for them, and it annoyed me every single time—but at least it meant I had the house to myself.

I put my stuff away as fast as I could before dashing up to my room, where my guitar was tucked away in its case under my bed. I unpacked and tuned it, then settled it on my knees. Then I remembered: my lucky pick.

Setting my guitar aside again, I darted over to my dresser, where I pulled open the bottom drawer of my jewelry box—the padded drawer made for holding rings. The one ring I had was currently safe in my pocket, so the drawer was empty, except for a single red guitar pick.

It wasn't anything special to look at, just a regular pick with a logo so worn that I couldn't even read it. But it had once belonged to Neko Case, my absolute favorite singer of all time. I'd spotted it lying at the edge of the stage after a concert a few years ago. Not yet knowing that people collected their favorite musicians' picks as souvenirs, I'd found a security guard and asked how I could give it back to Neko.

The guard had laughed at me, not unkindly. "Keep it, honey," he'd said. "Maybe you'll use it on that stage one day."

He'd probably been kidding, of course, but at the time I was floored. How had he known that I dreamed of being up there, too? Either he was psychic, I'd decided, or it was fate. So I'd put it in my jewelry box, telling myself that I'd use it when I could write songs that would make my favorite singer proud.

Holding the guitar in my lap and the pick in my fingers, I took a deep breath—and an image sprang into my mind. An image of tonight's rehearsal, at the exact moment I'd caught sight of Oliver up on the catwalk, and he'd smiled at me, and the cavernous theater had suddenly compressed itself into a tiny little universe that held only the two of us.

I grinned at the memory. And suddenly, the words came.

It was effortless. Clear, sharp phrases poured out of me, pushed forward and forward and forward by a guitar that suddenly seemed to have a life of its own. A verse, and second verse, a bridge and a guitar solo, a third verse, and another half verse that drifted into an unexpected ending. All within less than twenty minutes.

I opened my eyes. I didn't remember them closing, but I opened them. That was a song. It wasn't a finished song, not by a long shot, but it was a song that felt . . . real. Honest. Exhilarating, even.

How had I spent so many years singing songs written by other people? Musical theater songs, rock songs, folk songs, it didn't matter. Even the best of those songs had been shaped by minds other than my own, touched by other people long before I ever got to hear them. But now, for the first time, there existed a single piece of music that was mine and, until I chose to share it, mine alone.

I called it "Vertigo."

I spent Friday night and Saturday morning polishing "Vertigo" until it shone, and then headed downstairs, still in my pajamas, to join my parents for lunch. We consumed sandwiches and small talk, and it wasn't long before I started itching to get back to my guitar. "Can I be excused?" I blurted out, interrupting Mom mid-sentence.

She'd been going over the details of a road trip she and Dad were planning, probably to visit one of his many heinous relatives—I hadn't been paying attention, so I wasn't sure—and now she just blinked at me, clearly surprised by my rudeness.

"Sorry, I just, um, I have a lot of homework," I said sheepishly. But as I closed my door and settled my guitar on my lap again, I wondered at the lie I'd just told. Why hadn't I just said I was writing music?

Maybe for the same reason I hadn't told them right away about the cast list. Because they wouldn't understand how delicate a thing it was. They might say "That's nice, have fun," and keep planning their road trip; or they might gush their excitement, stalk me upstairs, and make me play them something before I was ready. And there was no way I could predict which one it would be.

The worst part, though, was this: Not too long ago, I wouldn't have thought twice about telling Mom the truth. When it was just her and me, without Dad around, she'd always known how to react to stuff like this.

Now, though . . .

I frowned, trying out a quick series of chords on my guitar. Settling on a sound that felt right for the mood I was in, I sang experimentally: "I am not Hayley Mills."

Then I laughed out loud at the ridiculousness of it.

But ridiculous though it was, for some reason I couldn't let the idea go. So I sang it a few more times, fiddling with the melody until I had something that actually worked: a musical phrase as inherently silly as the lyric I'd paired it with. And then I kept going. But while the music remained light and fun, the lyrics slowly became less jokey and more honest, growing sadder and darker until they stood in stark contrast to the quirky, bouncy melody.

I wrote without even thinking, letting the words flow through me just as they had with "Vertigo." Only when I was done, and I'd written all the lyrics down from beginning to end, did I let myself look at them.

I am not Hayley Mills.
First of all, come on, I'm hotter.
I do not have, for another thing,
A double waiting in the wings,
To step in and be your long-lost perfect daughter.

That was the first verse. It was a first draft with a false rhyme, but I could fix that later. I skimmed past the second verse, the bridge, and the third verse, letting my eyes settle on the lines that sat alone, intentionally unrhymed, at the very end.

> *You were enough for me, back then,*
>
> *So why wasn't I enough*
>
> *For*
>
> *You?*

I read those lines over and over, murmuring the words to myself. They were desperately sad, maybe even emo, but that wasn't what bothered me. What bothered me was the blatant, severe *truth* of them. How long had I felt this way about my mom? Since the third honeymoon? The first?

Since the wedding?

And what other thoughts did I have lying dormant inside me, waiting to be revealed in song?

The songs kept coming, one after another after another. Some tended toward the emo, like "Hayley Mills," but most of them, like "Vertigo," were sly and peppy and fun. But all of them were honest and, more than that, all of them were *good*. I even recorded "Vertigo" and played it back on my laptop, just to make sure I wasn't letting the pleasure of singing influence my opinion of the song. I wasn't. I sounded great, and so did my guitar, and now that I'd polished the lyrics to a shine, I was insanely proud of them.

That was when I decided I needed an audience.

Oliver was the first person I thought of, but that idea still made me nervous. Even if he loved my songs, he would know they'd come from a wish. A wish he'd granted, no less. No, what I needed was a truly unbiased listener.

"Heya," I said, when Naomi picked up her phone after only two rings. "Listen, sorry, I know you probably already have plans for today, but—"

"Don't be sorry, babycakes," she said with a laugh. "As it happens, I did have plans, but my stupid boyfriend had to pick up a stupid extra shift at his stupid job. So I'm all yours, if you want me. What's up?"

So I told her. Twenty minutes later, she arrived at my door.

"That's an interesting new look, McKenna," she smirked, closing my front door behind her.

"Huh?" I said, trying not to shiver in the blast of cold air that followed her inside.

Her only reply was a critical once-over that took in my bare feet, my mismatched pajamas, and my hair, which pointed in about a thousand different directions. Yet another reason to be glad I hadn't called Oliver first.

"Oh, this?" I said, trying not to let my embarrassment show. "I call it Insomnia Chic. Admit it: You're jealous you didn't come up with it first."

"Totally jealous," she deadpanned, pulling off her coat to reveal a stylish cowl-necked sweater over form-fitting jeans. "So, what's this I hear about new songs?"

Naomi called out a quick greeting to my parents, who were in the kitchen doing something mysterious with eggplants, and we ran upstairs. She settled herself on my bed, and I sat on the floor with my guitar nestled in my lap. She looked expectantly at me, but I refused to be nervous. So what if there was no absent songwriter to blame if Naomi didn't like what I played? I'd planned this performance. I'd practiced my new songs until they'd become second nature. I would be fine.

Of all the songs I'd written this weekend, my favorite was "Hayley Mills," the one I'd written about my mom. But as much as I loved it, it was awfully depressing—so I'd chosen "Vertigo" to play for Naomi first. With my eyes firmly on my fingers, I took a deep breath and began.

Only when the last note faded did I allow myself to look up at Naomi again. She was frowning, almost like she was confused.

"I messed up some of the chords," I explained, setting my guitar gently on the carpet. "It's just nerves—"

"Girl, you did not write that," said Naomi, like she hadn't even heard me.

My stomach twisted uncomfortably. "What? Yeah, I did. Like two days ago."

"For real?"

"Yeah. What?"

Naomi stared at me. "It's just . . . that's really good. Like, *really* good. Why the hell haven't you played me your stuff before?"

I felt my cheeks glow with relief. It was one thing to think my own work was good, but it was another thing entirely to hear someone else say so. I got up and joined her on the bed.

"Because that was the first song I ever wrote that's actually worth showing to anyone," I said truthfully.

She gave a low whistle and shook her head. "Must be a hell of a guy."

"What? What guy?"

"The guy you wrote the song about. Who is it?"

I felt my face go bright red. "It's not about a guy."

"Yeah right it's not," she said. "There was all that stuff about someone being inside your head, and that one line about, what was it, fingertips? And then the one where—"

"Okay, okay, fine," I said, waving my hands at her. "It's about . . . someone. But it's mostly about space. The space around people, how it's different, depending on—"

"Is it Simon?" she interrupted. "Holy crap, McKenna."

"No, it's not Simon," I said with a laugh. "It's not about anyone in particular, really. Just a feeling."

Which was, of course, a blatant lie.

But she gave me a knowing nod. "Ahh. It's the Imaginary Boyfriend." I could practically hear the capital letters as she said it.

"The huh?"

"Imaginary Boyfriend. You know: The longer you go without an actual boyfriend, the more you think about what your ideal boyfriend would be like. And you've gone, what's it been, three years since you dated Joey?"

I shook my head at the memory. Joey Priori and I had been an item for a few months of freshman year, after his amazing talent-show cover of "Life on Mars" and before he moved away. Well, an item by ninth-grade standards. Basically, I liked that he could sing, he liked that I had boobs, and we both liked kissing.

"That wasn't dating," I said. "That was making out in empty classrooms."

"And feeling each other up under the bleachers," added Naomi, giving me an evil grin. She'd witnessed that particular incident firsthand—accidentally, she claimed—and probably wouldn't ever let me forget it. "Point is, it's been a while."

"True that."

"You should play it for Simon."

"I should *what?*" I sputtered.

She gave me a look. "Come on, McKenna. You've had this raging mega-crush on the guy like forever. So do something about it. Serenade him. The song might not be about him, but you could totally make him think it is, and—"

"And it would make me look pathetic and desperate," I finished firmly. "No way."

"Okay, okay," she said. "Hide your songs under a bushel if you must. But I'm not moving from this spot until I get more. So what else have you got?"

"Song-wise, you mean?" I asked hopefully. "You want to hear another one?"

"Very perceptive, Nancy Drew. Now entertain me."

Chapter SEVEN

When Monday rolled around, the idea of going to school and leaving my guitar behind was almost too painful to bear. So I left it in the backseat of my car until the last bell, and then carried it up to the auditorium. I had a few hours before rehearsal, and driving home would only take away from the time I could otherwise spend writing more music.

So I sneaked into the stage manager's booth, which was probably the most secluded place in the theater, aside from the dressing rooms. It wasn't much: just some tall wooden boards that someone had painted black, nailed together in order to make a box, and stuck in the wings, just offstage. There was a music stand with a small light clipped on, where Naomi would stand with her copy of the script so she could call tech cues and give us lines if we needed them.

During chemistry earlier, I'd scribbled down a few lyrics about getting caught under the bleachers, and a few more about first kisses. Now, sitting cross-legged on the floor beneath the music stand, I began setting them to music, wondering what kind of song I'd end up with this time.

When I thought to look at my watch again, it was almost time for rehearsal. Not enough time to start something new. So instead, I played through a couple of the songs I'd written over the weekend. And then I played "Vertigo," which was slowly overtaking "Hayley Mills" as my favorite, for a second time.

Just as I was coming out of the bridge of the song, I heard footsteps. I hushed the strings with my hand, ending the song a verse and a half early. Maybe Oliver had arrived, with those bright green eyes and warm, warm fingers. What would he say when I played "Vertigo" for him? Would he be able to tell it was about him?

Fighting my nerves down, I put my guitar away and stood up—and came face-to-face with George the Music Ninja, who was leaning over the side of the booth.

Somehow I managed not to drop my guitar case. "You scared me!" I hissed. "How long were you standing there?"

"Couple minutes. Sorry," he added, although he didn't look it. "Whose was that? Don't think I know it."

"Whose was what?"

"That song."

"Oh. Um. It's mine."

"No kidding," he said, eyebrows shooting up. "You got more?"

I nodded.

"I want to hear them."

"Now?"

He looked at his watch. "Whenever Cass lets you guys have a break."

"Oh, um . . . sure. Definitely."

"Good," he said. With that settled, he clomped off across the stage, leaving me staring after him.

I was going to play for George during our break. That meant I had two hours, or maybe less, to figure out how to be the sort of person who was not at all terrified of playing her brand-new original songs in front of a professional musician who fronted his own band. Sure. Yeah. No problem.

By the time I collected myself enough to venture back out into the theater, a bunch of people had arrived, including Naomi. Her eyes fell on my guitar case, and she sprinted over to me. "You little minx," she whispered. "You're totally playing for Simon, aren't you."

"You wish," I said. And hesitated. "Actually, I'm playing for George. During break."

"For the Ninja? Seriously?"

"He asked me to," I said, and explained about him spying on me.

Naomi shook her head in disbelief. "Well, if you need moral support, you just tell me when and where." She paused, giving me a sly grin. "Although if you and the Ninja want some alone time, I completely understand. Older guys are so deliciously *experienced*."

"Oh, stop it." I laughed, and she ran off to join Miss Delisio.

I put my case down with the rest of my stuff, and looked around for Oliver. He wasn't there yet. He still wasn't there when Miss Delisio called places for the top of Act One, which wasn't like him. I just hoped he'd show up in time for break.

The stumble-through was about as painful as its name implies. Most of the individual songs and scenes were okay, but this was our first time stringing them all together. Despite George's valiant efforts, the transitions were terrible. Ryan hadn't learned his lines yet, and thus made a highly unconvincing villain. And of course, Vicky still had all the acting skills of a robot.

When MaLinda Jones accidentally knocked over a junior ensemble boy during the haircutting contest scene, a very frazzled-looking Miss Delisio finally conceded that we needed a break. She gave us twenty minutes.

As everyone hopped off the stage, Naomi appeared at my side, clutching her binder and looking very much like a tired babysitter at the end of a long night. I gave her a sympathetic smile. She had her work cut out for her.

"Thank you, Miss Toby," she said, "for knowing your damn part."

I grinned. "My knowledge of my part, Miss Stage Manager, is all for you."

"It better be," she said fiercely. "Where's the Ninja? I need a musical reward for all this crap."

"And Oliver," I said, without thinking. "I kind of want him to hear, too."

Naomi just looked at me. I darted away in search of George, mostly so she wouldn't see me blush.

Oliver was still nowhere to be found, so five minutes later, it was only Naomi and George who followed me into one of the empty dressing rooms backstage.

At Naomi's request, I played "Vertigo" first, managing to screw up only one small section of the bridge. George bobbed his head along to the rhythm, almost like he could hear invisible drums. Naomi leaned forward, elbows on her knees, grinning like a maniac.

When the song was over, the room was quiet for a moment, which made me want to hide under the table in the corner. Would that happen every time I played for someone new? That weird moment of limbo that hung in the air after the music faded away?

But Naomi came to my rescue: "Awesome, right?"

"Nice," said George, a thoughtful frown on his face. "Real nice."

I felt my face break out into a huge, doofy grin as relief flooded my entire body. "Really?" I said.

Naomi wiggled her eyebrows at me.

"Got time for another one?" said George, whereupon I think my heart actually skipped a beat.

"Yeah," said Naomi, glancing at her watch. "Barely, but yeah."

So I took a chance and played "Hayley Mills," even though it was slow and not nearly as catchy as "Vertigo." George's frown deepened as I played, but I tried not to think about that. I thought about my family, and about the feeling of loneliness that had led to these lyrics in the first place. About yearning to be understood.

The song ended, and there was that moment of limbo again. But before anyone could break the silence, the dressing room door squeaked open. Startled, I dropped my pick. My now-empty hand tripped over the strings, making an ugly sound as I turned to see who had come in.

"Everyone all right in here?" asked Miss Delisio, eyeing me suspiciously.

George looked pointedly at his watch. "Thought you said twenty minutes, Cass."

"I did," said Miss Delisio, raising a stern eyebrow. "That was twenty-two minutes ago."

Naomi immediately started apologizing for all of us, and I quickly packed up my guitar. Like children who'd just been scolded by their parents, we filed quietly out of the dressing room—but George stopped me at the door. "Stay after for a minute, okay? When we're done?"

He barely waited for an answer, but I managed to squeak out a quick "Um, sure" before he brushed past me and followed the others back into the auditorium. Without saying anything more about my songs.

Luckily for me, Tobias Ragg didn't care what George the Music Ninja thought about a couple of dumb songs written by some girl named Margo McKenna. He cared about his own songs, and that was it. He sang like a boy with too much confidence, and he assumed everyone liked him. Knowing all of those things, and forcing myself to act them for the next hour or so, was what got me through the rest of our rehearsal—at least until I made my last exit.

As I slipped out of Toby mode and became myself again, I found an empty seat in the auditorium, where the rest of the cast was gathered to watch Simon and Vicky close the act with "A Little Priest." Simon was fantastic, but almost the entire song depended on Mrs. Lovett's comic timing. So, needless to say, it fell pretty flat.

Not that anyone seemed to notice. Everyone applauded like they'd just seen the greatest performance ever. Or maybe they, like me, were just grateful to have forced their way through an entire act for the first time. Either way, Miss Delisio gave us a big cheer, promised to give us notes at our next individual scene rehearsals, and let us go.

Only two weeks till the Act Two stumble-through.

As everyone left in a flurry of adrenaline and exhaustion, I ventured slowly toward George, who was sitting at the piano, penciling notes into his copy of the score. "Oh, good," he said when he spotted me. "Come here a sec."

"What's up?" I said, relieved to hear my voice sounding much calmer than the rest of me probably looked.

He stood up, crossing his arms and looking down at me. "I told you to be straight with me. About your songs. You weren't."

"Sorry," I said meekly.

"Don't be," he said curtly. "Thing is, it would've been real easy for me to just write you off after that. Assume you weren't serious about writing. You know? So it's a good thing I heard you play tonight."

"It is?"

"Yup." He tilted his head to the side, his dark eyes narrowed critically at me. "You're not really a theater kid, are you."

I frowned at him. "Sure I am. I've been in every show since freshman year."

"Sure, every musical," he said. "You do the plays too?"

"Well, no."

He flashed a lopsided grin at me. "Me neither. You get what I'm saying?"

I nodded slowly. "You're in it for the music, right? Just like me."

"Well, that and the paycheck. But still. Yeah. Take the music out of a musical, and what've you got? Filler."

I grinned. "Glitzy, jazz-handed, and in this case cannibalistic filler."

He laughed and plopped back down on the piano bench. "So here's the thing. My opener canceled."

"Your . . . huh?"

"For my gig on Saturday." I raised my eyebrows in a silent question, and George sighed. "Cass?" he called toward the wings. "You post about the South Star gig?"

The South Star? My ears perked up instantly. I'd never been

there, but I knew the name. Everyone played there. Indie musicians on their way to bigger places, big-name bands that wanted a break from the Manhattan clubs, and everyone in between. I had no idea George's band was already big enough to play in a place like that.

Miss Delisio poked her head around one of the black curtains. "Yup. Band website, Twitter, Facebook, so on, so forth."

As she disappeared behind the curtain again, I gave George an apologetic shrug. "I don't go online much. Sorry."

George smiled. "Me neither. No big deal. But we got a gig this Saturday, up in New York. State, not city. Y'all are invited. Might be twenty-one and over, though, I'm not sure. Anyway, point is, guys at this bar expect me to bring in an opener. Had this guy lined up, sort of folky acoustic guitarist, kinda like what you do, but he bailed."

George paused, and I bit my lip. I was pretty sure I knew where he was going with this, but I didn't even want to think it until he said it. But my heart was already beating faster than a healthy heart should. Finally, I couldn't take it anymore. "And?" I prompted.

He grinned. "And, you wanna come open for me? South Star Bar, Saturday night? Short set, maybe five, six songs. Use our equipment if you want. I have a spare pickup if you need one. Don't need to tell me now. Think about it, let me know tomorrow."

George turned back toward the piano and began to gather

his music books into his black backpack. For a moment, all I could do was gape at his leather-clad back and try to figure out whether or not he was serious. An opener? Me? But . . . for these guys? Simon had emailed me a copy of the first Apocalypse Later album, *Pirates Vs. Ninjas*, last fall. It was a blend of sea shanties and death metal, and Simon thought it was totally brilliant. I thought it was a little weird, but when I'd said as much to Simon, he'd rolled his eyes and told me it was a *concept* thing and I just didn't *get* it.

But George knew better than me what his fans wanted to hear, and I couldn't just stand there and not say anything, so I made myself choke out, "Are you kidding me? I mean, are you freaking *kidding* me?"

"I am not freaking kidding you," he replied.

"But are you——" This time I made myself stop. If I asked the same question too many times, eventually I might get an answer I didn't want. "I mean, of course. Yeah. Of course I'll do it."

Reality began to sink in as I crossed the parking lot to my car. This was too much. I'd decided on the songwriting wish because I'd thought it would be the perfect balance of fun and safe: a means of self-expression, but one that wouldn't actually change my life in any unforeseen way.

But unless I'd hallucinated the last ten minutes, I'd just been offered an opening gig at the freaking South Star Bar. If that wasn't life-changing, then I didn't know what was. And had I really said yes, just like that? Without even thinking about it first? Who the hell *was* I?

Of course, only an idiot would say no to an offer like that. Especially since everything had fallen so nicely into place, what with George just happening to overhear me, and his opener canceling. A perfect series of coincidences.

I frowned to myself, slowing down my steps as a tiny red flag waved somewhere near the back of my brain. Coincidences, my ass. Where was Oliver tonight, anyway?

A few feet away from my car, I set down my guitar case and hiked up my coat so I could reach into my jeans pocket. Taking off my gloves, I gripped the ring between my thumb and forefinger. Three seconds passed, and Oliver appeared, right under one of the parking lot streetlights. Dust motes danced in the light above him, making him look sort of unearthly. His dark, messy hair seemed to glow. I wondered if he'd positioned himself that way on purpose.

"I was waiting for you to call me," he said, smiling in a way that made my heart jump.

"Well, I was waiting for you to show up on your own," I countered. "You weren't at rehearsal. I didn't see you in school earlier, either."

He shrugged it off. "Vicky doesn't want to see me. And I only went to school in the first place to keep her company. So it's official. I am now"—he spread his arms dramatically—"a high school truant. I mean, unless *you* want me to go to school with you? You're my master now, after all, not her."

"I don't really care, honestly. You aren't in my classes anyway."

Oliver clapped his hands together, grinning broadly. "Hallelujah. You have no idea how sick I am of high school. Watch out, Jackson High: This truant is about to become a dropout."

"Damn," I murmured. "I guess if you're a genie, graduation isn't a priority, huh?"

"My job does have its perks," he said with a shrug. "So, wish number two?"

I sucked in a breath. "Oh crap. Actually, no, I'm sorry . . ."

Something tightened in his expression, making him look a hell of a lot less ethereal than he had a moment ago. "You promised," he said.

A loud wolf whistle reached my ears, and I looked sharply over to see a small knot of people a little ways across the lot. Someone gave us two thumbs-up. I squinted: the thumbs-upper was Simon, and he was walking with MaLinda, Ryan, and Jill, three other seniors from the cast. Oliver and I both stayed quiet, watching as they got into someone's car and drove off.

"I'm so sorry," I said, once they'd left. "I've just been so distracted by the songwriting stuff, and . . . I'm sorry. I really am. But I need more time."

He pressed his lips together, but didn't reply, which just made me feel worse.

"I'm sorry!" I said again. "It's just that the first wish is so amazing—"

"Is it?" he said, visibly perking up.

"Holy crap *yes!*" I gushed, grateful that he'd finally spoken. "It's the most awesome thing in the world. The awesomest thing that ever awesomed. Except *even more awesome*. I mean, what did you *do*? Just, like, fire up some lonely little neuron cluster in the back of my head?"

"Sort of." His posture was suddenly serious and intensely focused, like when he'd told me about the mathematics behind Vicky's second wish. "It's like . . . okay, it's like this. Picture a river. On one side, there's you, along with every idea and feeling that you've ever wanted to turn into a song. On the other side, there's the finished product that you want to create. I just built a bridge between the two, and gave your brain a little shove in the right direction."

"Wow," I said. "That's so . . ."

"Magical?" he suggested, spreading the fingers of one hand like a firework exploding. He was smiling again, thank goodness.

"I was going to say vague."

"It's a little vague," he agreed. "But it worked, didn't it?"

"Oh, it more than worked." I put a hand on my hip. "So, tell me how George the Music Ninja ended up being part of my wish."

"George?" said Oliver, his face contorting into an expression of exaggerated surprise. "Why, whatever do you mean?"

I fixed him with my best no-nonsense stare. "You know exactly what I mean. Three days ago, I couldn't write a song to save my life, and just now he asked me to play a professional gig with him. And don't try telling me all that stuff happened by itself, because there is no way."

"Oh, that," he said. "It was nothing. Just a little suggestion here and there. I *may* have put it into George's head that he should *maybe* pay attention to the girl playing the guitar before the rehearsal started. And I *may* have arranged for his original opener to land a headlining gig at another venue on the same night. It was just a matter of creating the right circumstances."

"But I didn't wish for all that," I said, alarmed by how blasé he was acting. "What's the catch?"

"There's no catch," he said. "You have to understand, my magic is bound by the actual words you speak, but as long as I don't directly contradict those words, I can embellish your wish as much as I want to. I saw in your mind that you want to impress George, and since that was in keeping with what you wished for, I figured, why not?"

Oliver was right. I did want to impress George—I'd wanted that ever since the day I'd first met him and seen firsthand how talented he was, and even more since he'd complimented my work in *Sweeney*. But that wasn't the point. I'd thought so carefully about what I'd wanted that first wish to be, and he'd turned it into something else entirely.

"You could have warned me," I said, letting an edge of accusation creep into my tone.

"I thought it'd be a nice surprise," he said—then narrowed his eyes. After a second, he said, "Ah. You don't like being taken by surprise, do you."

I didn't reply. It was true, but when he said it out loud, it sounded kind of dumb.

"You like to know what's coming," he continued. "You like to have a plan for everything."

I lowered my eyes, embarrassed by how easily he was summing me up. "I'm just saying," I said, more to the pavement than to him, "you could have warned me."

"And you could have said no."

"What?"

"Just now, when George asked you to open for him. Just a hunch, but I'm guessing he didn't have a gun to your head. You could have said no." Oliver's lips curled into a smug smile. "But you said yes, didn't you."

"Well, obviously," I said, throwing my hands up in exasperation. "It's the South Star. Who says no to that?"

"Then you *do* want to play the gig?"

"Of course I do!"

"Then what's the problem?"

I stared at him, all smug and proud and still completely missing the point. But as I opened my mouth to give him a piece of my mind, I realized that somewhere in there, I'd lost track of what the point actually was. Here, in front of me, was a real live genie who'd not only granted my wish, but made it bigger than I'd ever imagined it could be . . . and I was annoyed about being taken by surprise?

"Why did you do it?" I asked, my voice coming out small.

"Well, this is kind of my last hurrah, so I wanted to do something big." He went quiet, his smugness falling away as he scraped the heel of one boot against the pavement. "And because I thought you'd like it. It was supposed to be a gift."

I blinked at him, completely floored. "A gift? For me?"

He rolled his eyes theatrically. "No, for George. *Yes,* for you."

And then, before I even knew what I was going to do, I was on my tiptoes with one hand curved around the back of Oliver's neck, and my lips pressed against his.

They felt like regular lips, without the tingling warmth I'd felt in his fingertips, but even so, a thrill rushed through me as I took in the thin shape of his mouth, the hint of roughness above his upper lip, and the way he was pushing into me—

Or pushing me away?

Oh crap, I thought, as I realized what I'd just done. I pulled away, taking a few hasty steps back to put some distance between us, and covered my mouth with my hand. "I'm so sorry," I said, even though I knew it would come out as an incoherent mumble.

Oliver looked baffled. His eyes were as round as quarters, and his hands hovered awkwardly in the air, like he didn't know what to do with them. "Oh," he breathed, all traces of theatricality gone from his demeanor.

"I'm so sorry," I repeated, this time without my hand over my mouth. "I didn't mean to do that. I really didn't. You were just doing your job, and I don't go around kissing people because they give me presents. That would be gross, and I don't want you to think that's the reason . . ."

It dawned on me that Oliver hadn't moved, and I forced myself to stop babbling. If that wasn't the reason I'd kissed him, then what was? On the one hand, there were those green eyes, which were sort of amazing—not to mention the way he'd held my hand in the park. But on the other hand, he was a genie, and he was granting my wishes because he was bound to me. It was his job, nothing more.

Right?

"Aren't you cold?" Oliver said uncertainly, breaking the silence that had gone on just a little too long. He stood perfectly still, but in a way that suggested barely suppressed movement. I wondered if he was thinking of disappearing.

Cold. Right. I probably was cold, even though my brain was too full to register it right now. "Yeah, sure," I said. My voice shook. "Listen, I . . ."

"You want to know if I mind," he said, letting his shoulders relax.

Well, that was a mild way of putting it. I did want to know that, but I also wanted to know if he'd enjoyed it, or if he totally hated me for springing that on him out of nowhere, or if he maybe, just maybe, wanted to do it again. . . .

"The thing is, I can't stay," he said, so quietly that it took me a second to realize the words had come from him, not my own muddled head. He looked sad. Worried, too.

"I know," I said, squeezing my eyes shut. "I know you can't. I'm sorry. I'm doing everything wrong. I promised you wishes in a day or two—and I planned on having them by now, I swear I did—but here I am, four days later, flaking out about the wishes and kissing you instead, which you totally don't need, and . . ." I took a deep breath, forcing myself to calm down. I opened my eyes again. "Oliver, do you want the ring back?"

"What?" he said, his eyes going wide again. "Yes. Wait. No. I mean . . . What?"

I held the ring out to him. "You need to leave. You said so, and all I'm doing is screwing everything up. You should just take it, before . . ."

"Before what?" he asked, looking from me to the ring and back again.

I opened my mouth, but there were those gorgeous eyes, right in front of me, and those lips, which had felt so good against mine, and I didn't know how to finish. But he shifted his eyes away, and I knew he'd heard me want something. I blushed.

Before I get too attached to you, I thought, knowing he wouldn't be able to hear me.

"Will you think about your last two wishes tonight?" he asked. I hesitated. "Are you sure?"

"Yeah," he said with a nod. "Another day won't kill me."

"You said that at the diner. How much time until he finds you?"

He smiled wanly. "I don't know. Five weeks. Five minutes. I just want to be long gone before it happens. But another day . . . I'll stay another day for you. For your wishes."

He covered the slip so smoothly that I almost didn't catch it. But catch it I did. He wasn't talking about my wishes. He was talking about me. Maybe he hadn't been pushing me away after all.

"Oliver, do you *want* to kiss me back?"

"Margo, listen," he began slowly, and I resisted the urge to shrink under his gaze. He flinched and sucked in a deep breath. "Yes," he whispered. "I really, really do."

Then I want you to do it, I thought at him. I saw the exact moment he heard me. He went still again, and indecision furrowed his brow. His pretty green eyes shone under the parking lot streetlight as they searched mine for . . . something. I didn't know what, and I didn't ask. I was too busy reminding myself to breathe.

And then he moved toward me. He leaned down, so his face was only inches away from mine. "Just for the record," he whispered, his breath fogging the night air between us, "this is a very bad idea."

Chapter EIGHT

It was a good kiss. I mean, a good freaking kiss. The kind of kiss where I didn't even care how much time we had together, because as long as I could feel his lips against mine, time didn't matter at all. He followed my lead, responding almost instinctively when I paused for breath, when I leaned into him, when I tilted my head just so.

And he kissed with his eyes closed, which meant I could peek at him without him seeing. Even when I couldn't see his eyes, he was . . . I didn't know what he was. I wasn't sure there was even a word for it.

But before I could figure out the language of my thoughts, Oliver's hand touched the back of my neck. It was a feather-light touch of fingertips on skin, but the surge of warmth that followed made me draw in a sharp breath. Just like when he'd held my hand in the park, only more.

Oliver broke the kiss, but he left his hand where it was,

brushing his fingers lightly up and down my neck. A sly, almost wicked smile was creeping across his face, which confused me until I realized why. I was thinking very hard about how I wanted him to keep doing that—and he could hear me.

I couldn't help it; I laughed. The sound quickly faded into a happy little sigh, and I took another moment to savor the strange feeling of magic on my skin, before pulling him down into another kiss.

His hand strayed from the back of my neck to the front, and it occurred to me that it was really too bad it was winter, as there were several bulky layers between Oliver's hands and the rest of my skin. But hey, at least I hadn't worn a scarf—or, even worse, a turtleneck.

When his fingertips began to trace the line of my jaw, I felt him go still. This time I pulled away before he could. "What's wrong?" I asked.

He cupped my cheek in his hand. "You're cold."

"I think I'll live," I said. I couldn't feel the cold at all. There were far more important things happening here.

But when he let go of me, all at once I did feel it. It was colder than before, if that was even possible. "Seriously," he said, "you should probably head home. I don't want you to get sick or anything."

I smirked at him. "Is that your way of saying *you're* cold, but you're too manly to admit it?"

"I'm not manly," he retorted, then paused. "That came out wrong."

"Of course it did," I said, fighting the giggles bubbling up inside me. "You are the most manly. The absolute manliest."

His eyes narrowed. "You're mocking me."

"Never," I said solemnly.

The corner of his lip curved, but he managed to keep his expression aloof. "What I meant to say is, I don't get cold. And even if I did, I'm not the one who has to worry about keeping my singing voice in good shape."

"Wait . . . you don't get cold?"

He shook his head. "Not unless I want to. My magic lets me shield myself from outside elements, at least physically. It gets too cold, I can warm myself up. I get a paper cut, I can mend my skin. Somebody chops my arm off, I can grow a new one. Well, probably. I haven't tested that one yet, and I'm not exactly in a hurry to."

"That's nuts," I said. Curious, I touched my hand to his cheek. He was just as warm as if we'd been inside this whole time. "Want to use some of that super-genie-magic to warm me up, too?"

"Do I want to? Yes. But sorry, no can do," he added apologetically.

"Oh, right," I said, remembering *Aladdin*. "No freebies. Sorry, it was probably rude of me to ask."

"No need to be sorry," he replied with a shrug. "Now, will you at least get in your car so I can stop worrying about you?"

"Only if you get in with me," I said. "Come on, let me drive you home."

Sitting in an enclosed space with Oliver was somehow different from standing with him in the school parking lot. The little car pressed down on us in a way that the streetlight didn't, making it feel like anything we said in here would mean ten times more than it would out there. So aside from a quick, halting conversation about how to get to his apartment (over on Crawford Circle, near the train tracks on the other side of town), neither of us said much of anything.

As I pulled up in front of his building, I racked my brain for a good parting line, something that would make me sound witty and thoughtful and, most of all, worthy of kissing again in the future. After a long moment, I finally came up with: "Um."

Oliver smiled hesitantly, twisting his hands in his lap. "That was nice." There was an unusual weight to his voice, like he was admitting a huge secret.

"Yeah," I agreed, before he could change his mind. "We should do it again sometime."

He laughed. "As you wish."

"Oh, you did not just say that," I groaned, shaking my head.

I unlocked his door from the driver's side, but instead of getting out of the car, he took my right hand in his left. He raised it to his lips and pressed a quick kiss to my knuckles. My breath caught. There were a lot of things I wanted to say to that, most of which ended in exclamation points, but before I could find the words, he gently turned my hand over and kissed my palm, too.

Fighting the urge to swoon like some corset-clad romance heroine, I said, "The gig is on Saturday. The South Star gig. I know I promised to make wishes before then, but . . ."

Understanding the question before I asked it, he let my hand go and shook his head. "I want to be there. I do. But I really, really have to leave."

My first instinct was to protest, but what could I say to a guy who'd just kissed my hand? That he didn't care enough? That he had to give me more time, even though he'd planned on being gone already?

So I made myself nod. "I'll make a wish tomorrow. I promise. For real this time, I promise."

Oliver smiled sadly. "Thanks for the ride," he said, and left.

When I pulled into my driveway, I turned the engine off and let the outside cold begin to creep in again. For a moment I just sat there, relishing the high of having kissed Oliver. But as it slowly settled into something that almost resembled calm, it left in its wake a nagging feeling of uncertainty about this whole situation.

Oliver had said this was a bad idea, and now that I was alone,

I was beginning to understand why. He had to leave before the week was out, and I'd probably never see him again. I'd known that right from the start—known perfectly well that whatever happened between us couldn't last—and still I'd kissed him. Why the hell had I done that?

A memory of Oliver's smug smile flashed through my mind, and I realized I already knew the answer. It was the same as the reason I'd said yes to George.

I'd kissed Oliver because I'd wanted to.

Maybe it didn't have to be more complicated than that.

I was almost surprised, when I opened the door, to hear Mom and Dad talking in the kitchen. The bright lights of the foyer made me squint. *Earth to Margo,* they seemed to say. *You do actually have a life beyond rehearsals and music and boys.*

"Margo, is that you?" called my mom.

"No, it's Batman," I called back. I shed my coat and boots, putting them away in their respective places as Mom wandered out to meet me in the foyer.

"You look happy," she said. "Have a good rehearsal? I hope so, if they're already making you stay this late." She glanced pointedly at the wood-framed clock on the wall. It was almost eleven.

"Yeah, good rehearsal," I said, and grinned. "But that is not why I'm happy."

Mom raised her eyebrows in a silent question, and it took everything I had not to shout, *I kissed a boy, I kissed a boy, I kissed an awesome and magical boy!*

111

"I have a gig," I announced proudly.

"A gig?" she repeated, tasting the word like she'd never heard it before.

"Yeah. You know George, our musical director?"

Mom nodded.

"Well, he's the lead singer of this band, Apocalypse Later. They have a show coming up, and their opener canceled. George heard some of my songs, and he wants me to open instead."

"Really?" Mom blurted out. "You're writing again?"

"What do you think I was doing in my room all weekend?" I said with a grin. The stunned look on her face told me that she hadn't bothered to give it much thought. Just as I'd suspected. "So that's the big news. Here's what I'm thinking. The South Star—that's where I'm playing—it's supposed to have the venue in back and a Mexican restaurant in front. I told George I'd meet him at seven, and the show's at eight, so I'm thinking we can all drive up together, and you guys can have dinner while I go and sound check or whatever, and then you can come see me play. I should invite Naomi too. You wouldn't mind driving her, right?"

"Whoa, whoa," said Mom, gesturing with both hands for me to slow down. "Start from the beginning. When's the show?"

"It's on Saturday. At the South Star Bar."

Her face fell. "Oh, honey. This Saturday?"

"What's wrong with this Saturday?"

"That's when we drive out to visit Aunt Sarah. Remember?

We're staying the night, and she's having a barbecue the next day."

I blinked. This was the first I'd heard of it. In fact, it was the first I'd heard of my aunt in years. "You mean crazy Aunt Sarah, who yelled at you over the phone when Dad left? The one who hates our guts?"

Mom wrinkled her nose and waved the words away. "That was ten years ago. We're a family again now. Time to let bygones be bygones, and all that."

"She called me a devil child, when I said I wanted to live with you instead of Dad! And she called you—"

"Bygones," she interrupted smoothly. "She was just defending your father. You can't blame her for that."

Yes, I could. But if Mom was determined to welcome Aunt Sarah back into the fold, there was no point in arguing. Time to try a different tactic. "Either way, you didn't tell me about this."

"We did tell you!" called Dad from the kitchen. I cringed as I realized he'd been listening the whole time. "Just a few days ago, remember?"

I did have a vague memory of them discussing a road trip of some kind, but the details were fuzzy and, to the best of my knowledge, did not include Aunt Sarah. "Did you put it on the calendar?" I asked Mom.

She sighed. "I didn't. I'm sorry. But you were right there when we were talking about this trip. You must have forgotten."

So she was allowed to forget to write down our plans, but I

wasn't allowed to forget what those plans entailed? "Not fair," I said.

"I'm sorry, honey," said Mom gently. "But there'll be other gigs, won't there? I'm sure George will ask you to open for his band again."

"Other gigs?" I swallowed hard. "But this is the *South Star*. Practically all my favorite singers have done shows there. You don't just say no to a gig at the South Star."

"Is that the place outside of Nyack?" she said, a tiny frown tugging at her lips. "The bar where that girl was kidnapped last year?"

"How should I know?" I replied. "Look, I'll stay safe. Even if you guys want to go to Aunt Sarah's instead, I can go with my friends. We'll be fine."

"We can't just leave you here on your own!" said Mom.

I laughed. "You leave me alone for weeks when you go on your honeymoons. This is just one night."

"That's different," said Mom, the lines of her face growing harder. "Those trips are for me and your father. This is a family weekend—"

"Dad's family," I cut in. "Not ours."

"—and you are part of this family, whether you like it or not."

"But George—"

"Oh, *George* again," said Mom, throwing her hands up in the air. "Wait a second. How old is this George of yours, anyway?"

"Thirty-one," I said. Then I saw what she was getting at. "Oh my god, Mom, it's not like that. He likes my *songs,* okay?"

"And that's all he likes, is it?"

"Mom—"

"I knew it. The second I saw that dreamy look on your face, I just knew it. But this . . . this is just inappropriate, Margaret. You should know better. More than that, *he* should know better. He's a teacher, for heaven's sake."

"Will you stop it?" I said coldly. "He's not a teacher, he's a musical director. And I already said it's not like that. You're just looking for excuses not to let me go."

Mom's eyes grew sharp, and I instantly regretted what I'd just said. But before I could figure out how to take it back, she said quietly, "You are part of this family, Margaret McKenna. And on Saturday, this family is going to visit Aunt Sarah and have a nice barbecue. I'm very sorry that you'll have to cancel on thirty-one-year-old George and his band, but you should have been responsible enough to check with us before you agreed to play."

"Cancel?" I echoed. "But you can't just make me cancel. You can't."

"Oh, I can't? Watch me."

"But—"

"You are not playing in that concert, and that is the end of this discussion."

"This isn't a discussion," I said, unable to help the whiny edge that crept into my voice. "This is you screwing up my life."

There was a pause that seemed to stretch on for ages. I heard the scrape of a chair moving against tiles in the kitchen. Dad was still listening.

"Go to your room," said Mom.

I forced out a laugh. "Are you kidding? I'm eighteen."

"You're eighteen, and you're about to go to your room, before I get really pissed off."

Another pause. I held her gaze, but she didn't back down. I seriously considered storming out of the house, getting back into my car, and driving away. But even if I did that, I would have to come home and face her eventually, and she would only be angrier than she was now. So I did the only thing I could do. I went to my room.

Chapter NINE

I ran up the stairs and threw myself onto my bed, burying my face in my vast collection of pillows. I should have seen this coming. I'd dared to do something spontaneous, and what had it gotten me? A fight with my mother, and a nice, old-fashioned "Go to your room." If only I could—

Oh, but I *could*.

The ring was still in my pocket, so I pulled it out and called Oliver, thumb and forefinger against cool silver. A few seconds passed and he appeared, just inside my closed door. I sat up board-straight, every muscle in my body humming with the need to make things right.

"What's up?" he said. Then he blinked, and his eyes darted around, taking in his surroundings. "Wait. Is this your bedroom?"

"Yes. I need you."

His eyes widened, and he put his hands up in a defensive

gesture. "Whoa, hold on a second. It was just a kiss. This is way too fast for—"

"I need to wish for—Wait, what?" I said, deflating a little as my brain caught up with what he was saying. Then it hit me. Oliver had just arrived in my bedroom, where I was lounging in a pile of pillows. Even though I was in jeans and a baggy sweater, which were not exactly sexy, it was an easily misinterpreted situation.

I burst out laughing and covered my face with my hands. "I'm sorry! I didn't mean *that*."

"No no no, it's fine," said Oliver quickly. When I looked at him again, he was still hovering near the door. His hands were buried in the pockets of his hoodie, and his face was beet-red. "I shouldn't have assumed, um, I mean, I just didn't expect you to call me here. Can anyone hear us?"

"Big house, and everyone's still downstairs," I said as my laughter faded. Somehow, Oliver's mere presence had taken the edge off my anger.

I slid down onto the carpet, crossed my legs, and patted the spot in front of me. I couldn't undo the fact that I'd called him here, but at least the floor was closer to neutral territory than the bed. Oliver sat down warily and arranged himself in a position that mimicked mine.

"Relax," I said. "I won't bite."

"Wouldn't be the first time," he said, rolling his eyes.

"But I never—oh, you mean your other, um, what is it, wish-makers?"

"Masters," he supplied smoothly.

"Right," I said quickly. "Okay, but biting? You mean literally, or . . ." I made a vague gesture toward the bed.

He let out a quick laugh. "Yes and yes."

"Huh." I took a moment to turn this information over in my head. "That's . . . huh."

"So, you have a second wish?" he said in a bright, businesslike tone. "What'll it be?"

"Second wish. Right." Distracted as I was by thoughts of Oliver and biting and questions I couldn't quite pin down, it took a moment for me to remember why I'd called him in the first place. "It's my mother. She won't let me open for Apocalypse Later, and I need to change her mind."

Oliver's eyes widened. "Whoa."

"Yeah. Whoa. I mean, I had it all planned out—the three of us driving up there, lots of family bonding, stuff like that—and she just shot me down. If it weren't for my stupid father—" But I could feel myself teetering on the brink of a rant, so I stopped. Shook my head. "Never mind. Wish number two. Let's go."

"Wait, wait, hold on a second," said Oliver, leaning away as I reached for his hands. "Don't say 'never mind.' What's going on?"

"Nothing," I said shortly. "I just want to make my wish."

"Wrong," he said. "It's not nothing. I can tell. Talk to me, Margo. You know you can talk to me." He narrowed his eyes. "And you *want* to talk to me. I can see it."

"No, I don't," I said. Or did I? I couldn't decide.

"Fine, then I'll do the talking." He sat back, cocking his head at me, just like in the diner, when he'd first read my mind out loud. "You want your mother to stop putting your father first all the time." I shifted uncomfortably, but didn't deny it. "You want her to understand you. You want to be happy that they're back together, but you're not—"

"Of course I am!" I interrupted. "Who wouldn't be? It's like the ultimate dream: Mommy and Daddy getting back together. That's what *everyone* wants."

"But you're not everyone," he said softly. "You're you."

I stared at him, suddenly unable to speak.

"And," he said, "you want your family back to the way it was."

That was exactly what he'd said in the diner. I'd misunderstood him.

Slowly, I nodded. "It's selfish, isn't it?" I said. "So many people want what I have. And here I am, wishing I didn't have it."

"That's not selfish," he said, so firmly that I almost believed him. "Have you talked to your mom about it?"

"No," I said, with a huff of laughter. "Of course not. I mean, what could I say? 'Please divorce Dad again, because I liked you better when you weren't so happy all the time'? She is, too. She's so happy, and she *deserves* to be happy. It's just . . ." I paused. There was that brink again. But Oliver nodded at me to go on, and suddenly I couldn't stop talking. "It's just, it took so long to put everything back together after Dad left. But we did. We had to. She turned herself into this strong, awesome person, and I molded myself after her, and we were like . . . like this force of nature, you know? Me and her against the world. We planned out what we wanted our lives to be, and then we damn well made it happen. Promotions for her, straight A's for me. Movie nights on Friday, chores on Sunday, study dates every school night after dinner. That kind of stuff."

"Sounds kind of . . . regimented," said Oliver.

"It didn't feel that way," I told him. "That's the thing. It would've felt that way if Mom had been a dictator about it, but she wasn't. Not at all. We planned everything together, and it made me feel like a grown-up. I loved it, actually."

"Ah," said Oliver, like someone who'd just fit two trouble-some puzzle pieces together. "How old were you?"

"When Dad left?" I said. He nodded. "I was nine. I know, poor me, parents divorcing during the formative years, right? But then last year, Dad comes back into the picture, and I . . . It wasn't part of the plan, you know? But Mom just went with it. And this is a woman who never just went with *anything*! Now she's taking all this time off work so she can go on honeymoon after honeymoon with him, and when they get back, it's not me and her against the world anymore, it's her and *him*, with me stuck back in this third-wheel little-kid role, like because there's two of them again, they can just go ahead and decide everything without even asking me, and I'm supposed to play along and make nice like I'm nine years old again, even though *I'm* the one, you know, cleaning the house and stuff, while they're off having fun."

My face felt hot. My whole body was tense with everything I'd just spilled out. I'd never told anyone this stuff—not even Naomi—and in the silent moment that followed, I began to regret letting myself explode at him like that.

"Sorry," I mumbled, my eyes dropping to the carpet. "Total overshare. I'll shut up now."

"Don't be sorry," he said with a smile. "So the problem here isn't your mother. The problem is that you're unhappy."

"I'm unhappy *because* of my mother," I said archly.

He laughed. "Fair enough. But do you really think using a wish on her will change that?"

I thought about that for a second. It would certainly change how Saturday night played out, but I knew that wasn't what Oliver meant. "I could wish bigger," I said slowly. "Like, maybe I could wish for her to treat me like she did before the wedding. We could go back to how we were, and she could still have Dad."

He shook his head. "Still not a good idea. Trust me: Wishes that affect other people aren't ones you should make lightly. I mean, look at what happened to Vicky."

I glared at him. "I'm not Vicky."

"Then stop acting like her!"

I reeled back at the force of his words, my jaw going slack.

"I'm sorry," he said quickly. "I didn't mean that. Really. It's just, wishes like that can have unpredictable consequences. You're my master, so if that's what you really want, I'll do it—but think about it first, okay? Give it a day or two."

"A day or two?" I repeated, frowning at him. "But you have to leave."

"I know, I know," he said with a frustrated sigh. "But I told you before: I want the last wishes I grant to be good ones. And I think you're pretty awesome, so I don't want my magic to screw up your life somewhere down the line. You know?"

Pretty awesome. That innocent little phrase brought me right back to the kiss under the streetlight, to his pretty eyes and warm hands, and to the moment he'd arrived in my bedroom, making assumptions about why I'd called him there. There must have been something about wanting mixed in, because before I knew it, Oliver was turning red again.

"God, I'm sorry," I said, putting out my hands like a shield between us. "I'm so sorry. Ugh, this mind-reading thing is . . . I'm really sorry."

"It's fine," said Oliver, still bright red. He reached one hand up and threaded his fingers through mine. The spicy heat of his fingertips warmed me, and he took a deep breath, like he was steeling himself. "I honestly don't mind it, coming from you. You're . . ."

He shook his head, like he was trying to think of the right word—but after a moment he decided against using words at all. Using our joined hands to pull himself closer, he kissed me softly. I closed my eyes this time, pressing one palm against the carpet to make sure I wouldn't float away.

When he pulled away, I kept my eyes closed, savoring the feeling as long as I could. "I'm what?" I murmured.

He laughed, and I felt his fingers touch my hair. "You're pretty awesome."

I sat back on my heels, opening my eyes with a grin. "You said that already. Are you really sure you're okay with another day or two?"

He hesitated, but only for a second. "Yeah. Yeah, it'll be fine."

"What about five?"

"Five?" he said, looking at me quizzically. "Oh, five days. The gig. I don't know."

"It's just . . . you should be there. You made it happen, so you should be there."

Oliver hesitated again, but before he could give me an answer, a sudden creak came from the hallway. Oliver looked at my door, then back at me, eyebrows furrowed in a silent question.

"Someone's coming upstairs," I whispered. "You should go."

"What about your wish?" he asked.

I bit my lip, thinking fast. As much as I desperately wanted my mom to change her mind, I couldn't make Oliver grant a wish when he didn't want to. Still . . .

Another creak.

"I'll think about it," I promised.

"Thank you," he said sincerely, just as the door started squeaking open. I froze, heart in my throat, expecting my mother to barge in, or Oliver to disappear, and wondering which would happen first. But when the door pushed open a crack farther, it was Ziggy's head that poked through. She strode into the room like she owned it.

With a relieved laugh, Oliver reached a hand out, palm up, for Ziggy to sniff. "And who is this?" he said, more to her than to me.

For a moment I wondered if she'd attack him or something, since cats are supposed to be sensitive to supernatural things. She didn't. She just sniffed him, decided he was harmless, and rubbed against his jeans a few times.

"That's Ziggy Stardust," I told him, leaning over to scratch behind her ears.

"Ziggy, huh?" he said, raising an eyebrow. "Nice. Good album."

"Yeah," I said. "My dad named her. She used to have a brother, too. His name was Sergeant Pepper."

Oliver chuckled, but stopped at the sound of another creak, much louder this time. "That is definitely not a cat," he said, mirroring my thoughts. "I should go."

Much as I didn't want him to, I forced myself to nod. "I'll see you soon, okay? Now get lost."

When he did as I told him and my room was empty again, a little coil of melancholy snaked through my gut. But my hand was still warm where his fingers had rested.

I tried to write that night, but with all the thoughts about Oliver and George and Mom and playing in a concert and visiting my stupid aunt slowly turning my brain to mush, it didn't go very well. Mostly I sat on my bed and strummed my guitar, humming melodies that were sometimes discordant and sometimes not, and singing whatever random words occurred to me.

But after the fourth or fifth time the words *green eyes* escaped my lips, I gave up. I was getting sappy and repetitive, and that was just pathetic. So I put my guitar away under the bed, then straightened up and looked around for my pajamas—

Something pricked at my skin, and I froze.

I don't think the hair on the back of my neck actually stood up, but it definitely felt like it. Like someone was watching me.

I peered quickly around the room, even in the closet, but of course there was nobody there. I went to the window; nothing was out of the ordinary. One lone car drove past my house without stopping, and aside from that, the neighborhood was quiet.

I closed the curtains and got into bed, but I was still jittery. So I grabbed my iPod off my bedside table and put my Neko playlist on shuffle, hoping that would take the edge off my nerves. When I finally did fall asleep, it was to the sound of a swaying, meandering melody, and words about dreams and the moon and forgetting my name.

Chapter TEN

True to my word, I gave my second wish some serious thought. I went back and forth, staging silent debates in my head. During a particularly boring chemistry class, I even imagined myself as a cartoon, with an angel on one shoulder and a devil on the other. I couldn't decide who should argue which point, though, so that didn't last long.

Oliver not wanting to grant my wish was a major sticking point, of course, but that wasn't what made up my mind. Actually, the moment of truth didn't involve him at all.

Since we didn't have rehearsal the next day, Naomi and I had planned a girls' night out: a trip to the movies, with dinner and frozen yogurt afterward, cold weather be damned. She met me by my locker, and as I tried to remember which books I needed to bring home, she told me about the travesty that was Callie Zumsky's latest rehearsal with Ryan Weiss. I listened eagerly, glad of the distraction from my own dilemma.

"And I guess he finally figured out that I get pissed when he forgets his lines and I have to remind him yet again. So he's stopped asking me. Instead he just kinda says what he thinks the line should be. Like, one time he goes, 'I . . . uh . . . uh . . . oh, Johanna, you're so friggin' hot, you oughta have my babies.'" This last was in a poor imitation of Ryan's deep jock-voice. "He starts grinding his hips, like this, and Callie's standing there onstage, mortified, and Miss Delisio doesn't know what the hell to do, and I'm just laughing my ass off . . ."

"Oh my god, poor Callie," I said, laughing.

"Poor Callie? Poor *me*. I didn't tell you the worst part." Naomi leaned over, implying that this was confidential. "Worst part is, Ryan comes up to me when we're done, and he's like, 'You're cute when you're laughing at me.' And he walks away."

"*What?*"

"McKenna, if I didn't know better, I'd say—"

"Ryan's got a thing for you," I finished, feeling just as bemused as Naomi looked. I usually saw Ryan Weiss in the company of girls who were tiny, fragile-looking, and bleach-blond. Naomi was none of those things. "Are you gonna . . . ?"

She rolled her eyes. "Yeah, right. When hell freezes over. Even if I wasn't with Diego, I wouldn't touch that with a ten-foot pole."

"You and anyone with half a brain," I said. "So when do I get to meet this Diego, anyway? I've been hearing about him since before Christmas, and it's already . . ." But I trailed off as I caught sight of Vicky Willoughbee walking timidly toward us. Naomi turned around to see what I was looking at, and greeted Vicky with a friendly arm around the other girl's thin shoulders.

"Hey, Willoughbee! What's up?"

"Hey, uh, Sloane," said Vicky, looking distinctly uncomfortable in Naomi's embrace. She said a quick hello to me, too, then asked Naomi something about the rehearsal schedule for next week. I tuned them out and went back to shuffling through my locker—until something Naomi said caught my attention.

"You sure you don't want to come see a movie? We've still got room in McKenna's car."

I looked up sharply. Surely my ears were playing tricks on me.

Vicky flicked a quick glance my way. "Nope, I still have plans tonight," she said with a tight smile.

"Aw," said Naomi. "Another time, though."

"Definitely," said Vicky, and scurried away as fast as she could.

"I didn't know we were inviting her," I said, keeping my tone as light as possible.

"Oh, yeah," said Naomi, like it was no big deal. "I just don't get to see her much outside of rehearsal, so I figured what the hell. Wait, you're not still pissed at her about getting Mrs. Lovett, are you?"

"Nah, of course not," I lied.

As I closed my locker, Naomi went back to chattering about

Ryan, but I barely heard her. All I could think about was Vicky and that stupid wish of hers. Everyone in the world wanted to be besties with her! They wanted to hang out with her all the time! They wanted to make her their queen and grovel for her attention and bring her delicious treats on silver platters and sacrifice her to their giant flesh-eating monkey gods!

Okay, maybe not the last one. But still, at that moment, I'd never been more grateful to be in the thirty percent of people unaffected by Vicky's wish. Because the more I thought about it, the more I couldn't stomach the thought of having a magic spell cast on me and not even knowing it.

And as mad as I still was at my mom, I couldn't imagine doing that to her, either.

As I drove us to the movie theater that afternoon, I told Naomi about George offering me the South Star gig. She shrieked so loudly that I almost drove right off the side of the road.

"For the millionth time," I said, once I'd recovered both my hearing and my sense of personal safety, "would you please not do that?"

"Sorry," she said quickly. "But holy crap, girl! How long have you known? Why didn't you tell me?"

"Only since yesterday," I said, slowing down as I saw a yellow light up ahead. "But I didn't tell anyone because there's some drama with my mom."

"Greeeeat. What kind of drama?"

"The kind where she's not letting me play the gig."

Now stopped at the red light, I glanced over at Naomi, who was looking at me in disbelief. "Whatever, McKenna," she said after a moment, waving away my mom's edict like candle smoke. "You're playing it anyway."

"How, exactly? I'm supposed to go with my parents to visit my stupid aunt in stupid Delaware for a stupid barbecue."

She paused. "What time are you leaving?"

"Kitchen calendar says six o'clock. It'd probably be earlier, but Dad has a golf thing."

She laughed. "Six? Oh, that's easy. Come over a few hours before that, and just don't go home. We'll leave from my house."

"You mean sneak out? I can't do that."

"Why not?" she asked. "Begging forgiveness beats asking permission."

Suddenly suspicious, I looked sideways at her. "You've done this before?"

She settled into her seat, a smirk tugging at her lips. "Sweetie-pie, you're like the only person I know who *hasn't* done this before. Trust me. I got you covered."

The light turned green again, and I stepped on the gas. She made it sound so easy, going behind my parents' backs. But what would happen when they found out? What kind of punishment would they throw at me? I had no idea, and that alone was enough to terrify me. No, this definitely wasn't worth the risk.

Then again, I already knew that changing my mom wasn't the

solution, and that left only one other option: changing myself. Maybe it was time for me to become a begging-forgiveness-instead-of-asking-permission sort of person.

"Let's do it," I said, shooting Naomi a sideways grin. "I'll dedicate my set to you."

"You sure you don't want to dedicate it to Oliver Parish?"

Between the smooth segue and the fact that I was trying to pass another car, it was a moment before I understood the question underneath the question. "No," I said, eyes firmly on the road. "Oliver's not the one helping me sneak out to the gig."

"Well, sure, but he can come with us, if you want. My car's big enough for five people. You and me and Diego, and Willoughbee, too, if Diego can get her a fake ID in time—which leaves one seat. I was gonna ask if you wanted to bring Simon along, but judging by what I've been hearing around school, I'm guessing Simon's not at the top of the list anymore."

Ignoring the part about Vicky, I gave her a sidelong frown. "What kind of things have you been hearing?"

"Oh, nothing," she said. "Just that Oliver was spotted in the parking lot last night, making out with someone who looked a whole lot like you. I didn't want to believe it, since you're *just friends* or whatever—but you, McKenna, are lobster-red right now, and since I somehow doubt you've managed to get a sunburn in the last three seconds—"

"Okay, okay, I kissed Oliver. Happy?" As I took a smooth right turn into a parking space near the movie theater, I tried to recall the details of last night. I knew a couple of people had seen us talking, but they'd all left well before the kissing had commenced. "Who told you?"

"Oh, I don't remember. MaLinda, maybe? Or, no, I think Yuki mentioned it in debate."

I wasn't sure what to say to that. The Yuki in question wasn't involved in the play, so she had no reason to be anywhere near the parking lot last night. Which meant this had actually reached rumor status. Even the thing with Joey under the bleachers hadn't gotten that far. *Crap.* What were they saying about me? And who, besides Yuki and possibly MaLinda, was saying it?

Naomi's elbow jabbed into my biceps, making me jump. It dawned on me that she'd just asked me a question. "Huh?" I said.

"I asked if he's a good kisser," said Naomi patiently. "And if he's less boring than he seems."

I tensed, ready to go on the defensive, but quickly realized there was no malice in her question. Just honest curiosity. "You think he's boring?" I asked.

"In an objective sort of way," she said with a shrug. "That's just how he comes off. Like he's trying to blend into the background. And he talks to people even less than you do, which is saying something."

I furrowed my eyebrows at her. "I talk to people."

"You talk to *me*, and *I* talk to people," she corrected me gently. "That's not the same thing."

She was exaggerating, of course, but not by much. Naomi

was the only person I really went out of my way to spend time with. Between schoolwork and the musicals, I'd never had the time to navigate the supposedly complicated high school social scene—and even if I had, it just wasn't my thing. I'd always preferred having one best friend to having lots of casual friends. I'd never thought Naomi had minded that about me.

"Huh," I said, somewhat disturbed.

"It's not a criticism or anything," she said, shrugging again. "I was just making a point. And the point is, that Parish kid is a quiet little thing."

"Well, he's definitely not boring," I said, smiling to myself. "And yes, he is a very, very good kisser."

"Then he has my seal of approval," said Naomi, nodding firmly. "And the last seat in my car, if he wants it."

"He doesn't," I said, taking off my seat belt. "He isn't coming."

I reached for the door handle, but Naomi stopped me with a hand on my arm. "Why the hell not?"

Turning to give her a tight smile, I said, "It's complicated."

She tilted her head to the side. "What's complicated? You just tell the boy he has to come hang out, or else he's not worth your time. Done and done."

I laughed. "Is that how it is with you and Diego?"

"Hell yeah," she said. "Boys have no idea what they want, so sometimes it's up to us to tell 'em. That's life, you know?"

"That's life," I murmured. Then I shook my head. "But not

this time. Oliver said he can't come, so he can't come. It's fine. Really."

She gave me a skeptical look. "You sure?"

I wasn't. Not by a long shot. But I gave her a sunny smile and said, "Totally sure. It's not a big deal. Come on, let's see what's playing."

Chapter ELEVEN

With my new top-secret plan for Saturday all ready to go, I used the rest of the week to work on my opening set. Thanks to the internet, I learned several valuable things about being an opener.

First, say a lot of nice things about the band you're opening for, because that makes the audience more inclined to like you. Second, play as many upbeat songs as you can, because when the audience doesn't know your music already, slow songs seem a million times slower. Third, play at least one cover song, because people like musicians who respect other musicians.

Oliver came over on Wednesday after school, and in the few hours before my parents came home from work, we sprawled out in the living room so he could listen to the songs I'd chosen for Saturday's gig. There were six in total, beginning with "Vertigo" and ending with a cover of "Stinging Velvet" by Neko Case.

"Nice choices," he said, when I was finished. "Except . . . are you sure you want to play that sad one? The third one—what was it called?"

"'Hayley Mills,'" I replied. "And yeah, why wouldn't I play it?"

"Well, it's about your parents, isn't it?" he said, shifting uneasily on the couch. "It's a beautiful song, but it's kind of a downer. You said you have a rule about sticking to upbeat songs."

"That I do," I said, sitting down next to him. "But it's a song about my mom not being around anymore, and she's not going to be there for the gig, so it's kind of fitting. Anyway, the melody's upbeat, even if the lyrics aren't, right?"

"Fair enough," he conceded. "Next question: Not to sound vain or anything, but is 'Vertigo' about me?"

I felt myself go red. "Um. Kind of, yeah."

"I see," he said, and then paused, licking his lips and not quite looking at me. "I see, I see. Okay. Last but not least: What made you pick that cover at the end?"

"It's my favorite song from my favorite album by my favorite singer," I said, grateful for the subject change.

He tapped his lip with one finger. "Understandable," he said thoughtfully. Then he grinned. "Though I'm more of a *Fox Confessor* fan myself."

I nearly dropped my guitar. "You like Neko?"

He rolled his eyes. "Who doesn't?"

I hesitated, suddenly suspicious of something I couldn't quite name. "Well, most people, actually. I know maybe one other person in the entire school who's even heard of her. Well, two, but the other one's a teacher, so that doesn't really count."

"What can I say?" he said lightly. "I am a man of discerning tastes. But seriously, why that song for the concert?"

"Why not?"

"Well," he said slowly, and I got the sense that he was choosing his words carefully, "I get why you want to do a cover. But why not end with something that'll get the audience on their feet? You've just spent the past five songs showing off your own stuff, so end on something everyone will know. Like the Beatles. Well, everyone does Beatles covers, but you know what I mean, right?"

As much as I wanted to spread the Neko love, Oliver had a point. So I tried out a few more covers on him. "I've Just Seen a Face." "Michelle." "Can't Buy Me Love." Eventually I moved on to non-Beatles songs, like "Closer to Fine" and "Jolene" and "Mr. Tambourine Man." Oliver was the perfect audience, laughing appreciatively at my Bob Dylan impression, singing along with the refrains he knew, and giving every single song a hearty round of applause.

After a while he suggested that I give my fingers a rest, and I handed my guitar over to him. He wasn't a great guitarist, but about halfway through the first verse of "The Rainbow Connection," I realized his singing voice was actually really good— although he just ignored me when I told him so.

"But listen to this one," he said. He closed his eyes, screwed up his face in concentration, and began to do an absolutely awful rendition of that "Genie in a Bottle" song. By the time he got to the part about rubbing him the right way, I was laughing so hard that I nearly fell off the couch.

When he was finished, I snatched the guitar back, slung the strap over my shoulder, and launched right into "Hound Dog." He retaliated with "Dancing Queen." I played "You Can't Hurry Love." He played "I Am the Walrus." And so we went, happily encased in our own little bubble of acoustic ridiculousness, until I looked at my watch and realized two things. First, it was nearly time for me to leave for rehearsal. Second, we'd come no closer to picking out a song for Saturday's gig.

"Which one should I play?" I fake-whined at him, kneeling down to pack my guitar away.

Oliver settled onto the couch next to me, looking thoughtful. "Any of them would work, really. You could even pick one when you're up onstage. Or make the audience vote. And whatever you pick, you'll have at least one person singing along."

I was about to ask who, when I realized what he meant. I looked up, and he was grinning.

"You're staying?" I nearly shouted.

"Just until Saturday night."

"For me?"

"For you," he said, with a dramatic sigh. "But only because you are remarkably terrible at deciding on wishes."

After Friday night's rehearsal, I left my guitar at Naomi's house, and she wished me luck as I drove away. Not that I needed it. I was a writhing mass of nerves when I told Mom on Saturday afternoon that I was going to Naomi's, but she barely blinked. She just reminded me to be back by six, and that was that.

With my bag hanging from my shoulder (containing a secret stash of tight jeans, a slinky black shirt, and my lucky guitar pick for tonight), I put on my boots and headed for my car. As I was fumbling for my keys, my phone buzzed. I dug it out of my pocket, figuring it was probably Naomi. Or maybe Oliver, although I was pretty sure he didn't actually have a phone. But it was an unknown number.

"Hello?"

"Hey . . . is this Margo?"

"Yeah, who's this?"

"It's, um, Vicky Willoughbee."

And this day had been going so well. Of course, I knew she'd been planning to meet us at Naomi's, but in a group of five, it would've been easier to ignore her. On the phone, not so much. Well, unless I hung up on her. But I wasn't *that* much of a jerk.

"What's up?" I said, very politely.

"Um," she faltered. I wondered if she could tell how much I didn't want to talk to her. "I kind of need a favor. If you don't mind. Naomi invited me to your show tonight, and I was supposed to meet her at her house, and my mom was supposed to drive me, but she forgot and she's out at the mall or something and she's not picking up her phone and Naomi's not picking up either and could I maybe have a ride?"

I let out a quiet breath, casting about for non-jerky reasons to say no. But it was a halfhearted effort. I already knew I was going to say yes, if only to make Naomi happy. "What's your address?" I asked.

"Oh, I'm actually at the McDonald's on Main Street. I just went for late lunch—anyway, you don't care about that." She gave a nervous little laugh, which set my teeth on edge. "Meet me outside?"

"Yup, give me five minutes." Without waiting for a good-bye, I hung up. And I breathed deeply, three times.

"I will be a nice person," I murmured to myself, as I stuck my key in the car door. "Nice, nice, nice."

Vicky was waiting for me in the parking lot, shifting nervously from foot to foot. I pulled in and popped the locks, and she slipped into the car, settling a small yellow purse on the lap of her wool coat.

"Thanks for picking me up." She looked sideways at me, like she was afraid I might smack her. Which, of course, made me want to smack her.

"Sure thing." I turned the radio up and merged back into the traffic on Main Street, heading toward Naomi's.

As I turned off Main and onto Elm, Vicky finally spoke. "Hey, Margo?"

"Yeah."

"Do you have Oliver's ring?"

My hands tightened on the wheel. "Why do you want to know?" I asked. But half a second later, I realized that I'd as good as answered her.

When I glanced over at her, she was smiling to herself—a contented, confident smile that I never expected to see on Vicky's face. "Did he tell you about me?" she said.

Two direct questions, right in a row. From anyone else, it would have been part of a normal conversation, hardly worth noticing. But from mousy little Vicky, it felt like an ambush. "Tell me what about you?" I asked, gripping the steering wheel even tighter.

Even with my eyes on the road, I could feel her looking at me. "Well, mostly that I never made my third wish."

She wanted the ring back. I should have known. But why now, on today of all days?

I made a quick right turn. "He did, yeah. He said you didn't want the third wish, and you left the ring on purpose."

"I kind of changed my mind," she said. Her voice took on an irritatingly sweet tone. "Could I borrow it? Not to keep, I promise. I just want to make my last wish, then you can have him back."

There was something unnerving about how she phrased the

question: like Oliver was a book or a pen, easily borrowed and easily returned. Did she have any idea how insulted he'd been when she'd left his ring on the windowsill?

"Actually, I think he'd want me to keep it," I said.

Vicky laughed. "Oh, Oliver won't mind. You're his master. You can do what you want with him. He knows that."

I looked sharply over at her—a dumb move that made me very grateful there wasn't much traffic on the road. She just kept on smiling. "Please?" she said.

"Look, Vicky," I began, making sure I sounded far more apologetic than I actually felt, "I'd really rather not. How about if I give it to you after I make all *my* wishes?"

"I'd prefer to have it now," said Vicky.

"I said no, okay? If you wanted your third wish so badly, you shouldn't have abandoned the ring."

"Give it to me," she said, all traces of sweetness gone from her voice. Something glinted from the space between our seats, and before I could stop to think, I looked down to see what it was.

Vicky was holding a switchblade. Its tip was mere inches from my thigh, and judging by the expression on her face, she was ready and willing to make that distance a whole lot shorter.

"What the—!"

I jerked the steering wheel to the right, bringing the car to a skidding halt on the narrow shoulder of the road. I had to get out. It was another mile or so to Naomi's house, but when the other option was being stuck in a car with a knife-wielding maniac, that mile suddenly didn't seem so long.

I fumbled for the door handle—but then something sharp pressed heavily into my leg. "Don't move," said Vicky.

I didn't move.

"What the hell is wrong with you?" I said, dismayed to hear a tremor in my voice.

"Nothing," she replied, eerily calm as she held the blade against my leg. "I just want the ring back."

As I struggled to process everything that was wrong with this picture, one thing stood out with crystal clarity: I could not give Oliver's ring, and by extension Oliver himself, to this psycho. But in this claustrophobic new world that consisted only of me, Vicky, and the switchblade, I couldn't see a way to keep the ring and avoid getting stabbed.

How long would it take to open the door and jump out? Could she outrun me? What were the odds she was bluffing?

Not nearly good enough.

Vicky's face grew harder, angrier, and I felt the moment stretch too thin. But just when I thought it would snap, my cell phone rang. "It's probably Naomi," I said quickly. "She's probably wondering where I am."

"Then answer it," said Vicky. But she pressed the blade harder against my jeans, a silent warning.

I fished my phone out of my pocket and flipped it open. I was right; it was Naomi. "Hello, uh, hi," I said, praying she'd hear the nervousness in my voice.

"Where are you, McKenna?"

I glanced at Vicky, who glared steadily at me. "I'm, um, on my way."

"Well, hurry your ass up!" she said. "Diego canceled, the bastard, but Parish and Willoughbee are here already."

For just a second, everything seemed to tilt sideways. "Willoughbee?" I echoed.

"Yeah, even the Queen of Late is here before you." Naomi laughed. "See you in a few!"

Naomi hung up. I pulled my phone away from my ear and stared at it, not daring to meet the eyes of the person beside me. I wasn't scared. No, scared didn't even begin to describe this. I felt hollow, like nothing inside me mattered anymore, and I was just a thin layer of skin that could be punctured and sliced as easily as paper.

"Well?" came from the passenger seat. The voice was still Vicky's—if Vicky were a little bolder and a lot meaner. The blade shone brightly between us.

I finally looked up. "Who are you?"

Chapter TWELVE

Her face turned sour for a split second, then settled into a contemptuous smirk. "I'm Vicky Willoughbee."

The blade stayed steady against my leg, and I tried not to look at it. I couldn't let her see how much it scared me. "Vicky's at Naomi's house," I said. "You're not Vicky."

"Well, aren't you Little Miss Smartypants."

"Come on. If I'm about to die, at least tell me who to blame."

The Person-Who-Was-Not-Vicky rolled her eyes. "For heaven's sake, you're not about to die."

I gestured with both hands at my thigh. "Then what's with the freaking knife?"

She prodded my jeans with the tip of the blade, almost playfully. "Oh, this old thing. Don't worry, I'll only use it if I have to. But as they say, there's a big difference between knife and death." She giggled, but before I could even process how terrible a joke that was, her face was stone cold sober again. "Now, for the last time, give me the ring."

"I don't have it."

"Yes, you do."

"I swear, I really don't. We'd have to go back to—"

"Stop lying," she cut in, sounding almost bored. "You have it with you. I know you do."

I curled my lip into a sneer. "If you're so sure, then why don't you just take it?"

Not-Vicky's face clouded over. "I can't take it until you've used all your wishes. Not unless you give it to me."

She couldn't steal the ring. That was interesting. Maybe I could use that to my advantage somehow . . . while not getting stabbed, of course.

"What would I get in exchange?" I asked.

She bared her teeth at me, and pulled the switchblade away— only to bring it slashing down across my thigh. The pain hit me so fast and so hard that it knocked the wind out of me. I held my breath as my jeans split, and the skin beneath the fabric did the same, all in slow motion, and red began to spill out, and the *pain*—

My chest heaved with the urge to cry out, but I bit down on it, holding my bottom lip firmly between my teeth. A whimper escaped instead, and I realized I was breathing too fast. I wondered if I was hyperventilating. People did that when they were hurt, didn't they? Would it help or make things worse? I pressed one hand against the wound, hoping that might stop the bleeding, or at least slow it. I looked up at Not-Vicky, who was eyeing the bloodied blade with distaste.

"In exchange," she said, once she saw that she had my attention, "you get my promise that I won't do that again."

I had to admit, from where I was sitting, it sounded like a pretty good deal.

"The ring?" she said, holding her free hand out to me. I looked at her hand and thought how damn easy it would be to pull out the ring and give it up. But then I thought of Oliver. If she could hurt me without a second thought, what would she do to him? Especially if she got hold of his ring?

Suddenly, I knew. I didn't know how it was possible, but I knew, deep in my gut, that this Not-Vicky person was the mysterious man that Oliver was trying to escape. The one he *would* have escaped, if I hadn't kept him here so long and screwed up his getaway plan.

This was my fault.

Forgetting the distances and the odds and the blade, I flung open the door, jumped out of the car, and ran. I'd always been a decent runner, for someone who didn't do it regularly, but my injured thigh wasn't helping. I tried to ignore it, to concentrate on breathing evenly and moving faster, but it burned. I could feel the open wound rubbing against my jeans. I could feel blood running down my leg.

I rounded the corner onto Valley. Just up ahead was Hamilton Park, and that meant people. It wasn't too cold or too late in the day, so there were bound to be some families hanging around, right?

But before I could get close enough to find out, something slammed into me from behind, and I fell hard onto the pavement, my wrists and knees thrumming horribly at the impact. For a moment I couldn't see anything, and all I could hear was the sound of my own breath, pounding like drums in my ears.

When the world came into focus again, Not-Vicky was crouched in front of me, smiling like an evil Pollyanna. "Give me the ring," she said again.

"You're crazy," I wheezed. Mustering all my strength, I scrambled to my feet, put on my best action hero face, and ran again. But an action hero I was not. I only made it a few feet before Not-Vicky tackled me again, this time sending me tumbling onto the strip of grass between the curb and the sidewalk. I landed on my back. My head thudded against the cold dirt, and my vision went dim for a second. I could try again—

Except Not-Vicky was sitting on my chest. I couldn't move. I yelled and flailed my arms, trying to scratch at her face, but she pinned my wrists against the ground. All I had left were my legs. I kicked as hard as I could, but aside from brushing her back with my bleeding thigh, it didn't do any good. Finally, in the face of her calm, cold determination, all I could do was let myself go still.

"Give me the ring," she said.

"What do you want with it?" I asked, still out of breath.

Her eyes narrowed in a mean, un-Vicky-ish expression. "The real question is, what do *you* want with it? Fame? Money, power, and a thousand beautiful men to worship the ground you walk on?" She paused, and her lip curled in distaste. "And, of course, your very own personal slave, until all your wishes are used up?"

"Slave? I don't even know what you're talking about."

Not-Vicky squeezed her eyes shut, shaking her head like she was a kindergarten teacher and I was the worst-behaved kid in her class. "No, you wouldn't, would you. You have no real idea of what that ring holds. None of you do. You just take and take and take, and when it's over, you long for what you still don't have." She opened her eyes again. "Give me the ring, Miss McKenna. I don't want to hurt you again. Quite the opposite, in fact. But you're making this very hard."

"How is slicing my leg open the opposite of hurting me?" I said. It was meant to come out louder than it did, but Not-Vicky's weight was pressing down on my lungs.

"For heaven's sake, that was just a scratch. Honestly. Suburban kids. If you only knew . . ." She let out a short, bristly laugh, and squeezed her thighs together, making my ribs ache. "The ring," she said again.

I breathed out painfully, and closed my eyes against the sight of her. "Okay. Fine. You can have the damn ring. I just need to get to my pocket. The right one."

"Thank you," she said, with what might have passed for sincerity had she not been sitting on top of me. Slowly, she let go of my right wrist. Slowly, I moved my hand down toward my waist.

And as quickly as I could, I balled my hand into a fist and hit her in the face.

It wasn't a good punch. Not surprising, since I'd never hit anyone in my life. But my fist connected with her jaw, and it shocked her enough that she rocked back, giving me the opening I needed. I heaved myself upward, but found myself pinned again, with my right arm squished against my side, held in place by a leg that was far too strong to belong to little Vicky Willoughbee. My left wrist was clamped between her hands.

"Help!" I called. It came out as a sad little wheeze, which I knew nobody would hear.

"We'll do this the hard way, then," she said, ignoring my pathetic cry. I shut my eyes. I didn't want to see what the hard way was going to be.

She lifted my left wrist with both hands. Something made a horrible *snap,* and pain exploded like fireworks in my left hand, and I screamed. Well, tried to scream. And I opened my eyes. There, held up by Not-Vicky's delicate fingers, was my left hand. More or less. All of my fingers were rigid with the same pain that was lancing like icicles through the rest of my body—except the middle one, which went up as far as the first knuckle, and then jutted awkwardly, unnaturally, out to the side.

I lost track of the scared, pained, animal noises I was making. I know I kept saying "please" and "stop," and at some point I'd started crying, but mostly I know that nothing I said or did had any effect on Not-Vicky.

"The ring, Margo," she said calmly.

"Fine," I said, gulping in as much air as I could between sobs. "You can have the goddamn ring. You can have it."

When she freed my right hand again, I reached into my pocket and grabbed the ring, making sure to hold it with my thumb and forefinger. If Oliver was going to find out that I'd given him up, at least he could see firsthand that I'd put up a fight for him.

One Mississippi. I pulled the ring out of my pocket as slowly as I could. Two Mississippi . . .

"You," came a voice from somewhere above me. A voice so warmly familiar that I would have started crying if I weren't already. "Oh god. Margo. What did you do to her?"

Something shifted in the air; I could feel it. Not-Vicky's iron grip on me loosened everywhere but my wrist, and she sat back like I was just a bench or something, not a person she'd just deliberately injured. "Hello, Oliver," she said. All the sugary-sweetness and all the menace had drained from her voice, leaving a strangely mild tone in their wake. "It is Oliver, isn't it? What was it last time—Daniel? Dmitri? Dylan? Something like that."

Oliver's voice, closer now: "I said, what did you do?" I twisted my neck around, but I still couldn't see him.

She gripped my wrist tighter. I whimpered as a fresh bolt of pain lanced up my broken finger. "I was negotiating with your *master*"—she flooded the word with contempt—"for your release into my custody."

"You have no right to interfere with me and mine," said Oliver, his voice harsher than I'd ever heard it before. "I want you to let her go."

There was a pause, and then Not-Vicky let out a breathy little laugh. "Ahh, I see, you *like* this one. That makes a change. All right, then."

She let my wrist go and gave my leg a little pat, right where the switchblade had cut me. I hissed in pain, but before I could do anything, she was already standing up and brushing the dirt off her jeans.

Oliver knelt swiftly beside me, and sat me up. His face looked uneven, and his eyes seemed supernaturally bright as they searched mine. His whispering voice was as loud as a chain saw. "Margo, are you . . . Is it just your finger?"

"My leg, too," I said dizzily, clutching my finger. "A knife."

His face went hard, and he held me tighter as he looked up at Not-Vicky, who stood over us, arms folded. "So it's time, is it?" said Oliver. "You want your third wish?"

Something strangely distant flitted across Not-Vicky's face, and she gave a curt nod. "It's time. You and I, we're the only ones left."

"I felt it," he said shortly. "Ten days ago."

"It was a long time coming," said Not-Vicky. "Come on, don't give me that look. I just want to talk to you."

Oliver's face twisted, and he laughed mirthlessly. "You really expect me to believe that, after last time? And after what you just did to Margo?" As if on cue, my finger throbbed, and a little moan of pain escaped me.

"Your little slavemaster will be fine," she said, annoyed. "And if you want me to leave her alone, then I will. You have my word. On everything that's holy: I won't touch her again."

"And me?" he asked skeptically.

"Oh, *Oliver* . . ."

"What. About. Me."

Oliver gave Not-Vicky the space of three seconds to answer, but she crossed her arms and remained silent. Letting out a breathy growl, he stood up and lunged toward her, hand raised in a fist. Not-Vicky sidestepped him easily, grabbed his wrist, and twisted—but only when she held the switchblade to his throat did he stop fighting her. He stood still as a statue but for his quick, shallow breaths. The sudden fear in his eyes shook me to the core.

Not-Vicky pressed the blade into the soft skin under Oliver's jaw. "Did you just try to hit me?" she asked, her voice low and dangerous. "Answer me. Did you?"

A small trickle of blood ran down Oliver's neck. "Yes," he said, through clenched teeth.

The word curdled in the air between them, and she smiled mirthlessly. How had I ever mistaken this person for the real Vicky?

"You should know better," she hissed. In one fluid movement, like something out of a martial arts movie, she twisted Oliver's arm around and knocked one of his legs out from under him. Oliver fell hard on his back.

He tried to get up again, but Not-Vicky's sneaker landed

squarely on his chest, keeping him where he was. He bit his bottom lip, but didn't cry out.

I heaved myself to my feet, still clutching my injured hand. "What the hell is wrong with you?" I said. My voice rang woozily in my ears. I didn't care. "You can't just—"

"I can't just what, Margo?" Not-Vicky said evenly, her gaze cold and calculating as she looked at me with interest. She leaned forward, shifting even more of her weight onto Oliver. He still didn't make a sound, but his face contorted in pain. Not-Vicky smiled. "Please, enlighten me."

I ran at her. My good hand firmly against the center of her chest, I shoved her with all the strength I could muster, and she stumbled backward, leaving Oliver gasping for breath on the ground. Her surprise gave me enough time to answer her question:

"You can't just show up out of nowhere, pull a knife on my boyfriend, and expect me not to kick your ass for it."

Not-Vicky's eyebrows shot up, and for a second I was terrified she'd call my bluff. Even without the bleeding leg and the broken finger, I wasn't exactly well-practiced in the art of ass-kicking.

But she didn't attack me again. She just smiled. "Interesting," she said, and disappeared.

Chapter THIRTEEN

Oliver knelt beside me and reached for my damaged hand, but stopped himself before he actually touched it. "We need to get you to a hospital."

"Me? What about—" But when I managed to focus on him, the words died in my throat. The skin of his neck was as smooth and unmarked as ever, and there was no sign of blood. "What . . ."

"I told you: Chop my arm off, I'll grow a new one. Turns out, the same applies to necks and lungs. No problem."

"But she hurt you," I insisted. Even with the blood gone, his face looked pinched and pale, probably from the effort of healing himself.

He just shook his head. "She hurt you worse, and you can't heal yourself like I do," he said firmly. "Where's your car?"

"My car," I said dizzily. Now that the threat of further injury was gone, and Oliver was more or less okay again, I felt my heartbeat slow to a normal pace. The chilly night air seeped in everywhere. My tailbone hurt where I'd landed when Not-Vicky had knocked me down. My head hurt, for so many reasons. My knees and my thigh hurt. And my hand . . .

"I need to get this fixed." Then a sob escaped me as I remembered: "The gig. I can't play like this. I can't—Oliver, my left hand, I can't play my guitar—and I have to—"

"Shhh," he said, threading his warm fingers through my hair, holding my head steady. "Don't worry about that. There'll be other shows. Your finger will heal."

"But not right now," I said frantically. "I need it to heal *right now.*"

"Just show me where your car is, and I'll drive you—"

"No. No hospitals. Naomi's house, then the South Star. I lied to my mom to get to this gig—I *lied* to her—and there is no way I'm just gonna go back home. No way. I have to—I have to—"

But my breath was coming shorter now, and my jeans were soaked with blood, and the whole world felt so tilty that I knew I couldn't stand up again, let alone stand on a stage in front of an audience and play music, because I'd just been attacked by a disappearing person who looked like Vicky but wasn't, and nothing made any sense except that I had to play, it meant everything. . . .

I held my injured hand out to Oliver. "You have to fix it," I said through clenched teeth. "I need to play tonight."

"Margo, I can't—"

"You can if I make a wish. Right? Can't you heal me if I wish for it?"

He sat back on his heels and paused. And then flinched. "Yeah, I can," he said quickly. "But I don't think—"

I held the ring up with two fingers, and he fell silent, setting his lips into a grim line. Remembering the last time I'd done this, I pressed the ring between my right hand and his. "Oliver," I said, looking him in the eye, "I wish for you to heal all the injuries I have."

The sound of screeching tires reached my ears, and I looked frantically around, half expecting to see a manic Vicky clone, frothing behind the wheel of a monster truck, ready to run me over. But all I saw was an unfamiliar car, which sped past us without stopping.

Panic jolted through me. "Wait," I whispered to Oliver, shoving the ring back into my pocket. "We have to get farther away from the road first. Someone might see."

He shook his head. "I can't put it off. You made the wish, so I have to grant it, or— Come on, I'll do it fast. Just breathe."

Oliver seized my injured hand. I gasped at the pressure, but in less than a second, my finger was whole again. The pain was gone, leaving only Oliver's warm touch behind.

"Ohh," I moaned, nearly crying again out of sheer relief as I curled my newly healed fingers around his.

"What?" he asked, alarmed at my sudden grip. "You okay?"

"Uh-huh. Very okay. You're . . . you're amazing, Oliver, and . . ." I trailed off, seeing him clearly for the first time since Not-Vicky had vanished. His whole body radiated tension, like he was trying to steel himself against the memory of Not-Vicky and the switchblade. I could still see fear lingering just behind his eyes.

"She *hurt* you," I whispered. He didn't reply. "You have to go. Right now. Hide, or whatever you need to do. Should I make a third wish, or should I just give the ring back, or—?"

I fumbled for my pocket, but Oliver put a hand on my arm, stilling me. "Don't," he said firmly. "It's too late now. Just let me finish your second wish."

He let go of me, freeing his hands to work. He moved one hand to my thigh, and I fought the urge to squirm as he gently touched two fingers to the worst part of the slice in my skin. Soon, again, there was just pleasant warmth where the pain had been. Very pleasant warmth indeed.

Eyes narrowed in intense concentration, he moved his hands over the rest of me, hovering an inch or two away from my clothing. Occasionally he stopped and let out a deep breath; every time he did, I felt another scratch disappear, another little bit of aching pain seep away.

"You were pretty quick on your feet back there," he said, running a hand over a scrape on my palm and making it disappear. "Were you really going to kick her ass?"

"Huh?"

"That's what you said." He smiled up at me. "You also said I was your boyfriend."

I shrugged, suddenly self-conscious. "Sometimes I open my mouth and words come out. It's a problem."

"Not a problem for me." He sat back on his heels, giving me a once-over before he said, "There. Good as new."

I felt so light, so whole, that I wanted to cry. Or to pin Oliver to the ground and kiss that unreasonably attractive smile right off his face. Or to make him tell me why his mysterious knife-wielding nemesis looked like Vicky. But I heard the sound of another car approaching, and I remembered:

"Oh no," I said, heaving myself to my feet. "My car. I left it on the side of the road. What if it got stolen, or hit, or—"

"I'm on it," said Oliver, and promptly disappeared. Seconds later, my car rounded the corner toward me, shiny and undamaged, with Oliver at the wheel. He parked it, disappeared again, and immediately reappeared next to the passenger-side door, which he opened for me. "Your carriage, my lady."

"Thanks," I said. "You're a lifesaver. But I'm good to drive."

His smooth, gentlemanly demeanor faltered a little. "Are you sure?"

"Positive," I said, heading for the driver's-side door. I reached for the handle, then hesitated. "You said it's too late for you to run and hide."

He nodded, his face settling into a somber expression again.

"I'll explain everything later, Margo. I promise I will. But it's a long story, and you're running late."

"But—"

"Later," he said firmly. "You just made me grant you a second wish, for the sole purpose of playing this gig tonight. So let's just get you to the South Star, okay?"

Naomi's house was the first stop, and she greeted us with blatant disapproval. "What took you so long?" she said, stepping aside so we could come in. "Does it really take that long to un-stall a car?"

Oliver shot me a quick look: a silent hint that I should go along with the stalled-car thing, even though I could have figured that out on my own.

"I'm just lucky it's running at all," I said, arranging my features into what I hoped looked like relief. "Thank goodness Oliver fixed it."

He gave Naomi a sunny grin. "What can I say? I'm good with my hands."

Naomi let out a loud bark of laughter, then gave me a quick nod of approval. Apparently Oliver had just proven that he wasn't boring. Score.

"Okay," I said. "Naomi, you can do my makeup, right?"

"Like I'd let you do it yourself," she said with a smirk.

"Awesome, thanks," I said. "Then I just need to change, and—oh."

My throat closed up, and my hand pressed reflexively against my chest. There, half hidden in the shadow of Naomi's epic staircase, stood Vicky. She watched us silently, like she was trying to blend into the background. *But this is the real Vicky,* I reminded myself. *She is not going to cut me open or break my fingers or attack Oliver.*

"You okay, McKenna?" said Naomi. "You'd better not puke on my floor."

"No, I'm fine," I said, pulling myself together with a long, deep breath. As long as nobody else stabbed me tonight, freaking out again was not part of the plan. "Let's get upstairs."

In addition to being an amateur fashionista, Naomi also had the largest makeup collection I'd ever seen. She knew how to use it, too. When we got upstairs, she sat me in the section of her room that she'd dubbed the Vanity Corner, and began applying her vast collection of expensive powders and pencils and glitter to my face. While Vicky busied herself perusing Naomi's bookshelves, Oliver hovered protectively over me, occasionally touching my shoulder or passing Naomi the items she needed, but never speaking. He was clearly still dwelling on Not-Vicky. Not that I blamed him. I was, too.

We all jumped when my phone rang. The display showed my home number. I thought about letting it go to voicemail, but for some reason, getting stabbed made dealing with my parents seem a lot less scary by comparison.

"Where are you, sweetie?" said Mom when I picked up.

"About to get into the car."

"Oh, good." There was a muffled noise, and the sound of voices. "We're ready to leave as soon as you get back."

Steeling my nerves, I took a deep breath. "I'm not coming back," I said. "I'm going to the South Star."

A sharp intake of breath. "Margaret, we agreed——"

"No," I said calmly. "You and Dad agreed. I didn't agree. You guys can still go visit Aunt Sarah, but this is my gig, and I'll play it if I want to. I've got some people coming with me, and we promise we'll be safe. Love you."

Before she had time to reply, I clicked the call off. Everyone was staring at me. Finally, after a few long moments, Oliver said, "Nice."

Mom didn't call back.

A little way up the New York Thruway, traffic slowed to a crawl. George had asked me to arrive at seven for sound check, but it wasn't looking good. It was almost six forty-five now.

After silently convincing myself that it would not help if I got out and ran, I mumbled that I should probably call George and update him—which would have been easier if he'd ever given me his number. Vicky tried calling information, but he was unlisted. I suggested that Naomi look up the South Star on her smartphone, but of course she'd forgotten it at home, which left Vicky calling information again. But after three rounds of calling, specifying that the number was for a music venue, and being connected to a Cuban restaurant anyway, we gave that up too. Without any other options, we sat back and tried to pretend we weren't all ready to tear our hair out. Naomi turned the radio up louder. It didn't help.

Almost an hour later, the traffic finally let up, and we drove like crazy. It was five minutes to eight when Naomi's GPS told her to make a left turn, then proclaimed robotically that we had reached our destination. We turned into a parking lot, passing a run-down supermarket, a discount clothing store, and a couple of takeout places. I frowned. Five minutes to go, and somehow we'd ended up at a seedy strip mall.

Then Vicky said, "There it is!" Craning my neck around Naomi's seat, I spotted it at the very end of the strip: a flickering green neon side that said *OUT TAR*. There were cars parked in front. A lot of cars.

The outside wasn't what I'd been expecting, but I shivered just thinking about the inside. That was where the magic happened. I knew; I'd seen pictures. Once you walked through the restaurant in the front, there was a short hallway that opened out into a room with a stage, bare except for whatever the band brought with them. I couldn't wait to see it for myself . . . to stand on that stage . . .

Naomi's car squealed to a halt, right up against the curb. She reached down, and I heard the sound of the trunk popping. "Get in there, McKenna," she said. "We'll be in as soon as I park."

"Thanks!" I scrambled out of the car, retrieved my guitar

from the trunk, and flat-out ran up to the door, where a heavily muscled bouncer stood guard.

"ID?" he asked, bored. He was wearing camo pants and no jacket, and his close-cropped hair gave him a military look—but for all that, he didn't look much older than me.

"No ID," I panted. "I'm on the list. For Apocalypse Later. I'm opening for them. Margo McKenna?"

The guy gave me a mystified look. "Honey, the opener's already onstage."

I froze. "What?"

"I said the opener just went on. Now, you got ID or not?"

"But I," I sputtered. "How could . . . that's supposed to be me. I was supposed to open. It's not even eight yet!"

He made a show of checking the thick watch around his wrist. "It's two minutes after. Listen, sweetheart, there was only three people on that list tonight, and they're already inside. So either you show me an ID says you're twenty-one, or you go have yourself a nice milkshake down the street."

I hated this guy. Hated, hated, hated him.

"Sorry, I'm not into milkshakes," I said with the sweetest smile as I could muster. "But there's been a mistake. Could you maybe check with—"

"I don't check with anybody about nothing, you got that?" His face grew ugly as he gestured toward himself, muscles flexing under his tight T-shirt. "You're either twenty-one or you're not, and if not, I'm sure as hell not gonna lose my job over it."

Between my encounter with Not-Vicky and the interminable car ride that followed, I'd had plenty of time to envision all kinds of things going wrong once I got here. And for each problem, a solution. Audience not paying attention? Make stupid jokes and play more covers. Sound system screwing up? Jump into the crowd and lead a campfire-style sing-along until someone fixed it. Stage catching on fire? Stop, drop, and roll.

But this? I hadn't planned for anything like this. I just gaped at the bouncer and backed slowly away, putting as much distance as I could between him and me.

"What's wrong?" asked Oliver, jogging over to meet me.

"The opener's already on," I replied.

"The hell?" said Naomi, right behind him. "But you—"

"I know," I said flatly, and explained what had just happened. Naomi looked over my shoulder in the bouncer's direction, and grimaced.

"Back entrance," said Oliver. "There has to be a stage door or something. Sneak in and find George."

That was the first thing that made sense since I'd arrived here. "Yes!" I said, pointing at Oliver.

I ran around the side of the building and, sure enough, there was a door there. But when I got inside, it became evident that this wasn't a stage door. Amid the steam and the sizzling noises and the smell of deliciously fattening food, a short guy with a thick accent yelled at me to get out, get out, *get out,* blah blah blah health code violation blah blah blah.

I backed out of that door, too. Clinging tightly to the handle of my guitar case, I looked around for some other way in. But this was the only other door. Other than this and the front, there were just a few narrow windows, and—

And suddenly, the unmistakable sound of an electric guitar reached my ears.

One of the windows was open a few inches, held in place from the inside. The view was obscured by a thin, dusty curtain. But I could hear well enough. And what I heard was . . . questionable. Very, very questionable.

A girl was playing and singing. Her voice was thin at best, and she kept trying to reach for notes that were well out of her range. The worst part, though, was her guitar, which was so wildly out of tune that it made my teeth hurt. Why had George replaced me with this girl? Even worse, why hadn't he told me? It didn't make sense.

But then, a gust of wind made the curtain flutter, and for just a split second, I saw the stage over the heads of the audience inside. And I saw the singer, playing a gorgeous red electric with all the finesse of a particularly dull-witted four-year-old.

The singer was me.

Chapter FOURTEEN

I t was him again. He'd been Vicky before, and now he was me, and I had no idea why. Not to mention *how*.

Someone tapped my shoulder. I jumped, but it was just Naomi. "No way in?" she asked.

I set my guitar down on the pavement, positioning myself between her and the window. There was no way I could let them see this. "Bouncer was right," I said. "He found someone else to open." Nobody replied. The singer went flat on a particularly high note, and I let out a sharp breath, like someone had just punched me in the chest.

"Someone else who completely sucks," said Naomi, wincing. "I thought George had better taste than that."

"I guess he didn't have a lot of options," I said. "And it's my fault for not showing up on time."

"Still," said Naomi. "He could've given you five more minutes. . . ."

But my attention wasn't on her. I was looking at Oliver, mentally replaying what I'd just seen, desperately wanting it not to be true. After a few seconds his eyes widened, and I knew he understood. But he didn't say anything.

Inside, the song screeched to a halt, and a smattering of polite applause followed in its wake. Outside, we all leaned in to hear. "Thank you!" said the singer, her sugar-high voice booming as she got too close to the mic. My hand drifted almost unconsciously toward my throat. She went on.

"Thanks, I'm *so* glad you liked that one. I wrote it for my dad. Next I'll play you one that I wrote for . . . well, someone very important to me," she said, with a little laugh. "Now, I'm still looking for that *special someone,* if you know what I mean. But until then, I've got my eye on a guy who, unfortunately for all of us, exists only in the pages of a book. I wrote this song especially for him. I call it 'My Immortal Amour.'"

That was it. I could not listen to this anymore. Practically tripping over myself in my haste to get away from the window, I stalked back toward the front of the bar, and kept going. Right past the knot of people smoking their cigarettes on the corner, past the sour-looking bouncer, past the darkened nail salon next door . . .

Finally, I stopped in front of a dry-cleaning place. There wasn't anything special about it, but it had a stoop to sit on, and it was far enough that I couldn't hear that awful excuse for music. Did George really think that was me up there? What in the world would he say? Would he kick me out of *Sweeney Todd*? Would I be banned from every self-respecting music venue in the entire United States?

And how the hell did that guy look like me?

Looking back in the direction of the South Star, I saw three figures approaching rapidly. Oliver was leading the way, and Vicky was holding the guitar case I'd left behind, but Naomi's was the first voice I heard.

"—some nerve to pull a switch like this. We're gonna storm this place and get McKenna up there where she belongs. You hear me, Parish?"

But Oliver paid no attention to her. He strode up to me, sat right beside me on the stoop, and clasped one of my hands in both of his. "Margo, I'm so sorry," he said, leaning heavily on each word. "Are you okay?"

"I'm fine," I said, even as I willed my hand not to shake in his. "Oliver, who *is* that asshole?"

Oliver didn't reply. Instead, he looked pointedly at Naomi and Vicky, then back at me—and after another second, he flinched and squeezed my hand harder. His magic was trying to force him to answer me, and he clearly didn't want to. But I was way too freaked out to care.

"What asshole?" said Naomi.

Oliver shot me a pleading look, but I didn't take the question back. Finally, he gave in. "Xavier," he said, and let out a breath of relief. "That's what he called himself, last time I saw him. He's, um. He's like me."

"Like you," I echoed in disbelief. "You mean——"

"Don't ask," said Oliver, before I could finish. "Not now. I'll answer anything you want later, but please"——his eyes flicked nervously up to Naomi and Vicky again——"don't ask me now."

"Right. Sure. Sorry." But I already knew the answer: This Xavier was a genie, too. Oh, this just kept getting better. I squeezed my eyes shut, pinching the bridge of my nose with my fingers.

"What's going on, Oliver?" said Vicky softly.

"Good question," said Naomi, her anger tinged with suspicion. "What the hell are you two talking about?"

Dropping my hand abruptly, Oliver stood up. "Nothing. Never mind. What we *should* be talking about is how Margo is obviously upset, and staying here isn't going to make things any better. We need to leave."

I desperately wanted to force the rest of the Xavier story out of him, but I already felt bad enough for not taking back the one question I'd already asked. Besides, he was right: We needed to get out of there. So I played along, putting on my best obviously-upset face and nodding miserably. "Yeah," I said. "Please, let's just go home."

Back in the car, Naomi clicked over to a satellite radio station that was playing '90s hits, then immediately turned it down enough that she could easily talk over it. "Okay, so is anyone gonna tell me why we're not going in there and kicking the Ninja's ass?"

Oliver and I exchanged a look, but it was Vicky who spoke first. "Well, for one thing, that bouncer would probably kick our asses first."

"And I don't want to make a scene," I added. Oliver reached over and took my hand again. "I'll just ask him on Monday."

"Fine, take the coward's way out," said Naomi, and pulled up to the red light at the edge of the parking lot. "I mean, I only set this whole thing up for you, after all. But if you want me to drive all the way back home after we just got here, then fine. It's totally your call."

She met my eyes in the rearview, and for the first time I felt the full weight of her disapproval. She was right: She'd gone to a lot of trouble for me, and I'd turned the whole mission around without even giving her a good reason. For a moment I thought about telling her that I'd been stabbed just a few hours ago, but the warm heat of Oliver's fingers reminded me that I couldn't. Not without giving away his secret. And I knew he didn't want that.

So I just said, "I'm really sorry," even though the complete lameness of the apology made me want to spork myself in the eye.

"Whatever, I'd've kicked his ass," she said, and pulled out into the street.

An uncomfortable silence descended, softened only by the feeling of Oliver's touch—until Vicky saved us by reaching over and turning the radio up. "I like this song," she explained apologetically. Moments later we were all singing along to Ace of Base. And then Alanis Morissette. And then R.E.M., and the Cranberries, and so on, all the way back to Oakvale.

Naomi dropped Vicky off first, and then asked where Oliver lived. I got the distinct feeling that she wanted to get me alone for a minute before I went home—but while I wanted that, too, just so I could make sure she and I were going to be okay, talking to Oliver was my absolute number-one priority right now. So I insisted on switching cars at her place so I could drive Oliver home myself. "We just need to talk about some stuff," I told her. "But I'll call you tomorrow, okay?"

"Talk, sure," said Naomi, somewhat sourly. "But it's cool. I don't like an audience either. Have a good one."

"An audience, huh?" said Oliver, in the passenger seat of my car. I'd parallel-parked in front of his building, but he hadn't made a move to get out. Which was good, because I didn't want him to. "What does Naomi think we don't want an audience for?"

I shook my head at him, bewildered. "How are you making sex jokes at me right now?"

He grinned. "Ohhh. Sex. That's what it is."

I shifted in my seat, angling myself to face him directly. I spoke slowly and clearly. "I mean, I got stabbed tonight, and there is an evil shapeshifting genie out to get us, and my head is inches away from exploding, and you are making *jokes*."

His grin faded almost instantly, and he leaned forward, rubbing at his forehead and looking more tired than I'd ever seen him.

"I'm sorry I made you answer me before."

"Don't worry about it," he muttered. I couldn't tell if he meant it.

"But you have to tell me what's going on," I said. Somehow I kept my voice from shaking. "I haven't freaked out yet, and I'm trying really hard to keep it that way, but he . . . he looked like me, Oliver. Exactly like me."

"I know," he said, squeezing his eyes shut. "I know, and I'm sorry."

"What's the third wish he wants to make?" I asked. "What the hell kind of wish is worth stabbing someone you've never even met?"

Oliver glanced over and met my eyes. "He wants to wish me free."

My jaw dropped. "You mean he wants to *kill* you? Why?"

"Because I'm the only one left to kill."

It's time. I could still hear Not-Vicky's voice echoing in my ears. *You and I, we're the only ones left.*

"You mean . . ."

He nodded, watching the realization dawn on my face. "I

mean he and I are the last of our kind. There were hundreds of us once. Not anymore."

"He killed them?" I said, my voice high with shock. "All of them?"

Oliver gave a huff of something that wasn't quite laughter. "Well, not all. He had some unexpected help in the early nineties, when a certain movie convinced a whole bunch of people that freeing genies was a good idea . . ." He paused, taking in my horrified look, and cleared his throat. "But yes, most of them. He was responsible for most of them."

"But *why?*"

He gave me a cold look. "Better to die free than live in slavery," he said, his tone almost mocking in its bitterness.

"Slavery?" I echoed. "But you're not a slave."

"No, I'm not," he said. "But it's a fine line, if you look at it in a certain light. We're bound to one master after another, and we have to use our magic to serve them. I call it a job. Xavier calls it slavery. And he's been taking steps to end it. Wishing us free, either through our own vessels or the vessels of others. I've been feeling them vanish, one at a time." His face contorted with sorrow. "Two of them were by my own hand."

I drew in a sharp breath. "Because you granted two wishes for him already."

He nodded miserably. "I never even met them, the two others. They were just images I saw in Xavier's mind when he made his wishes. But I still . . . I had to do it, once the wishes were made. He was my master. I didn't have a choice. And then, when I thought he was going to free me too, he gave my ring back. So he could save me for last."

"But you could still leave, right?" My voice came out thin and desperate. "You could still hide. You could—"

"It's too late," he said. The quiet finality of his tone made me want to cry. "He knows where I am. He knows who my master is. The moment you make your third wish, or the moment you return my ring to me . . ." He made a swift grabbing motion. "He'll be there, and he'll take it."

"Then I'll keep my third wish for as long as I can."

But even as I said it, I knew the plan was no good. Even if Xavier couldn't steal the ring from me, he could easily attack me again, forcing me to use my last wish to heal myself.

"I wish you could keep it forever," said Oliver, with a small smile that almost eased the oppressive tension permeating the car.

"Me too," I said. Then I imagined having Oliver in my life forever, and what that would mean. More people offering me gigs, or more people stabbing me in the leg? The uncertainty made me nervous all over again, so I put it out of my mind, focusing instead on the topic at hand.

"Oliver, how long have you known this would happen?" I asked. "How long have you been running from him?"

Oliver twisted his hands together in his lap. A moment passed, and his shoulders squinched up, just like before. Maybe he didn't want to talk about it. Maybe it was too recent. Hadn't he said something about ten days?

"Never mind," I said quickly. "I take it back. You don't have to answer."

Another mirthless huff of laughter, as his body loosened again. "Thanks, but you don't have to do that. You can ask me whatever you want, as long as we're alone. It's my fault if I don't answer you right away."

"But if it hurts you—"

"A hundred and sixty years."

All at once, everything seemed to stop. I stared at him, unable to make sense of what he'd just said. Only when he hesitantly met my eyes did I manage to force a word out: "What?"

He smiled tightly. "Xavier made his first two wishes on me over a hundred and sixty years ago."

The world seemed to tilt as I tried to reconcile the number with what I knew of Oliver. My brain refused to process it. "But you're a sophomore."

He shook his head. "Not true. Technically, I am now a high school dropout." Seeing the look on my face, he cleared his throat and continued: "Also, technically I'm a teensy bit older than most sophomores."

"Oh god, I knew it," I moaned, covering my face with my hands. "I mean, I didn't really, but you've been dropping hint after hint after hint, and I should have known. I really should have. Oh god. I'm one of those girls."

"What girls?" he asked, perplexed.

"*Those* girls. The ones in all those books and TV shows. Some dumb high school girl falls in love with some supernatural guy, and he's all, 'Behold, I am five million years old!' and she's all, 'Oh my god, how can you ever love pathetic little me!' and he's like, 'Because of destiny!' or whatever. It's just so . . . ew. You know?"

There was a pause. When I finally chanced a look up at him, he was biting his lip, like he was trying really hard not to laugh.

"What?" I said defensively.

"You're in love with me?"

"Pfft. No. I've known you for like a week." Another pause. "You're a really good kisser, though."

Finally, he laughed. "As are you."

I felt like I should laugh with him, or at least acknowledge the compliment, but I just couldn't get past that number. I narrowed my eyes, taking a good look at him. His eyes, and how his lashes shadowed them. The shape of his jaw, and the way his dark hair curled a little bit over his ears. His hoodie, bunching up between the collar of his coat and the skin of his neck. Everything about him was so very high school.

He watched me, with a calm that seemed forced, as I studied him. Finally, I asked, "So how old are you?"

"Sixteen. Biologically, anyway, at least at the moment. But I was born in 1822, so if you want to go by that, then chronologically I'm . . ." He paused, silently moving his lips as he calcu-lated.

"Almost two hundred years old," I breathed, feeling very dizzy all of a sudden. "But that's not possible. Is this some kind of . . . are you undead? Please tell me you're not undead."

That night in the parking lot came rushing back to me—the streetlights, the cold, Oliver's eyes. Except this time, I was pic-turing rotting zombie lips, slowly moving toward my own. I shuddered.

"I'm not undead. I promise."

I narrowed my eyes at him. "Okay, then you're a dirty old man who tells people he's a teenager. Except in real life instead of online. And with magical powers."

"I'm not—" But he snapped his mouth shut, frowning at me. I raised my eyebrows, and he began again: "I'm not dirty. You kissed me first, remember?"

A loud laugh escaped me, and I leaned forward until my fore-head rested against the top of the steering wheel. I couldn't believe I was actually having this conversation.

"I'm sorry, Margo," he said. "I really didn't expect you to take the age thing quite so hard."

"Of course you didn't," I murmured. "Because it's obviously such an easy thing to hear."

He didn't reply. My hands started fiddling nervously with my seat belt.

"How much more haven't you told me?" I asked.

"A lot." He looked uneasy. Almost scared.

"Do you want to tell me?" *And do I want to hear it?*

"I . . ." He trailed off, looking out the window, then down at his hands, then up at the ceiling of the car. "Yes?" Then something sharpened in his expression. "Actually, yes, I do. If this is my last . . ."

"Your last time granting wishes?" I supplied.

He nodded. "I want to tell someone," he said simply. "And it should be you."

I gripped the seat belt tightly to keep my hands still. Whatever he wanted to tell me, I would not become a giant ball of exploding nerves over this. I would handle it like an adult. I would be calm.

"Okay," I said, bracing myself for the next big revelation.

But Oliver just said, "Come upstairs."

"What?" I asked. "Why?"

"Because I think it's a good place to start," he said. Then he rolled his eyes. "Yes, I can see what you're thinking, and no, I won't try anything funny. Just come up."

A good place to start. I had a sudden vision of piles upon piles of magical artifacts, all stuffed into a tiny little Crawford Circle apartment. It looked suspiciously like a suburban version of the Cave of Wonders from *Aladdin,* but I never claimed to have an extensive frame of reference when it came to genies.

"All right," I said. "Let's go."

Chapter FIFTEEN

"**C**an you wait here a second?" he said when we reached his front door.

"Hah!" I said nervously. "Want to get your dirty underwear off the floor before I come up?"

"I don't leave my underwear on the floor, thank you." Oliver sniffed. "Besides, it's not that. It's more about, um, how I don't exactly have a key. Just wait here. I'll buzz you up. Second floor, apartment C."

"What do you mean—"

But he'd already disappeared.

A minute or so passed by—not long, but long enough to make me wonder whether Oliver was setting up mood lighting or hiding dead bodies. Or if someone was up there waiting to stab me again. Or if someone was up there waiting to hand me a crown and tell me I was the long-lost Princess of Genovia. Or if I'd tumble into a pit of lava, only to get saved at the last second by a flying carpet.

Just when I thought my skin was going to peel off from the agony of not knowing, the front door buzzed. I pushed it open and went up to the second floor. Oliver was there, holding open a door with 2C on it in fancy gold letters.

"Come on in," he said, and stepped aside for me.

With my mind full of oil lamps and magic carpets, I stepped over the threshold. And inside . . .

I gasped.

As far and as high as I could see, there were piles and piles of . . . well, *treasure*. Gold glinted everywhere, in so many different shapes and sizes that I could barely tell one object from the next. Brightly colored jewels winked in the dim light. Dark sculptures of fantastical creatures loomed majestically over me. Thick Persian rugs and long strings of pearls were draped carelessly over everything.

I looked down. The marble floor was strewn with gold coins. A silver crown, woven with gold and studded with rubies, lay at my feet.

And standing in the middle of it all, clad in rich, colorful fabric that made him look like a prince from a fairy tale, was Oliver.

"You like it?" he asked, gesturing expansively at the overwhelming opulence that surrounded us.

I took a step forward, taking care to avoid the crown. "This is . . ."

"Exactly what you were imagining?" finished Oliver with a smile. "I know. Here, have a seat."

He indicated a chair that I hadn't seen before. No, not a chair. A throne. An actual throne, made entirely of gold.

I began to move forward again, but I couldn't bring myself to walk across this gleaming floor with feet covered in muck from outside. I unzipped my boots and stepped out of them, and then moved toward Oliver, who regarded me with regal pride.

As I arranged myself on the throne, I looked around the room in wonder. There were at least three vases, so delicate that I was afraid I'd break them just by looking at them. There was a chandelier, lying uselessly on the ground and reeking of decadence. There was soft, gorgeous light, but I couldn't tell where it came from.

I looked up, trying to find its source, but there was only more treasure, piled higher than I could see. Was there even a ceiling? I actually couldn't tell. And of all the craziness in that room, that was the thing that finally brought my nervousness creeping back in. We were on the second floor of a five-story building. I wanted to know the ceiling was there. I needed to see where the room ended.

"I'm sorry," came Oliver's voice, cutting into my whirling thoughts. "I didn't realize. Maybe this will help."

He raised one hand and gracefully unfurled his fingers. The space above me opened up, and suddenly I could see the clear night sky. Stars twinkled cheerfully, and a crescent moon bathed the piles of riches in pale, clean light. Oliver watched me expectantly. Every muscle in my body tensed, silently protesting how completely wrong this felt.

"This is," I began again. My mouth felt dry. I swallowed. "This is weird. This is not right. Whatever you're doing, please stop it."

Oliver made a grand, sweeping motion with his hand. A comet appeared, blazing through the sky. It grew brighter and brighter until everything was eclipsed with white light and for a moment I forgot to breathe—

And then it was gone.

I was sitting on a metal folding chair in an empty apartment.

I leaped up, blinking rapidly as I looked around. Where there had been piles of gold a moment ago, there was now a faded blue couch with sagging cushions. A lone, threadbare carpet adorned the middle of the floor, its green and white stripes reminiscent of a beach towel. There was a thing against one wall that looked like a shoe rack, but it was hard to tell since there weren't any shoes on it.

Beyond those things, which all had a distinctively Ikea-ish air about them, there were only bare walls, a wood floor, and three closed doors. Kitchen, bathroom, and bedroom, I guessed. A perfectly average apartment, if you didn't expect anyone to live there. And if you didn't count Oliver, who was standing in the middle of the room, his princely attire looking cartoonish now that the treasure was gone.

"The furniture isn't mine," he said cheerfully. "The last tenants must've left it. Take the couch, if you want. It's more comfortable. I'd offer you something to drink, but I don't have any glasses. Can I take your coat?"

No glasses. In mere seconds, we'd gone from silver crowns and Persian rugs to bare walls and shoeless shoe racks and no drinking glasses.

Moving mechanically, I unzipped my coat and handed it to Oliver, and as he slipped it into a closet behind the front door, I sank down onto the couch. Squeezing my eyes shut, I pressed my palms against my temples. I hadn't gotten stabbed again. That was good. But while the attack had scared the crap out of me, it had also brought a clarity of purpose: Get away from Not-Vicky, get my finger healed, get to the gig. And Oliver had been right there, helping me do those things, giving me a steady sense of security amidst all the chaos.

But now, even Oliver didn't feel safe anymore. In the vast sea of my confusion, he'd suddenly become the biggest question mark of all—and that scared me far more than a switchblade ever could.

The cushions moved slightly, telling me that Oliver had joined me on the couch. After a moment of silence, I chanced a look at him. He was still wearing those distractingly colorful clothes. They made him sit up straighter than usual. They also made him look like a stranger.

"What was all that?" I asked. "Where were we?"

"We were right here. We've been here since you walked through my door."

"But . . . but that was . . ." I paused and forced myself to take a deep breath. "What was that?"

He gave me a timid smile. "You wanted to see something fantastical when you came inside. Something out of a movie. So that's what I showed you."

"But why?"

"Because that's what I do, Margo. It's who I am. I show my masters what they want to see. I show them things that will comfort them, or dazzle them, or at least make them trust me with their wishes. Almost none of the magic I do is real, at least not without the power of a master's wish behind it—but I can create the illusion of real magic."

"The café," I said, remembering the night I found his ring. It seemed so obvious in hindsight. "That was an illusion?"

"Yes," he said. "A French café for you. A walk on the moon for someone else. Everyone wants to see something different." He paused long enough to sweep his hand over his elegant clothes. Right before my eyes, his princely costume shimmered, transforming itself into faded jeans, a black T-shirt, and that familiar gray hoodie. The same outfit he'd worn earlier. He met my eyes again. "And that includes me."

"You?" I said, utterly confused.

Oliver crossed his legs underneath himself, relaxing a little now that he was back in his normal clothes. "Before, in the car, you called Xavier a shapeshifting genie. And while you're right, the part I didn't tell you is that he's a shapeshifter *because* he's a genie. We can all change our shapes. It's part of the job."

My breath caught. I shook my head. Oliver, a shapeshifter. But he couldn't be. He was *Oliver*.

"I've been a lot of things to a lot of people," he continued. "Whenever I have a new master, I have to become part of their life. That takes a lot more than just moving from place to place. It's moving from identity to identity, too. Clothes, haircut, money, paperwork, you name it. I create a new confidant for each of them. Someone they can trust with their secrets. And the masters I've had are all so different. They want such different people in their lives. One person wants a best friend who always shows up at her door with a bottle of wine and a shoulder to cry on. Someone else wants a girl who reminds him of his estranged daughter. They want mentors, or secret pen pals, or knights in shining armor, or—"

"Lovers?" I cut in softly, thinking of Oliver in my bedroom, assuming so quickly that I'd called him there to sleep with him.

He paused, but only for a second. "Sometimes," he said carefully. "I've definitely had masters who were most comfortable confiding in a . . . well, a boyfriend. Or a girlfriend."

That gave me pause. "A girl? You've been a girl?"

"That's the weirdest part to you?" he said with an odd smile. "Yes, I've been a girl."

I stared at him. It took me a moment to find my voice again. "But . . . but you're a boy," I said stupidly.

"Yes, I am." He shrugged and leaned back against the couch. "And sometimes I'm not. I told you, I'm a shapeshifter. I can be anyone."

An image of a switchblade flashed through my mind. "Could you be me?" I asked. "Like he was?"

He thought for a moment. "Probably. Yeah, if I wanted to. But replicating real people is a hell of a lot harder than starting from scratch. Although Xavier's good at it, like you saw. Scary good. I don't do it, as a rule. At least, not if I can help it. I mean, there was one time at a Bowie show in '72, but there were . . . extenuating . . . I mean . . . that was a wish, so . . ." He trailed off with another shrug.

"But aside from wishes, it's all illusion," I repeated, mostly to myself. For some reason, I suddenly remembered that night in the parking lot, when I'd asked him to warm me up. He'd said no. I'd assumed it was because he didn't want to, or wasn't supposed to, or something. It honestly hadn't occurred to me that he couldn't.

The list of things that hadn't occurred to me was suddenly getting far too long for my comfort.

He scooted closer to me on the couch. "I know this is a lot

to absorb, Margo, but you asked. And I wanted you to know. I wanted *somebody* to know me, not just as this"—he ran his thumb over his fingertips, reminding me of the magic he held there—"but as me."

In the space of a breath, I took it all in: the feel of his magic, the earnest look on his face, and the way his eyes studied mine, like he was silently urging me toward an understanding I hadn't reached yet.

And all at once, it came crashing down. The huge thing that lay at the center of this whole conversation, even though he hadn't said it out loud. The reason why he was nearly two hundred years old, but he looked sixteen.

"You're not real, are you," I said, jerking my hand away from him. "Oliver Parish doesn't exist."

Oliver's gaze grew sharp. "Well, I wouldn't put it quite like that," he said, with a belated attempt at a smile.

I stood up. "How would you put it?" I said, my voice going taut as I looked down at him.

He regarded me with an expression that looked a lot like fear. "I would say . . . I mean, *I'm* real. I am. And I created Oliver, so—"

"But Oliver isn't real," I said. "You just—you invented him! All week long, we've been— And you spring this on me now? You never thought maybe you should tell me?"

"You didn't ask!" he countered hotly. "Nobody ever asks. You all just assume!"

"Assume you're who you say you are?" I said, dumbfounded. "Well, who the hell wouldn't? And you just let me!"

"Yes, I did. It's part of my job."

"Your job." That was what it came down to, in the end. I was just another job. "So, what, you looked into my head and decided I was just another one of those people who needed a boyfriend to confide in? And you became *this*?" I gestured broadly at his familiar form, suddenly so alien. "Someone two years too young for me, who always wears the same goddamn hoodie, for heaven's sake? Which one of my thoughts told you I wanted any of that?"

Oliver was silent for a moment. His Adam's apple moved as he swallowed. Then he took a breath and said, "None of them. I created Oliver for Vicky, not you."

Of course it was for Vicky. Even now, everything came back to Vicky. Suddenly, I didn't know which was worse: the idea that he might have created Oliver just for me, or the fact that he hadn't.

He continued quietly, evenly: "The night you found my ring, I thought it was Vicky calling me. By the time I saw it was you, it was too late to become someone new, unless I wanted to shift right there in front of you. So I tried to get you to return my ring, so I wouldn't have to worry about who you'd need me to become.

"It almost worked, too, but then your director startled me. I panicked, and I jumped. And once you'd seen my magic, I knew you wouldn't let me go that easily. So when you called me to the diner, I looked into your head to see who you might want me to be. I saw that you wanted someone quiet. Someone safe and comfortable and easy to talk to. Someone who wouldn't judge you poorly for being a bit of a control freak."

I folded my arms tightly around myself, suddenly feeling young and garish in my stage clothes and sparkly makeup. "Stop."

"Friend, boyfriend, it didn't matter, as long as he'd encourage you, entertain you, support you, listen to you—"

"I said stop it."

"I thought I could be all of those things, and still be Oliver. I made the choice in a split second, Margo. I'm sorry if I chose wrong."

My mouth hung open. Sorry, my ass. I wanted to throw something at him. Something heavy. Something that would fill up this awful hollow feeling . . .

"It does matter," I said, fighting to keep my voice even.

His eyes narrowed. "What does?"

"The friend-or-boyfriend thing," I said. "It matters a lot."

"Sure, if you say so."

"You *kissed* me." The words slipped out of my mouth before I could stop them. They sounded pathetic and needy, and I hated them for it.

"You wanted me to," he replied.

"I asked, though!" I said. "I asked you, and you said—"

"I said it was a bad idea," he finished flatly.

Tears stung the corners of my eyes. Enough halfhearted accusations and evasive answers. If I just asked him directly, he would have to answer me.

"Do you even like me?" I asked shakily.

"Of course I do!" he exclaimed, throwing up an exasperated hand. "Otherwise I wouldn't have—"

"As a friend, or as something else?"

"Both." His eyes fixed firmly on mine, like he was willing me to believe him.

I hugged myself tighter, not sure what I should believe anymore. "But you . . . you programmed yourself like that. You made Oliver like me, because it was your job to become part of my life." Silence. "Am I right?"

His eyes went wide, and for a moment he just stared at me, like I'd spoken to him in ancient Greek. But the moment went on too long, and he flinched. "Yes," he said quickly. "I mean, sort of, but—"

"Oh my god. Oliver." I stared at him, amazed and appalled that I'd been right. "This is . . . I can't . . . I have to leave."

But as I bent down to stuff my feet back into my boots, Oliver unfolded himself from the couch and moved hesitantly toward me. "Margo, don't. I can—"

"If you say you can explain, I swear I will kill you." Gritting my teeth, I yanked at the zipper on my left boot. Then pulled it down and yanked again when it got stuck. It still wouldn't go up. I left it alone and grabbed the other boot.

Oliver came over to me and knelt on the floor, positioning himself so he had to look up to see my face. "Just listen, okay? I'm sorry. I didn't know you'd react like this. I should have, but I didn't."

"React like what?" I asked, zipping up the other boot in one satisfyingly vicious yank. "Like a control freak?"

"That's not what I—"

"So if you *had* known I'd react like this, then you probably wouldn't have told me, right?" I stood up straight and glared down at him. "Seriously. Direct question. Would you still have told me?"

He hesitated. "I don't know."

"You don't know," I muttered, and shook my head. "I thought you had to give me honest answers."

"That *was* an honest answer," he said. "Margo—"

"Just shut up."

Oliver sat back on his heels, like I'd just physically hit him. I stalked over to the closet and found my coat inside, hanging on one of three mismatched hangers. The other two were empty.

When I closed the closet door again, Oliver was still on the floor, watching me like he couldn't believe I was really about to go. I ignored him, zipped myself into my coat, and headed for the door.

"Just be careful, will you?" came Oliver's resigned voice as my hand turned the knob. "Xavier's still out there, and I don't want you to get hurt again."

"He doesn't want me, remember? He wants you." I turned and fixed him with a glare. "I only got *hurt* because of you and your stupid ring."

His expression tightened, but he replied without missing a beat: "And as long as you still have the ring, Xavier will have his eye on you. No matter what you heard him promise."

"Then maybe I should ditch the ring, huh? So you don't have to be my slave anymore?"

Oliver drew in a short breath, his face falling. "Margo, no matter what you think, I still . . ." He shook his head, his expression turning stoic. "Never mind. It's your decision, not mine. If that'll make it easier for you, then go ahead. Give me the ring. You won't have to worry about Xavier anymore."

Not moving from where he knelt on the floor, he held one hand out toward me, palm up: a gesture that managed somehow to be a demand and an offering at the same time.

I watched him, trying to figure out if he was bluffing, but his face gave nothing away. I turned back and walked out the door, the ring still in my pocket. I just wanted my third wish. That was all.

Chapter SIXTEEN

Only when I was halfway home and my anger had cooled a little, did I realize that Oliver was right about Xavier. He knew who I was, where I lived, and even where I kept Oliver's ring. And he could become anyone. What was to stop him from coming after me again, whenever he wanted? Sure, he'd promised to leave me alone, but how much could I really trust a guy who attacked me and stole my identity?

So even though it was almost midnight, I called Naomi and asked if I could sleep over. I knew it wasn't any better than spending the night alone in my house, but at this point I'd settle for even the illusion of safety. I drove over as fast as I could, then made absolutely sure her lawn was empty before dashing for the front door.

When she let me inside, the remnants of her earlier annoyance still lingered in her face. But before I could even muster up an excuse to avoid talking about Oliver or George or the South Star, she shook her head and said, "You look like the walking

dead, McKenna. Let's get you some jammies so you can crash."
And that was what we did.

But as comfortable as Naomi's pillow-top queen-size mat-
tress was, and as many times as I'd slept over before, I couldn't
calm down enough to sleep well. I tried telling myself that at
least Xavier probably didn't know where Naomi lived, and
wouldn't he be surprised when he jumped into my bedroom
that night only to find me gone—but somehow, that wasn't terribly comforting.

After the third time some tiny sound jerked me out of that
hazy, heavy place just before sleep, I decided to give up. Sliding
silently out of the bed, I crept across Naomi's room by moon-
light, took her laptop, and went down to the living room. After
a quick look through my email, I typed *Oliver Parish* into Google
and began to scroll through the results.

There were a few people who shared his name, but a quick
look at each link revealed that none of them were the Oliver I
knew. I went to page after page, but my search just confirmed
it: As far as most of the world was concerned, he didn't exist.

When Naomi woke me up in the morning, I was curled up
on her couch, and her monitor displayed the decidedly useless
results of a search on *Oliver Parish Xavier*. She just shook her
head and wordlessly carried the laptop back upstairs.

I got home around ten thirty, expecting to find an empty
house—but both of my parents' cars were in the driveway. I

almost turned around and went straight back to Naomi's, but somehow I forced myself to park and go inside. *It will not be as scary as getting stabbed,* I told myself firmly.

But when I came face-to-face with my mom, I wasn't sure about that anymore. She didn't even speak to me at first; she just looked at me like she couldn't decide whether to hug me or yell at me. After a moment of the most awkward silence ever, she pressed a cup of coffee into my hands, steered me into the kitchen, and said, "Sit."

I sat.

"Well?" she said, easing herself into the chair opposite mine. Even in her fluffy pink robe, she looked willing and able to commit murder.

"I thought you'd still be at Aunt Sarah's," I murmured, even though that obviously wasn't what I was supposed to say.

"We didn't go," she said curtly. "We went to the South Star Bar instead, to see you play."

I went very still. "You . . . you saw me play?"

She took a sip of her own coffee, and let out a long sigh. "Yes. Which doesn't change what happened. Margaret, I understand that this concert was important to you, but that does not mean you can disobey us whenever you want to."

"I'm sorry," I said automatically.

She eyed me. "Are you, really? Or are you just saying that because you think it's what I want to hear?"

I was definitely sorry about most of what had happened last

night, so it wasn't a complete lie when I lowered my eyes and said, "No, I really am. I am really, truly, honest-to-god one hundred percent sorry."

I waited for her to lecture me, or to yell, but after a few moments of eerie quiet, I realized there was nothing else she could say. I'd done what I'd done, and she couldn't change it. Because I'd made my own decision for once, and damn well stuck to it.

Somehow, that didn't make me feel as good as I'd hoped it would.

"So you really came to the gig?" I asked, clutching my mug tightly.

She nodded. "Your father and I tried to catch you after the show, but you must have left before that other band was done. Apocalypse . . . whatever it was. They were strange. But your performance . . ."

My throat went dry, and I braced myself for the worst, already racking my brain for an excuse. I had a migraine. Someone spiked my drink. I ate some really questionable food that mysteriously altered my entire personality.

But then, Mom smiled at me. "It was adorable," she said. "Your songs were . . . and your stage persona! So different from what I ever would have expected of you. But you're just full of surprises, aren't you? Do you remember when you used to put on your own concerts for us? Gosh, it's been such a long time."

I remembered all too well. I was seven years old, and I'd just gotten my first piano—if you defined "piano" as "small battery-powered instrument with eight color-coded keys." I wrote my first songs on that thing, usually with lyrics about the various woes of my many stuffed animals, and performed them for my parents in a series of well-received living room concerts.

I'd absolutely lived for those concerts. Nowadays, I tried not to think about them too much. Mostly because, as I was redis-covering right now, the memory made me want to crawl under the kitchen table. And this was what Xavier's performance had reminded my mother of? At least, if she'd criticized it, that would've meant that she thought I could do better. But this . . . ?

"It's definitely been a long time," I said numbly.

Mom gave me a soft, wistful look, clearly more comfortable dealing with the memory of little-kid-me than with the me sit-ting in front of her. "You used to write all kinds of songs when you were little. I loved it so much. But after your father and I separated, you just got so serious all of a sudden, and . . . well, I'm just glad you're doing something that makes you happy. I'm proud of you, honey. We both are."

"Thanks . . . ?"

Standing up with her coffee cup in hand, she pointed her spoon at me. "But if you ever do that to me again," she said, "you are grounded for the rest of your life."

Grounding me now would work just about as well as forbid-ding me to go to the South Star, and she probably knew it as well as I did. But with all this guilt weighing me down, I wasn't about to argue the point. I nodded firmly and said, "Aye-aye, Captain."

She headed upstairs, and I slumped over in my seat. Yet another thing I hadn't planned on: my parents ditching Aunt Sarah and actually showing up to my gig. Maybe it was for the best that they hadn't heard my real songs. After all, what would I have done if Mom had actually heard my emo masterpiece, "Hayley Mills"? Would she have understood that it was about her? Would she have called me on it?

But all those questions were pointless, because she'd seen Xavier instead of me. And he'd proven singlehandedly that my parents had been right all along: We really were living in *The Parent Trap*. Just not the part where I'd wanted them to get back together.

No, we were living in the part where my identical twin had replaced me, and my own mother hadn't been able to tell the difference.

Instead of waking me up, as I'd hoped, the coffee just made me feel vaguely queasy. After finishing it and putting the mug neatly in the dishwasher, I trudged upstairs, found Ziggy, and locked us both safely inside my bedroom. For one crazy moment I thought about calling Oliver, but dismissed the thought just as quickly. I couldn't deal with him today.

Hell, I could barely deal with myself today.

The moment I'd picked up that ring, I'd started losing track of who I was. First I'd become the sort of person who believed in magic. Acceptable, since magic was apparently real. But then I'd become the sort of person who agreed to play a professional gig with only five days' notice, without checking with her parents first, and without ever having played for a real audience in her life. Then, the sort of person who sneaked out. Who lied to her best friend. Who apologized to her mother and didn't even mean it.

And I'd done it all because I'd trusted Oliver Parish: a boy who didn't even really exist.

My fingers itched with the urge to transform this gut-wrenchingly awful feeling into a song, but I stopped myself before I could reach for my guitar. Songwriting would only make me think of my first wish, and Oliver, and that amazing day we'd shared in the park. I didn't need that right now.

So I opened up my laptop and started working on my AP English essay. At least, I tried to. For every sentence I typed, I spent a good ten minutes staring listlessly out the window— until I remembered that I was supposed to be working and started again.

The fifth time this happened, something caught my eye. A flicker of movement from the window.

Remembering the night Oliver had been here, and the creepy feeling of being watched, I stood up and peered nervously outside. Just below my window, half hidden in the shadow of my house, someone was standing. Waiting. I sucked in a breath, my right hand moving instinctively to cradle my left. Xavier. It had to be.

But then he looked up, and I saw that it wasn't Xavier at all. It was Oliver. Or was it? Could Xavier take Oliver's shape as easily as he'd taken mine?

Smiling hopefully up at me, he pointed first at himself, then at my window. The gesture was clear: *Can I come in?*

Oliver, then. Surely Xavier wouldn't bother asking. Still, I shook my head. *I want you to leave me alone,* I thought firmly at him, knowing that he could easily hear me.

His face fell. But he made the same gesture again, this time mouthing one word: *Please.*

My chest felt hollow, like my lungs were shrinking. It actually hurt to look at the desperation in his face. But I just couldn't bring myself to let him into my room. Not this soon.

Pressing my lips together, I thought firmly, *I want you to go.*

It took a moment, one very long moment, but Oliver nodded. Giving me a small, tight smile, he vanished from the yard.

Chapter SEVENTEEN

I thought about faking a cold on Monday, so I could stay home sick. But then I thought about another day at home, alone, stuck inside my own head, with nobody but Ziggy to protect me if Xavier dropped by for a visit. So I dressed in the most comfortable outfit I could find, drove to school, and braced myself for the worst.

I arrived at my calculus classroom early , but I wasn't the first one there. Simon was already in the room, iPod on, using his desk as a pillow. A jolt of nervous energy shot through me, and I paused in the doorway. Xavier wouldn't disguise himself as Simon and fall asleep in a classroom. Would he?

I eased into the room. Simon opened one bleary eye and pulled one of his earbuds out.

"You're here early," I said, moving warily toward an empty desk.

"Nnngh," he said. "Moron Morton failed me on the quiz last

week. Wanted to ask about extra credit." He sat up straight, blinking rapidly. "Which means I should probably be awake when he comes in."

"Probably so," I said with a cautious smile.

Simon stretched his arms over his head. Then looked sharply over at me. "Hey!" he said. "Where'd you go after your set?"

My heart sank. This was really Simon, which was great. But if he meant what I thought he meant, that was a lot less great. "My set?" I asked.

"Saturday night," he said. "Duh. I was looking for you. Did you leave early?"

I dropped my backpack and sank into my seat. This day sucked. I hadn't even been at school for ten minutes, and this day totally and completely sucked. "Yeah, I did," I said. "Sorry. Wait, how did you even get in?"

"Friend of mine. You don't know him. Scored me a fake ID so we could go."

"Ah. And, um . . . was it just you and your friend?"

"Yeah." He shrugged. "I asked MaLinda, and she would've come, and Danny Q would've come with his boyfriend, too, except we only found out on Friday, and everyone already had plans."

I let out a sigh of relief. Only one person I knew had been there. That was one more than I wanted, but it was still manageable.

"But don't worry," Simon continued. "I took video with my phone and put it all up on YouTube!"

I stared at him in horror. "No. No, no, no! Why would you do that? You can't do that. You have to take it down."

"Why?" he said. "You put on a good show! You deserve to be seen!"

"But I . . . Wait. A good show?"

"Really good!" he said, grinning. "I mean, like, horrible, but in this totally ironic way. The ultimate commentary on the state of the music industry today. Like in that one song? Where you had the part that just went 'sparkle sparkle sparkle sparkle' twenty times in a row? Effing hilarious."

He held out a fist toward me, like he was trying to punch me but someone had hit the pause button right in the middle. I gave him a confused look, and he rolled his eyes. "Fist-bump, dude."

"Ah," I replied, and dutifully bumped fists with him. "Um. Well, thanks. Did your friend think it was hilarious, too?"

"Nah, I don't think he really got it. I mean, whatever, he's not a music person. He ditched me to chill at the bar for, like, the entire show. But it's okay." He leaned in, like he was about to tell me a secret. Like he'd done at the *Bat Boy* cast party, right before we'd kissed. "You and me, dude, we know what's what."

"Simon," I said slowly, enunciating each syllable as I leaned away from him. "You have to take the videos down. Now."

He blinked at me. "How? Bell's about to ring."

"I don't care. Just do it."

A pause, and then he shrugged. "If you say so. It's your music, after all. I have study hall third period, so I'll do it then. But I'm just saying, leave it up and this could go viral. You could be famous."

There were so many things wrong with that idea, I didn't even know where to begin. But luckily, Naomi chose that moment to walk in, followed closely by Kara and Eli, two other seniors I didn't know as well. Naomi strode right over to my desk, her smartphone in her hand.

"What the hell, McKenna?" she said, practically radiating fury.

I recoiled at her expression, which was one she usually reserved for actors who still didn't know their lines by final dress rehearsal. "What? What'd I do?"

She thrust the phone at me, then crossed her arms and waited. A video was playing on the screen. A video of someone who looked an awful lot like me, playing an out-of-tune guitar and singing lyrics that I couldn't make out.

"Oh," I said, my throat suddenly dry. "That's . . . that's . . ."

"That's you," she said. "That's you, playing at the South Star Bar, uploaded on Saturday night at exactly eleven forty-two p.m."

I tried and failed to come up with an explanation that didn't involve magic. But all my brain could cough up was, "That can't be right. That's not me."

"Shut up, that's totally you," said Simon, leaning over Naomi's shoulder. "That's my vid. Isn't it awesome?"

I hadn't thought it possible for Naomi to look angrier, but apparently I'd been wrong. "Saturday at quarter to midnight, which, I might add, is around the same time you called and asked me if you could sleep over. *Without* telling me that after you ditched me and Willoughbee, you and your little dropout boy toy turned around and went back to New York to, I dunno, play a late show or whatever it was."

"No, no, no!" I said quickly, holding my hands out defensively. Simon, finally sensing that he had no place in this conversation, backed slowly away.

"Then what happened?" said Naomi, snatching her phone back and pointing to the screen. "Explain."

That's not me, I wanted to shout. *Why can't anyone see that's not me?*

But I couldn't say that. I couldn't tell her the truth. Unfortunately, that didn't leave me with a lot of plausible options. None, in fact, except the story she'd already come up with on her own.

"I'm sorry," I whispered. "I didn't mean anything by it. I just wanted—"

"You wanted me not to be there," she finished darkly. "You know, you could've just said so."

"Said so . . . ?"

"Yeah. You know, 'Hey, my bestest gal pal, thanks for wasting your Saturday night on me, not to mention all the gas money it took to get to New York, but I'd rather hang out with Simon Lee and my stupid camera-happy sophomore boyfriend tonight.' See what I mean? Like, if you're gonna be a terrible friend, at least don't lie to my face about it."

Everyone was watching us, mouths open and eyes wide. I wanted to crawl under my desk and die.

"I thought you were gonna turn out cool, McKenna," said Naomi. "But you seriously need to grow the hell up."

I knew my face was beet-red, and I could feel my heart pounding. But I kept my voice steady and sweet as I said, "Grow up? I'm not the one starting fights in the middle of school."

Her expression grew stormy, and I knew I was in for it—but then the door swung open and Mr. Morton, our calc teacher, came in. He didn't even seem to notice the tension in the air as he walked to his desk. Naomi stared at me, clearly torn between speaking her mind and avoiding detention. After a moment, she just shook her head and stalked away to sit on the other side of the room.

"Late show?" I heard Simon murmur. Nobody answered him.

True to his word, Simon took the videos down during third period, but the damage had already been done. People looked at me funny in the hallway. Five different students, three of whose names I didn't even know, whispered "Sparkle sparkle!"

as they passed me. And Naomi didn't speak to me for the rest of the day.

Since that night was the first meeting of the *Sweeney Todd* tech crew, Miss Delisio had her hands full with set-building preparations, which left the cast in George's hands. As I came in, I saw our esteemed director near the back of the stage, gesturing expansively at a ragtag assortment of students while Naomi took notes. The cast remained in the audience, looking on with vague curiosity, but there wasn't a single person among them I wanted to talk to.

"Margo!" called a voice, and I whipped around, an image of a blade flashing in my mind. Sure enough, Vicky was heading toward me. My heart started pounding, but I willed it to calm down. This was Vicky, not Xavier. Probably.

"I've been looking for you all day," she said breathlessly, as soon as she was close enough to speak quietly. "I saw Simon's video last night. I saw it, and I thought, that explains why she was so upset on Saturday. Not that you wouldn't've been upset anyway, but that wasn't really you, was it?"

The one person who could tell me apart from Xavier's version of me, and it was Vicky Freaking Willoughbee. Awesome.

I nodded.

"I knew it," she whispered. "But who was it? Oliver said someone like him. Another genie?"

Her eyes were wide, and everything about her radiated nervous energy. Okay, not Xavier. I sighed, letting my shoulders slump. "Another genie," I said. "He made himself look like me. That was the second time I saw him. The first time, he looked like you, and he stabbed me in the leg with a switchblade. He wants Oliver's ring."

Vicky gasped, and her hand flew to her mouth. "He was me? But how did . . . oh no." Her face went pale.

"What is it?" I asked.

"There was this guy," she said, and swallowed hard. "Um. This guy, a couple weeks ago at the bowling alley, he made some comment about Oliver's ring." She paused, and I tried and failed to picture her bowling. "I was wearing it, so I didn't think it was weird, but he asked if he could see it, and then he got really mad when I said no."

"That sounds like him," I said. "What did he look like? Anyone we know?"

"I didn't recognize him. He introduced himself, but I don't remember the name he said."

"Xavier?" I asked.

She shook her head. "I don't think so."

An intense feeling of claustrophobia crawled up my spine. He'd used another name: yet another reminder that he could be anyone. He could be Miss Delisio, or Naomi, or George, or . . .

"How'd he know to look for me?" Vicky asked softly, interrupting my fit of paranoia. But I didn't have an answer for her.

And I didn't have time to think of one, because that was when George walked in and beckoned me over to the piano. Mouth suddenly dry, I left Vicky behind and slunk toward him. I could feel the eyes of at least half the cast watching me, but hey, at least they'd be witnesses if he turned out to be Xavier in disguise.

"Different songs, huh?" he said, eyeing me as he pulled his *Sweeney Todd* score out of his bag and set it on the piano.

"Um," I said stupidly. As many times as I'd imagined this conversation over the past two days, I'd spent all my energy envisioning what George might say to me. Not once had I thought about what I'd say back. What had happened to the Margo who always had a plan? And who was this idiot standing in her place?

He quirked an eyebrow at me. "Not what I had in mind when I asked you to open." His voice was as calm and even as ever, but underneath it was the very thing I'd been searching for in my mom's reaction.

Disappointment.

"I know. I'm sorry. I was terrible. I . . . I don't even . . ."

"It was my fault," came a quiet, steady voice from beside me. My heart leaped into my throat. Oliver was there, a flash drive in one hand and a contrite look on his face. "I shouldn't have let her get up on that stage," he said.

"What do you," I began, but he gave me a look that told me plainly to shut up and let him talk.

"That so?" said George, settling himself on the piano bench.

"Yeah," said Oliver. "See, we were on our way to the South Star, and Margo got this horrible migraine. I had some pain medication in my car, so I gave her some. I think she must have been allergic or something. Her speech was slurring, and she kept saying her vision was funny, and I asked if she still wanted to perform, and she said she was perfectly fine, and . . . I'm so sorry, I really am. I should have known better."

George looked dubiously back and forth between Oliver and me. I kept my mouth shut. The story sounded far-fetched at best, but it was a hell of a lot better than saying a genie had stolen my identity and taken my place.

"Pain meds?" said George.

"Yes," said Oliver, his tone as meek as his expression. He was a damn good liar. But of course, I knew that already.

As much as I hated giving Oliver any credit right now, I played along: "I don't even remember half of what I played that night. But the ones I do remember . . . god, I'm so embarrassed. I wrote that stuff when I was like twelve. I'm so sorry you guys had to hear any of that."

George was starting to look mollified—even amused. Finally, he just shook his head. "No worries, I guess. Just retire those songs, okay?"

"Consider them retired, shredded, burned at the stake, and shot with silver bullets. I'll do better next time. I promise."

"Next time?" he said mildly, turning back to the piano.

Of course. This gig had been a trial, and in his eyes, I'd failed spectacularly. Panic surged through me, and I grabbed his leather-clad forearm.

"Give me one more chance," I said. "I can do better. You know I can. I'm just really new at this. Please."

George looked at my hand on his arm, then back up at my face. There was sympathy in the smile he gave me, which just made things worse.

"I have to start rehearsal," he said, and shrugged my hand off.

I left George and the piano behind, feeling oddly numb. But when I reached my seat in the third row and started to rearrange my stuff, I realized that Oliver had followed me. He stood a few feet away, not quite looking at me, obviously waiting for me to speak first.

"What?" I said.

He looked up, eyebrows furrowing. "You're welcome," he said pointedly.

Simon, a few seats over from mine, looked curiously over at us. So did a few other people. I decided not to care. "For what?" I said coolly. "You got me into this mess in the first place."

Which was not only mean, but also mostly untrue. Still, it felt good to say. Well, a little bit good. Also a little bit horrible. But I didn't apologize.

"What are you even doing here, anyway?" I went on. "I thought you dropped out."

"I did," he said evenly, and held up the flash drive. "I just stopped by to give Miss Delisio the pictures for her slide show. And to find you. Can I talk to you for a minute?"

I narrowed my eyes and lowered my voice. "As Oliver, or as you?"

"Both," he replied, clutching the flash drive harder. "I know you're angry at me. I'm not saying you shouldn't be. But I do think you deserve an explanation."

"I deserve one, or you deserve the chance to give me one?"

He hesitated, then said again, "Both."

I moved my backpack to the floor and sat down, ignoring him. I was being childish, and we both knew it, but I didn't know what else to do. There was no script for what to do when you find out that the boy you like isn't real. Especially when the boy in question, real or not, was standing over you, his pretty green eyes silently pleading with you to forgive him.

After a moment, he sighed. "Okay. I'm going to give this to Miss Delisio, and I'm going to leave you to your rehearsal. If you want to talk, call me when you're finished. If not . . ." He shrugged expressively, but didn't finish.

I gave him a single, quick nod to let him know that I'd think about it. But as he walked away, I already knew I wanted to hear what he had to say.

Chapter EIGHTEEN

Only when rehearsal ended, two hours later, did I let myself think about Oliver again. Spending most of the rehearsal as Toby had done good things for me. It was the first time since Saturday that my head felt clear. So I went immediately to Tom's Diner, where I snagged the same back-corner booth, the one under the framed fajita picture, and touched the ring. Almost right away, Oliver appeared inside the door—just like the first time I'd called him here, not even two weeks ago.

As he slid out of his coat and into the seat opposite mine, a waitress plunked two menus down on the table and asked if we wanted anything to drink.

"Just a hot chocolate," I said. "No whipped cream."

"Belgian waffles," said Oliver. "Everything on them. Oh, and lemon tea, if you have it."

"Tea," I said dryly as the waitress left. "How very healthy of you."

He nodded gravely. "You may have noticed that I am a very health-conscious individual."

Pointedly ignoring his attempt at wit, I took a breath and said what I'd come here to say: "You wanted to talk. So talk. And don't you dare think about turning this place into a French café again."

He frowned at me. "Margo, are you okay?"

"Of course I'm not okay," I snapped. "You lied to me."

Oliver's eyes flicked downward, just for a second, and I could tell I'd caught him off guard. "I didn't lie, Margo. Not to you, at least not the way you think. You never gave me a chance to explain myself." It wasn't an accusation. Just a fact. "You asked if I programmed myself to like you. I did, and that's the truth, but it's not the whole truth."

This sounded like the beginning of a speech. I wondered how many times he'd practiced what he would say to me tonight. Something inside me softened a little, and I nodded for him to continue.

"The thing is," he said, "I have to do that. Every time I create a new identity, I'm creating a brand-new version of myself. I add things here and there, depending on who my master is. Like, say my ring gets picked up by some German expat living in Japan. I'll probably want to make myself fluent in German and Japanese, you know? But that's just little stuff. The big stuff doesn't change. It's always me. Different-looking versions of the same person."

"Okay," I said slowly. "So Oliver is just a version of the real you. A version based on what you thought Vicky needed in her life—which happened to be a cute guy."

Oliver grinned. "At least you still think I'm cute."

I folded my arms protectively across my chest, like that would somehow stop me from fixating on those eyes of his. I couldn't have this conversation now; I wasn't finished being mad at him. "Cute by Vicky's standards, is what I meant. Not that I—I mean, it's not like I even know her well enough to say what her standards are. But like, cute by anyone's standards. Just sort of generally . . . I mean, not *my* standards. That's not what I'm saying. It's not like I have . . . standards. . . ."

I frowned, wondering exactly where that train of thought had derailed.

Oliver took a well-deserved moment to smirk at me, but thankfully didn't drag it out too long. "Okay, here's the thing. Vicky's best friend is someone she's never met."

"So?"

"His name is Devon. He lives just outside of London, and she met him online. They talk nearly every day, usually about his girl troubles or the plays they've seen. She loves him like a brother. So I took her mental picture of him, changed it enough that it wouldn't freak her out too much, and went from there." He gestured down at himself. "And here I am."

"So, you're Vicky's new fake online brother."

"Yeah," he said. "Well, it's not as precise as that, but starting out with a brother-sister–ish relationship was a way for me to connect with her. Making sure I like my masters, that I have some kind of connection with them, is the one thing I change about myself every single time, before I do anything else. Even if I'm one hundred and five percent sure I'll come to like them anyway. Otherwise, odds are as good as any that I'll end up bound to someone I can't stand." He smiled. "That's why I said yes to your question. I did program myself to like you, but not in the way you think. It's just habit. A safety precaution. It's part of my job."

"Like a magic bike helmet."

He grinned. "Sure, something like that."

"But it isn't always a brother-sister connection. You said so yourself: Some people confide most easily in, um . . ." My entire body tensed, and I tried to start again. "With me . . . you made yourself into a boyfriend for me. The perfect boyfriend. You kissed me exactly the way I wanted. You practiced songs with me. You even liked my favorite singer. And you let me think it was real."

"I tried to create a friend for you, Margo," he said earnestly. "That was all. I promise."

"Then why—"

"I don't know why!" He almost shouted the words, but then snapped his mouth closed, looking startled at his own tone. Leaning over, he rested his forehead in his hands. "I'm sorry. I hate having a sixteen-year-old body. Sometimes you just don't know how to *say* things." He took a deep breath. "I saw your audition."

"What?" I said, confused.

"When Vicky was my master, she wanted me to go with her to the musical auditions. She wanted me to tell her she'd done well, because she thought nobody else would. So I watched her, and I watched everyone else, too. That's when I first noticed you. Singing. Long before you found my ring, and long before I had to . . . to program myself, and . . ."

His eyes met mine. Something sharp crackled in the air between us, and he gave a little shake of his head. "Screw it. I had this whole speech planned out, but—listen, here it is, plain and simple. I don't fall for people. Ever. I don't let myself, not anymore. I go in, do my job, and leave. But you can't always plan for the side effects of having different bodies. I mean, as Oliver, who knew I'd end up craving waffles all the time? I sure didn't." He took a short breath. "Just like I didn't know I'd fall head over heels for you."

A mug of hot chocolate clinked onto the table in front of me, making me jump. I looked up sharply, and there was our waitress, grinning her face off as she arranged our orders in front of us.

"Need anything else?" she said. "Or should I, ah, leave you two alone?"

"We're fine," I said, in what I sincerely hoped was a dignified voice. "Thank you for asking."

The waitress gave Oliver a pointed once-over, then gave me a wink before she walked away. An actual wink.

Oliver saw it, too. "Ah," he said, and scooted farther into his side of the booth. "Come sit over here. We can whisper."

With a low laugh, I gratefully did as he asked. He slid his waffle over to where he now sat, and took a quick bite. A blissful expression flitted across his face, for just a fraction of a second, as he swallowed.

"You didn't plan on liking waffles this much, huh?" I said.

"No," he replied, giving me a timid little smile. "I didn't plan on a lot of things."

"Same," I said, grabbing my mug from across the table. I rolled it back and forth between my palms, letting its heat focus me. "I definitely didn't plan on getting involved with someone so . . . um."

"Charming?" he supplied hopefully.

I shot him a look. "Unpredictable."

His smile faltered.

"You just said so yourself," I continued. "New bodies for every master, with different side effects every time. I mean, if you changed into someone else right now, right this second, would you still . . . you know . . . want to eat waffles?"

He paused, his fork hovering just above his plate. He looked at the waffle in question, and then back up at me. "That was the real reason I decided not to change. Not because I didn't have time, although that was part of it. It was because I already liked, um, waffles." He laughed, squeezing his eyes shut for a second. "I'm sorry, I can't do this. This is a terrible metaphor. I already liked *you*, Margo, and I liked liking you, and I didn't want to risk ruining it."

"But liking me was still just a side effect," I said. "You might have changed your mind about me if you'd changed into someone else."

"I thought so at first," he said, pressing his fork between his palms. "But it's not. I checked. That night in the parking lot, the first time we kissed? After you left, I shifted. I changed into as many of my former selves as I could remember, and every single one of them felt the same way about you. It isn't a side effect, Margo. It's real."

"Oh," I said, suddenly feeling incredibly stupid, and more than a little embarrassed. "But . . . ever since my audition? Really? That was before I even met you."

Oliver nodded. "Your audition, and everything you've done onstage since then. You're so . . ." He paused, his face going red as he searched for the right word. "I'd say talented, but that isn't enough. There are talented people in this play, Margo, but nobody else does what you do."

I shrugged, trying to hide how enormously flattered I was. "It's just singing. We've got plenty of good singers in this cast. Look at Callie and Dan. Hell, look at Simon."

"Sure," he conceded, "but they always look like they're trying too hard. You sing like you talk—like it's natural for you, even when you're playing someone else. You're just so full of joy when you're up there, like you're losing yourself in the performance, and you slip in and out of character like you're not even trying, and it's so . . . anyway." He bit his lip. "Plus, you tried to give my ring back. Twice."

I frowned, thinking back. "So what?"

He looked surprised. "So what? So everything. Margo, I've been a genie nearly my entire life. I've lost count of how many people have found my ring. Not counting Xavier, this was the first time in my entire life that someone offered it back to me."

"Are you serious?" I said, dumbfounded. I'd only offered the ring back because I didn't want to piss him off by taking too long to make my wishes. It wasn't supposed to be some grand, magnanimous gesture. Surely he knew that.

"Totally serious," he said, smiling as he pointed his fork at me. "You were the first."

My cheeks flushed. I couldn't help it. "Nearly," was the first thing I managed to say. "You said nearly your entire life. You haven't always been a genie?"

"I was born human," he said. "All of us were."

Born human. *Born real,* came an insidious, unwelcome little thought. I clutched my mug tighter.

"How did you become a genie, then?" I said, and then tried for a little smile. "Did another genie bite you?"

He laughed. "No, no, nothing like that. It was my choice, actually. I made a fourth wish."

"A fourth . . ." I trailed off. "What?"

"A fourth wish," he said again, smiling at me. "I was a genie's master, too, once, back when I was human. I found his coin—his spirit vessel—completely by accident, just like you did. I made my three wishes, and then . . . well, then I made a fourth."

"You can do that?" I asked.

He nodded gravely. "You can. Only if you're willing to trade your human life for it, but you can. And I did."

I frowned. "Why?"

"For the sake of someone dear to me." His expression grew strained, and he looked down at his hands. "The wish was for my fiancée. Maeve."

"Fiancée?" I repeated, louder than I'd intended. "You have a fiancée, and you didn't tell me?"

"I *had* a fiancée," he said, smiling sadly. "She's . . . It was a very long time ago. When I was human."

"Oh, right, duh," I said sheepishly, embarrassed by my outburst. "You said that already. So . . . that means you were older, right? Older than you are now? Unless, did sixteen-year-olds get engaged back then?"

"Some did," he said wryly. "Some still do. But no, I was twenty-three when I asked Maeve to marry me. And when I made my fourth wish."

"Oh," I said, frowning to myself. He'd been twenty-three and engaged, *and* he was a two-hundred-year-old magical being. The fact that he still looked sixteen was becoming more and more unsettling.

"And my name was Ciarán," he said with a hint of an accent. I repeated the name, tasting the unfamiliar cadence of it, and he nodded. "Do you want to hear more?"

"Yeah," I said. "I do. Ciarán—is that Scottish?"

"Irish." He twisted slightly in the booth and steadied himself with one elbow on the table, so we were face-to-face again. "When I was human, I lived in Dublin with my family. My mother, my father, sisters, grandmother. I went to school and then got a job at the brewery when I was old enough. Went to church on Sundays, painted pictures when I had time, drank some. And I had Maeve."

"That sounds . . . normal," I said, frowning. "Why'd you give it all up? What happened?"

"Well." He dragged the word out a little. "Okay. How much do you know about Irish history?"

I gave him an apologetic shrug. I barely knew my own country's history, let alone anyone else's.

"Okay. But you've heard of the Great Famine, right?"

"The Gr—" I let my head fall into my hands as I realized what he was talking about. "You mean the potato famine? You were actually alive for the freaking potato famine. That's just . . . That's . . ."

It wasn't even a real thing, is what it was. It existed in textbooks and bad Irish jokes, not in the personal histories of people I actually knew.

He nudged me with his shoulder. "Yeah, I'm old. Rub it in, why don't you."

I winced, but when I looked back up at him, there was a sly smile on his face. "Okay," I said. "Potato famine. Go."

"Right. So, we were already hearing about crop failures out west. It wasn't bad for us yet in the city, but we all knew it was just a matter of time. So when Niall—that was what my genie called himself, Niall—when he told me I could make three wishes, I used them all to keep the people I loved from starving when the famine came. My family. My friends. Maeve and her family, too."

I looked down at my hands. I'd wished for musical talent and a healed finger, and this guy had saved people from a famine. "Uh-huh," I said weakly.

"Once Niall had granted all my wishes, he told me that I had two choices. One: I could give his coin back to him, and he would just vanish. No more master, no more body." Seeing the stricken look on my face, he rushed to explain: "It's not like we stop existing. It's more like . . . we're invisible. Like ghosts."

"So, wait," I said, holding up a hand. "That's it? You grant three wishes, and you just disappear? Then what?"

"Then I get a vacation," he said, with a grin that looked forced. "But usually not for long. I don't exactly enjoy not having a body."

I tried very hard not to think about returning Oliver's ring and watching him vanish—watching him become a ghost. "Then how do you find a new master? Do you get to pick who it is?"

"I can try," he said. "But it's always a gamble. I mean, even if I drop my vessel in the middle of your bedroom, you might not be the first person to find it. And that's assuming my previous master returns my vessel in the first place. Some of them pass me along to their friends, which is just . . ." He trailed off, shaking his head.

"Rude?" I suggested timidly.

"That's one word for it," he said darkly. "Especially if they don't ask first. You'd be surprised how many people don't ask first."

I thought of Vicky, leaving the ring on the bathroom windowsill; I wasn't surprised at all. "Okay, so my first choice is returning your vessel. What's my—I mean, what was your second choice? The fourth wish?"

If he caught my little slip, he didn't acknowledge it. "No. I mean, yes, but he didn't tell me about that right way. The way he told it, my only other choice was to just hold on to the coin, so he'd get to stick around. Not for long, mind you. Without wishes to grant, his magic would fade him away in a week or two, and his vessel would find its way out of my hands. But he'd still get a little while. So that's what I did. He and I had become close by then. He went to the pubs with my friends. My mother practically adopted him. And Maeve . . . they grew fond of each other, too. She was the only one besides me who knew what he really was.

"But Maeve got hurt. There was a fight in the street one night, and there was a carriage, and panicking horses, and . . ." He looked up at the ceiling, blinking fast. I touched his arm, just to remind him that I was there. "It was my fault. I was right in the path of the carriage, and she pushed me out of the way. Would have gotten away herself, too, if the carriage hadn't swerved like it did. It fell over, and she . . . Even if we'd had time to get her to a doctor, I don't think . . . and I'd already used up all my wishes. You have to understand, Maeve was everything to me. I watched her dying right in front of me, and it felt like I was dying, too."

When he finally met my eyes again, his whole body looked weighted down with the memory. I reached for his hand and held it, savoring the tingling warmth of his touch.

"That was when Niall told me about the fourth wish. So I did it. I saved her life, just like she saved mine." He smiled crookedly. "And they all lived happily ever after. The end."

I frowned, hearing something sour in his tone. "Not so happily ever after?"

"Well, at first, maybe," he said, suddenly very intent on studying his mug. There were hairline cracks in it, just like there were in mine. "I vanished in seconds after I made that wish. But soon I was bound to my first master, which let me create a new body for myself. From then on, whenever I had a body but wasn't granting wishes, I spent all my time with her. I became Ciarán again, for her sake. I told her about my . . . my adventures, she called them." A wistful smile tugged at his lips. "She thought it was romantic, at first. But I'd vanish every time my master called me, and sometimes I'd be gone for days at a time, or weeks, and . . ."

He'd pulled his hand out of mine, and was pressing his fingertips hard against his tea mug, like he couldn't decide whether to absorb its warmth or crush it. I remembered the stricken look on his face that night in the parking lot, when I'd kissed him—and how quickly he'd reminded me that he couldn't stay.

"She tried to make it work," he said. "We both did. But in the end, she wanted a real husband. A family. Daughters. I couldn't give her any of those things."

She'd wanted a normal, safe, predictable life. Who could blame her? But Oliver, on the other hand . . . no wonder he never let himself have feelings for normal, mortal people.

No wonder he never told anyone who he really was.

"Oh," I said, feeling entirely inadequate. "I'm sorry."

He blinked at me, then let out a little laugh and ran his hands over his face. "No, I'm sorry, Margo. You didn't ask for all this. I came here to tell you how I feel about you. Not her."

I sat up straight, fixing him with a glare. "Don't you dare apologize. What, you think I'm going to start being jealous of her now or something, just because you loved her a frillion years ago?"

He shrank back a little, his cheeks going red. "I didn't mean that."

"I know, I know," I said, closing my eyes and willing myself to calm down. "Saturday night, you said you wanted me to know who you really are. And all this stuff, Maeve and Ireland and the shapeshifting and the fourth wish—this is what you meant. Isn't it."

He nodded slowly, like he was waiting for me to pass judgment on him.

"Right, then," I said, resolutely steering us back toward what I'd come here to learn. "So where does Xavier come into all this?"

"Ah," he said, shifting uncomfortably in his seat. "Well, you know I wasn't originally called Oliver."

I nodded.

"Niall wasn't my genie's real name, either."

My jaw actually dropped. "What? So he made you a genie and now he wants to kill you? Or, wait, does he want to kill you *because* he made you a genie? Because that's pretty sick."

"No," he said quietly. "My being his . . . protégé . . . that's the only reason he let me live this long. He could have wished me free the first time he got hold of my ring. He didn't."

"He saved you for last," I murmured. Somehow, that troubled me even more.

"Hey, it's better than the alternative," said Oliver, giving me a grin that completely failed to reassure me.

I shook my head. "But you said you were friends!"

"We were," he said, his grin fading a little. "But that was when I knew him as Niall, and when he was showing me how to use my magic. Everything was fine, and then he just disappeared. Twenty years passed, and when he found me again, he was . . ."

"Xavier," I supplied, and Oliver nodded. "So what the hell happened? Something must've happened. Twenty years is a long time."

"I wish I knew. I really do. But he never told me."

Looking away from me, he drained his tea like a shot. I shakily downed the last of my hot chocolate. It had gone cold. When I looked at him again, he was studying his empty mug, a dark look on his face.

"God, Oliver," I said. "I had no idea. But you have a plan, right?"

"A plan?"

"To get rid of him. Or at least get away from him. What are you gonna do?"

"Margo, there's nothing I can do."

"But—"

"Look," he said firmly. "We've got two scenarios here. In the first, Xavier waits to take my ring until you've made your third wish of your own accord, like he promised. But let's face it: That's pretty unlikely. In the second, Xavier bullies you into making your third wish, so my ring unbinds itself from you and he can steal it. Either way, he's coming back for me. I'd venture to guess he won't wait very long."

I stared at him, chilled by his matter-of-fact tone. "And you're okay with that?"

"Of course I'm not okay with it! But it's not up to me anymore. If I'd gotten away before he found me, then maybe I'd have had a chance. I could have taken my vessel and hidden . . . but it's too late now. There's nothing I can do. Excuse me, ma'am. Could we have the check, please?"

The waitress came over and put the check down in front of Oliver. I didn't even protest when he paid for my hot chocolate. As we made our way past the defunct jukeboxes and out of the diner, he took my hand again; the spicy tingle of magic snaked up my arm. But this time, it wasn't reassuring.

Oliver gave my hand a little squeeze as we headed for my car. "You shouldn't worry about it, Margo. I've been lucky. I've had a hell of a lot more time than most people do." He slowed us to a stop next to my car, then stepped in front of me so we were face-to-face. "I'm serious. I know you want to do something about Xavier. I can hear it." He touched one finger to my temple. "But trust me. Leave this one alone."

"Leave it alone?" I repeated incredulously. "How can you say that? How can you just . . . just put your life in someone else's hands like that?"

"I can because I have to," he said simply. "I've always had to. That's what it means to have a master."

"Maybe so, but none of the others were out to kill you," I said, which actually made him laugh. "Wait. Oliver, I have one wish left. I could use it on him. Make him change his mind about wishing you free."

He smiled sadly. "You think I never thought of that? I don't have enough power. I can grant a wish to change my own mind, or a human mind, but the mind of another genie? Not a chance. Believe me, I've tried."

I frowned. "Fine. Then I'll wish him free, before he comes back for you."

"What?" he shouted, his eyes going wide. "No. No, absolutely not."

"Why not?" I said.

"Because I can't just kill him, Margo. I can't."

"But it wouldn't be you," I said slowly. "If I made the wish, it would be me."

For a moment everything was quiet, except for a few cars zooming past, just beyond the parking lot. Slowly, Oliver reached out and took me by the shoulders. He spoke in a low, even voice. "Margo, listen to me. I've been a genie for a long time now. And I love it. Honest, I really do. I love giving people what they want, changing their lives for the better in those tiny little ways.

"But I've done things . . . There are people who honestly want nothing more than to hurt other people. Sometimes you can talk them out of it, but not always." He ran both hands through his hair, agitated and tense. "Have you ever wished a slow and painful death on someone? Have you?"

"N-no," I stammered, trying to remember. "I don't think so. Not out loud, anyway. And I've never actually meant it."

"There are people who do mean it," he said. "They're few and far between, but they're out there. I've met them. One of them—a man from Kiev—he said those exact words to me. He wished for someone to die, and I quote, slowly and painfully. I was bound by those words. He didn't have to decide how. He didn't even have to watch. He could just make his wish and consider it done. I was the one who actually had to make it happen. It was one of the few times in my life where my job really did feel like slavery."

"Couldn't you just—"

"Refuse?" He let out a grating laugh. "No. You can't refuse. I learned that the hard way. If I refuse, my magic will take over and grant the wish for me, using me as a conduit. It would still be my hands doing it, and my eyes watching, but I wouldn't have any control over it. So whatever the wish is, you get it over with, and you hope your next master just wishes for a healthy baby, or a huge promotion, or a billion dollars."

He slid his hands down and threaded his fingers through mine. His voice was unsteady. "But what you're talking about . . . that wouldn't just be you using me as a weapon. That would be me agreeing to it. Benefitting from it. I can't do that. And if you feel anything for me at all, please don't force me to do it. I know you're my master, and you can if you want to . . . but please don't."

He clutched my hands so hard that it almost hurt. But I squeezed back, even harder. "Oliver," I said, like I could put everything I was feeling into that one word. It came out choked. "I wouldn't force you. I won't. Of course I won't."

Relief washed over him like a calming wave, but I couldn't feel what he felt. How could I possibly be what he needed me to be? How could I open myself up enough to accept the truth of him, only to let him disappear from my life without a fight?

I didn't know.

I didn't know anything anymore . . . except that there he was, and here I was, and there was too much space between us. So I wrapped my arms around him, wove my fingers into his soft, dark hair, and pulled him close, anchoring myself in the familiarity of his touch. When he leaned down and pressed his lips to mine, I could feel an urgency in his kiss that matched my own. He pulled me even closer, pressing himself against me like he wanted to disappear into me.

And I let him, because it was the only thing I could do. I just hoped he could hear, somewhere in my thoughts, how sorry I was. Not just for wanting to use him to wish Xavier free, but for not understanding until now that no matter how much I'd trusted Oliver, it didn't begin to compare to the amount of trust he'd placed in me.

Chapter NINETEEN

The next day, after French, I leaned against a bare stretch of hallway wall, keeping a sharp eye out for the person I needed to find. "Vicky!" I called, when I finally spotted her. I waved, and she fought her way through the crowd to get to me.

"Hey, Margo," she said, suspicion edging her tone. "Um. What's up?"

"I need to ask you a favor."

The phrase came out awkward and forced, and Vicky couldn't have looked more surprised if I'd said I was secretly a Martian and I'd come to take over the world. "I . . . what, really? Me? Why?"

Leaning in closer, I lowered my voice. "Because you've seen Xavier before."

She hunched down into herself, like she wasn't sure whether or not I'd just accused her of something. "Oh, you mean at the bowling alley. Yeah. Why?"

"I need to know if he was with anyone when you saw him. Like, someone who might be his master."

Vicky frowned thoughtfully. "I don't know, um . . . No, I don't think so. I mean, he could have been, but I wasn't really paying attention. I'm sorry."

I blew out a sigh. That would have been way too easy. So much for Plan A.

"No worries," I said.

"Sorry," she said again. "But I promise I'll keep an eye out if I see him again, okay?"

"Thanks, Vicky," I said.

I started to move past her, but she stopped me with a hand on my arm. "Hey, wait a second," she said, and nervously licked her lips. "Can I ask you a favor, too?"

"Really?" I said, before I could stop myself. "I mean . . . sure. What is it?"

Vicky fidgeted with the straps of her backpack. "Um," she began—but before she could say anything else, some boy walked by and nudged her shoulder. She jerked back in surprise, and he gave her a very obvious once-over, then grinned as he walked away.

"Who was that?" I asked, looking after the boy. The hallway was getting less crowded. The bell would ring soon, which meant I would be late, but I couldn't bring myself to care.

Her whole body seemed to sag. "I have no idea. But it happens all the time. It's the stupid wish. That's why I need a favor, Margo. I just—" She stopped abruptly, peering at me. "Wait. Oliver did tell you what I wished for, right?"

I nodded.

"That wish was the stupidest idea I ever had in my life," she said, sounding like she wanted to hit something. "And it's so embarrassing. I can't even tell anyone. The only good part is, it didn't affect everybody. And now I'm going around avoiding the people who suddenly want to be all over me, and seeking out the ones who don't give a crap about me, because they're the ones who make me feel normal."

Vicky raised an eyebrow. "And then there's you."

A knife flashed in my mind, and I tensed at the memory of Saturday night in my car. *That wasn't her,* I reminded myself firmly. But my voice still came out squeaky when I said, "Me?"

"Yeah," she said. "You hate me."

"I don't hate you," I said automatically, but if the words sounded as false to her as they did to me, then I was in trouble. I tried to remember if I'd ever acted as nasty to her as I'd felt. I didn't think I had, but you can never be sure of those things.

"Okay, maybe not hate. But you don't like me—and that's fine. I really don't blame you. I mean, Naomi's your friend, not mine. Uh . . . I mean, you guys are still friends after Saturday night, right?"

Honestly, I had no idea if we were. Naomi still wasn't speaking to me, and the idea that she might have complained about me to Vicky was . . . I didn't know what it was, but it certainly wasn't good. But I didn't have time to think about that now, so I just shrugged, trying my best to look nonchalant.

"Well, whatever," said Vicky. "I'm just saying, she only hangs out with me because of the wish. And I knew you wanted my part in the play. I just wanted to be in the chorus, but the wish . . . I shouldn't have gotten that part. And nobody seems to know it but you and me. And George, I think, but he's too nice to say anything."

This was it. She was going to ask to use her third wish to undo the second. Everything would go back to normal, and maybe Miss Delisio would even recast the show. All I had to do was loan her the ring.

It was Saturday night all over again.

Oliver could tell the difference between Real-Vicky and Xavier-Vicky, but I couldn't. This was him again. I was sure of it. I should be running. Why wasn't I running?

Vicky let out a deep breath, which sounded almost like a hiss in the quiet hallway. "Would you give me acting lessons?" she asked.

"But I—" I paused. Rewound. "Wait, what?"

She ducked her head a little, blushing. "Acting lessons. I know I'm doing everything wrong, but Miss Delisio won't give me notes except if I'm standing in the wrong place or something. She just says I'm doing great, and I know I'm not, and . . ." She sniffed. "And we open really soon, and I don't want to suck."

I let out a breathy laugh, giddy with relief. This was definitely not Xavier.

"Yeah," I found myself saying. "Sure, I can do that."

"For real?" said Vicky, her eyes going wide behind her glasses.

I laughed. "Yeah, for real."

"Okay!" she said. "Awesome! When are you around? Is tonight all right?"

"Actually, I'm seeing Oliver tonight." I hadn't made any actual plans with him, but I wasn't sure I could figure out how to be a good teacher on a few hours' notice. "How's Thursday?"

"Oh, um, okay. Oliver. Right. So you and he are really . . . ?"

She looked keenly at me, and I smiled. "We're something. Yeah."

"Good," she said. She pressed her hands together, smiling to herself. "That's good. He's nice."

She seemed gratified, which didn't make sense. "Yeah, he is," I said. "But if you think he's so nice, why'd you abandon him like that?"

Her eyebrows shot up, and she pushed her glasses up her nose. "Abandon him?"

"Well, yeah," I said, with a wry little huff of laughter. "You gave up your third wish and left his ring in the girls' bathroom, remember?"

"I didn't want another wish," she said defiantly. "You saw how much my second one backfired. Can you really blame me? And I did not abandon him. I left it there so you could find it. I mean, I would've just given it to you, but . . ." She shrugged. "I wasn't sure you'd take anything from me."

"You *wanted* me to have it?" I said, bewildered. "Why?"

She shifted her weight, dropping her gaze to the floor. "Well, I made you mad when Miss Delisio gave me your part in the play. And I made Oliver mad when I didn't like the second wish he granted for me. So I figured I'd try to make it up to both of you at the same time. Give you three wishes of your own, give him more time with you."

"More time with me?" I repeated. "What do you—"

"Come on," she laughed. "Like you didn't know. Ever since he watched the auditions, you were all he could talk about. 'What class does Margo have third period?' 'Has Margo always been able to sing like that?' 'What's Margo's favorite band?'" She sighed. "Speaking of which, has he had a chance to impress you with his newly accumulated knowledge of Neko Case yet?"

"That was you?" I blurted out. I'd assumed that Oliver had snapped his fingers and made himself a Neko fan for my sake, like the musical equivalent of becoming fluent in my language. But he'd learned about Neko the real way. Without magic.

"Yeah," she said. "It was just a guess that she was your favorite, but I mean, your entire Facebook page is her song lyrics, so . . ."

"Oh," I said. "I don't even know what to say."

She shrugged. "I'm just glad it worked out, that's all. You guys seem . . . Anyway, I have to get to class. I'm already late."

Before I could even get the words *me too* out of my mouth, she was gone.

And I was no closer to finding a way to save Oliver.

Chapter TWENTY

A mandatory college-centric meeting with my guidance counselor kept me late after school. It didn't last too long, but by the time I left, the student parking lot was mostly empty. I desperately wanted to call Oliver, but there was the small problem of his being able to read my mind. Now that I was looking for solutions to the Xavier problem, when he'd explicitly asked me not to, I didn't exactly want him peeking into my thoughts.

The way I saw it, the simplest plan would be to find Xavier's master, take his vessel, and make a wish. It would be clean and easy, and I wouldn't have to involve Oliver at all. The only problem was, I had no way of finding out who his master was.

Lost as I was in thought, I didn't register anyone coming toward me until a hand waved right in front of my face. Startled, I stopped in my tracks. "Earth to Margo," said Simon with a smirk. "I said hello."

"Oh! You scared me."

"I can see that," he said. "Listen, I just wanted to say I'm sorry."

"Don't worry about it. We're cool—as long as those videos never see the light of day again. Ever."

He blinked. "No. I mean the kiss. I'm sorry about the kiss."

Wrapping my arms around myself, I forced a laugh. "Oh, great. Just what every girl likes to hear."

"No, I mean I'm sorry I didn't say anything afterward."

I sighed. "It was my fault, too. But whatever. It doesn't matter. It was a whole year ago, and I'm over it, and I have Oliver now. Let's both just forget it, okay?"

His face fell, and his lips twisted in a pout just a little too exaggerated to be genuine. "I'd rather remember it," he said. A feeling of uneasiness crept over me, though I didn't know why—until he leaned over, cupped my cheek in one gloved hand, and kissed me.

I'd crushed on Simon for so long, it actually took me a second to remember that I'd lost the desire to kiss him. But when that second was over, I shoved him away as hard as I could. "What the hell?" I said, wiping my lips on my sleeve.

"What?" he said, spreading his hands to expand the question. "I thought you wanted—"

"No, I didn't want!" I cut in. "God, Simon, did you hear anything I just said?" His only response was a blank look, so I pushed past him and strode toward my car.

But I'd only gotten a few steps before his voice called out, "Give my best to Ciarán."

I stopped. Slowly, I turned around to face Simon. He was still standing there calmly, regarding me with a detached sort of curiosity as he idly turned something over in his palm. It glinted in the weak afternoon sunlight.

The switchblade.

"You," I said.

"Me," replied Xavier, in Simon's voice.

Suddenly I couldn't move. My leg tensed in memory of long-gone pain, but I lifted my chin and glared at him. "What do you want?"

He cocked his head to one side. "Actually, I should be asking you that. What do you want. Let's see. Well, there's something about finding out who my master is, something about a coin, something about a wish. Come on. Do you really think that will work?"

"What? How can you . . . !" I sputtered. Then I narrowed my eyes at him, realizing what was going on. "I thought only Oliver could read my mind."

Xavier smiled at me. "And you'd have been correct, if you hadn't given me permission to enter your mind, too."

"Permission?" I echoed.

He lifted the switchblade, turning it idly in his hand as he showed it to me. "You don't remember our little conversation in the car? I offered you my blood in exchange for access to your thoughts. You accepted by offering your blood to me in return. A blood exchange of this nature is a contract between us, valid for as long as you remain Ciarán's master."

A blood exchange. Suddenly I remembered: He'd given me a

pat on the leg. At the time, it had seemed like a pointless gesture, if a cruel one, but it would have been easy for him to nick his hand and mingle his blood with my own.

"I didn't offer you a damn thing," I seethed.

"Perhaps you did, and perhaps you didn't. Aren't loopholes fascinating?" He let out a little laugh. "But I'm not here to talk business, Margaret McKenna. I am here because you have a plan—a stupid plan, but a plan nonetheless—to end my life."

"What?" I said indignantly. "I do not."

"As if I haven't already warned my master against those who'd seek to take my vessel," he sneered, taking a step toward me, the blade steady in his hand.

I took a step back. "I just wanted to change your mind," I said frantically, feeling my heart pound in my chest. "I don't want to kill you. I don't want anyone killing anyone! That's the whole point!"

Something softened in Simon's—Xavier's—face. "Ah. I take it our dear Ciarán has filled you in on how I'm secretly Johnny the Homicidal Maniac." He chuckled, like that was the silliest thing he'd ever heard.

"Doesn't seem like that big of a secret," I said. "And I should warn you: Stabbing me again won't get me to make my third wish."

I nodded toward the switchblade, and he did an exaggerated double take, like he was surprised to find himself holding it. "Stabbing you?" he said, closing the blade with another little laugh and sliding it into his pocket. "Why would I do that? It's not like another blood exchange would do me any good."

"Then why are you here?" I asked.

Xavier held up both of his hands to the sky. "Finally! She gets to the heart of the matter. I am here, Miss McKenna, to ask you ever so nicely if you would please do me the honor of making your third wish and releasing Ciarán's vessel."

"The honor . . . ?" I echoed, disgusted. "No. Absolutely not."

He paused, peering at me like I was a particularly colorful insect. "Look at you. So protective." A cruel smile spread slowly, Grinch-like, across his face. "In that case, let's dispense with asking. Give me the ring by sunset tomorrow, Miss McKenna"—he patted the pocket where his switchblade rested—"or else I will force it from your hands."

The finality of the statement chilled me, but I refused to let him see. "Force it? By what, stabbing me again? I thought you swore you wouldn't touch me."

"That I did," he agreed. "But I daresay I don't need a blade to get what I want from you."

The air around him suddenly shimmered, and before I could even blink, I wasn't looking at Simon's face anymore. There, right in front of me, was . . . me. A mirror image of myself, from her mussed brown pixie cut right down to the mismatched blue and green shoelaces on her Chucks. I stared. Was my nose really that pointy?

I glanced quickly around—half hoping nobody else was seeing this and half hoping somebody was—but we were alone.

Xavier watched through my eyes as I took in the sight before me, and all that it implied. He smiled as he saw me understand. "Saturday night was a warning, Margo. I felt like performing for an audience that night, and I *happened* to be wearing your image at the time. Nothing you couldn't handle, am I right? But if I *happen* to look like you next time I want to, say, rob someone? Shoot someone? Or better yet . . ."

Suddenly, Oliver was there, right next to Xavier. I froze. He blinked a few times, like he was trying to orient himself, and then he noticed Xavier and smiled. "Hey, Margo," he said to Xavier's copy of me.

But there was something off about him. It took me a second to put my finger on it, but it was definitely there. Maybe the inflections in his voice were different, or maybe his hair fell the wrong way, but it was enough to make me look closer. Close enough to spot the slight shimmer that rendered him just short of lifelike.

"He's an illusion," I said. "The blood exchange. You can get into my head, so you can make me see things. Well, I have news for you: Your illusions suck."

Disappointment flickered across his face, but disappeared just as quickly. "Of course they do, to your eyes," he said placidly. "The connection we have isn't nearly as potent as the one you have with your dear Oliver. But I merely want to demonstrate something. A path your future might take, should you ignore my warning."

He turned back to Fake-Oliver. "Hello, darling," he said, in my voice. Oliver just kept smiling at him, like I wasn't even there. God, this was creepy. "Want to play?"

"Yes, please," said the Oliver illusion. "Did you bring the knife?"

Xavier stretched my face into a grin. "Why, as a matter of fact, I did," he said, and held up the switchblade. "What would you like me to do with it?"

"That's up to you," said Oliver, his voice so sweet it made my teeth clench. "What does my master command?"

Xavier nodded thoughtfully. "An interesting question. Well, what I really want is to wish you free. Nice and clean, no mess, no pain. But since your real master declined the opportunity to give me your vessel and let you go easy, we'll do it the hard way."

"I understand," said Oliver, nodding sadly. Then he knelt down in front of Xavier, just like he'd done on Saturday night, when he'd offered to take the ring back from me. He tilted his head to the side. Xavier leveled the switchblade at Oliver's neck.

This is not my Oliver, I told myself firmly. *This is not real. It's just an illusion.* As if in response to my thoughts, the image of the false Oliver began to go transparent, almost like a hologram.

But my hands still wouldn't stop shaking.

Bright red bloomed across Oliver's neck, following the path that Xavier's switchblade carved. Xavier held his head, and I watched, I actually watched, *it's not real it's not real it's not real,* as the life bled out of Oliver's eyes. Xavier let him go, and he crumpled unceremoniously to the ground.

"It's not real," I whispered aloud.

"No, it's not," agreed Xavier. "But it could be, very easily. And hey, look on the bright side: With Oliver out of the way, all your problems would go away. Poof!"

Tearing my eyes away from the Oliver illusion lying lifeless on the pavement, I looked Xavier in the eye. "Oliver isn't my problem. You are."

He rolled his eyes. "Oh, I know, I know: I'm the big bad villain and Oliver is your sweet and innocent little boy toy. You love him and you want to save him and all the rest of that mushy crap." He paused, narrowing his eyes at me. "But don't kid yourself into thinking that's all you feel for him. It's all right there in your head, Miss McKenna. I can see it. You resent him for dragging you out of your precious little comfort zone. For leading me right to your doorstep. Perhaps even for making you fall in love with him, when you both knew he wouldn't be around much longer. Am I wrong? Do tell me if I'm wrong."

"You are," I said hotly. "You're very, very wrong."

But he wasn't nearly as wrong as I would have liked. And the sharp smile on his face told me that he knew it. But I changed the subject before this could go any further: "And you can't kill him with a knife. He said so. He'd just come right back."

"He would, it's true." As if on cue, the false Oliver stirred, then slowly climbed to his feet again. The blood was gone. The gash across his throat was gone. He was whole again, just like Saturday night. He looked at Xavier. Xavier looked at me. "But it would still hurt. More than you can imagine."

"What next?" asked Oliver, smiling patiently at Xavier. "Would you like to kill me again?"

"Stop," I said hoarsely. "I get it, okay?"

"Do you?" he said, peering at me. Beside him, the Oliver illusion shimmered into nothingness. "Do you really understand what will happen if I don't have that ring by sunset tomorrow?"

I forced myself to nod. Then I took a deep breath. "Yes," I said, when I was sure I could keep my voice steady. "I understand just fine. What I don't understand is why. You said you want Oliver to be happy. Just now, you said that. If that's true, then why not, you know, just not wish him free?"

He hesitated, pursing my lips in a way that made my face look downright ugly.

This was too much.

"And stop looking like me!" I blurted out. "Who are you, anyway? You must have made a fourth wish once. Who were you before that?"

Xavier let out a harsh laugh. "I was nobody of import. One sad, mortal man in a land full of sad, mortal men."

"But what's your name?" I pressed. Oliver had wanted so badly for me to know him, to know his history. Surely Xavier wanted to be known, too. Surely that could help me somehow.

But he just stared at me. "The name I was born with is no

longer mine. At the moment my name is Margo. And before that, Simon. Vicky, once, as you may recall. These days, I am usually a boy called Shen, who shares his master's admittedly strange tastes in video games, athletic teams, and pornography. I've been count-less different people, you know. But maybe this will do. . . ."

The air shimmered again, and there stood a tall, pale young man with black hair, a generous helping of chin-scruff, and deep-set eyes that were an eerily light shade of gray.

"Meet Xavier," he said, holding his arms out with a flourish to present himself. His voice was deeper than I'd expected it to be. "This is who I was when Ciarán was bound to me."

"What about Niall?" I asked. "Can I meet him? Oliver said you were friends back then."

"Oh, we certainly were." Then he twisted his face into a smirk. "We were even better *friends* when I was Xavier."

I bristled at the implication, but I crossed my arms over my chest. I couldn't let him see me react. "Fine. Whatever. But I still want to know why you're after Oliver."

He snickered. "You really are a tough girl, aren't you? No won-der Ciarán likes you so much. He's always had a soft spot for tough girls. That Maeve—he did tell you about her, didn't he? She was a firecracker."

Despite the overwhelming urge to hit him, I clenched my teeth and refused to rise to the bait. "Right," I said acidly. "You go ahead and list all the people he's ever loved. I'll see that I'm not a special snowflake after all, and I'll have myself a little sobfest while you stand over me and practice your supervillain laugh. Can we skip to the part where we both get over it, and you tell me why you want to wish him free?"

He laughed. "Miss McKenna, while I appreciate that you want to know, there are many things about this life of ours that you can't even begin to understand."

"I understand that Oliver wants to keep living it."

"Living?" he said, regarding me with an expression I couldn't quite read. "Did he actually use that word? Living? Because this"—he gestured down at his body as he stepped closer to me—"is not living. This is a shadow, an echo of what living should be. People used to love us. They worshiped us and feared us. They put us in stories and songs, built legends and myths around us. We were gods. Tricksters. Angels, devils, creatures of fire. Those who knew us, called us the djinn."

At first I thought he'd said "gin," and it took me a moment to realize what he was talking about. "Oh, *djinn,*" I said. "But wait, isn't that just another word for genies?"

"Well, aren't you the clever one," he said, bringing his hands up to give me a slow, mocking clap. "Don't you just know everything. It's merely a different placement of the tongue, isn't it—a quirk of translation. Arabic, English. Djinni, genie. The same thing." He was closer to me now, looking down at me with such intensity that I had to fight not to back away. "Listen to me, Margaret McKenna. Is the ocean the same as a cup of water? A cup of water is something you can toss away, or boil and flavor to taste, or consume without a drop left over. The ocean, though . . . the ocean consumes *you*." He smiled. "Or it doesn't. But the choice is never yours."

He closed his eyes, drawing in a deep breath and letting it out. "We were oceans, once. Now we're just tap water, easily used and easily discarded. That isn't living."

I frowned, trying to piece together everything he'd said. "What do you mean?"

"I mean we had true magic," he said patiently. "Magic unbound by the wills of masters. And then it was lost."

"Lost?" I said, taken aback. "How can magic be lost?"

He stepped away, laughing as he threw his hands up to the sky. "How the hell should I know?" he cried, so loudly that I looked around to see if anyone was listening. "Some believe it was taken from us. Some believe it was cast off by one of our own kind. And others . . ." He paused to make sure I was listening. "Others believe it left of its own accord. It knew the world was changing, and true magic would soon be stifled by chemicals and wires and screens. So it abandoned us and moved on to the next life, leaving behind only enough of itself to bind us to our vessels, and remind us of how much we'd lost."

With his head slightly bowed, he let the words float away into the evening air, as solemn as a sermon. True magic, possessed and then lost—the idea of it made me feel uncomfortably small.

I tried to steer him back to more familiar territory: "And what does Oliver believe?"

"Oliver." He snorted. "Ciarán's still young. To him, this life of slavery is still whimsical and thrilling, even when his masters force the most horrible of wishes upon him. The things I've seen him do . . ."

My stomach turned, remembering how Oliver had said the same thing.

"The last time I found Ciarán," Xavier continued, "his vessel had landed somewhere in eastern Europe. He called himself Dmitri, and he belonged to a bitter old man who treated him like dirt. I offered, back then, to unbind him from his vessel, but he said no. He wanted to see who he could become next, when this was all over.

"Ciarán throws himself into this with his whole heart, reinventing himself time and time again, making himself newer and prettier for every master he has. Falling in love with each of them, in his own way." He gave me a pointed look, which I tried my damnedest to ignore. "But the day will come when he'll realize there's no substance to this. He's only playing different versions of the same part, over and over, with no end in sight. He can deal out life and death, but only at someone else's whim. He's nothing more than a slave. He can't even die without a master to wish it so."

"In other words," I said slowly, "he can't choose when to die, so you get to do it for him? What kind of sense does that make?"

Xavier gave me a tight, disappointed smile. "The kind of sense we immortals understand," he said, almost kindly, "and you do not. It's a matter of honor."

That rankled, but I kept my face as neutral as I could. Xavier sighed. "I encountered the one who made me, shortly after our true magic left us. She was called Dunya, and she was old. Six thousand, seven thousand years, maybe. One of the most powerful djinn I ever knew. She asked me if I'd felt the loss, too, and she asked if I would wish her free. She said that our time here was nearly over—that there was no longer a place in this shrinking world for great beings like us.

"So I did as she asked, and do you know what she said to me? She said 'Thank you.' She smiled, and she burned until she was nothing but air and light." He shook his head slowly, reverently. "I've never seen anything so beautiful."

"But that's different," I said. "She was *ancient*. Oliver isn't even two hundred!"

"I knew you wouldn't understand." He gave a little shake of his head, like he was horribly disappointed in me. "Ciarán does, though, even if he won't admit it to you. Maybe he doesn't even want to admit it to himself. But he does understand."

"But—"

"But nothing," he said gently. "Sunset tomorrow, Miss McKenna. I won't ask again."

Chapter TWENTY-ONE

Years of after-school rehearsals had accustomed me to being alone in the dark mostly-empty school parking lot, but after my encounter with Xavier, nothing seemed familiar anymore. Shadows were deeper. Edges were blurrier. A pink-orange sunset stretched across the sky, only to be cut off by the pine trees that bordered the lot, but I could imagine it stretching on and on, beyond the reach of my vision, continuing forever and ever and ever and . . .

I zipped my coat up and wrapped my scarf tightly around my neck. Then I reached into my pocket, grabbed Oliver's ring, and called him. It seemed like eons before he arrived.

"Margo!" Oliver jogged briskly toward me, his cheeks flushed, his hair messier than usual, and his camera clutched in one hand. The sight of him looking so happy, so *alive,* made me want to grab him and hold him tight and never let Xavier near him again.

"Listen," he said, "I found the greatest spot, just a couple blocks away, and there isn't a lot of sunlight left, so I should get back, but if you want to meet me . . ."

But as he drew closer to me, he trailed off with a frown, and before I knew it, he'd pulled me close and wrapped his arms around me. I closed my eyes and leaned into him, breathing in the warmth of his soft gray hoodie and yearning to keep that third wish forever.

After a few breaths, he pulled gently away. "Now, why was that the first thing I saw in your mind? Is everything okay?"

Worry clouded his face, eclipsing the happy, excited Oliver of a moment before, and just then I hated that he could read my thoughts. I had to tell him. I had to say, out loud, that Xavier had given him one more day to live—but I had no idea how. I hadn't had a plan beyond making sure Oliver was still alive.

"I'm fine," I said instead. "You were in the middle of something. Something fun? You should get back."

His eyes narrowed. "You're not fine. There's something you don't want to tell me. What is it?"

I hesitated, clenching my jaw. But the moment was lost anyway. "Xavier found me."

"What?" Taking me by the shoulders, he gave me a hurried once-over, like he was checking me for more broken bones and knife wounds. "What happened?"

"Nothing," I said, shrugging irritably out of his grasp. "He didn't do anything. I just wanted to see you, but you were in the middle of something. You said sunlight . . . ?"

He squinted up at the sky. "It's not important."

"Yes, it is," I said. He gave me a questioning look, but I wasn't sure how to explain. How could I possibly tell him how important it had felt when he'd appeared, all windblown and smiling and full of life, just minutes after Xavier had killed him right in front of me?

But something in my head must have told him that I really meant it, because he gave me the tiniest nod. "All right," he said, smiling again. "Get in your car. Meet me at the end of Lombardi Boulevard. You know where that is, right?"

"Sure, yeah. But why—"

"Good. See you there!" Giving me a cartoonish salute, he disappeared without waiting for my reply.

Lombardi was a short street that ended in a cul-de-sac. It used to be nearly identical to Naomi's street, a quiet place with a small handful of big houses—but a few years ago, someone had decided to tear down the big houses and build *really* big houses in their place. For whatever stupid money-related reason, though, construction always seemed to be halted, which meant there was a street full of half-finished houses in a ring around the cul-de-sac. A lot of people called them ghost houses.

As I got out of the car, I spotted Oliver on one knee in front of the center house, right by the chain-link fence that bordered the property. Backlit as he was by the setting sun, his features weren't clear. My stomach clenched in sudden panic, and I snaked my hand into my jeans pocket, touching the ring with my thumb and forefinger. Almost instantly, Oliver straightened up, his shoulders going stiff as he looked around, and relaxed again when he spotted me.

"Why'd you call me?" he said, waving me over. "I'm right here."

Relieved, I crossed the lawn to meet him. "Just making sure it was really you," I said, trying to sound as nonchalant as possible.

His expression darkened, but he must have understood that I didn't want to talk about it further, because he just nodded and knelt down again. He pointed his lens upward, adjusted it a few times, and snapped another picture. He looked at the result on the screen, then held it out to me. "See? It's not every day you see sunsets like this one."

Even on the tiny screen, I could see that the picture he'd taken was absolutely gorgeous. By themselves, the bones of the ghost house were dark and flat and foreboding, but the bright colors of sunset shone through where the walls would eventually be, giving the structure a vibrant depth. I squinted up at the real house. The sunset colors weren't as bright in real life. Frowning, I looked back at the camera screen.

"Backlighting and no flash," said Oliver, smiling proudly. "Plus I fiddled with the saturation. Cool, right?"

"Very cool," I said. "You're actually really good at this."

He raised an eyebrow. "I've been doing it a long time."

"Oh," I said, suddenly flustered. "Um. How long would that be?"

He tilted his head thoughtfully. "Since . . . the twenties, maybe? The thirties? I put off using cameras for a long time, because I thought painting and drawing were just *so* much more *dignified*." He rolled his eyes at himself. "But I like to remember where I've been, and who I've been, and this is the easiest way. And then, of course, digital cameras came along a few years ago, and they are absolutely the coolest things ever, and will you stop giving me that look?"

"What look?" I said quickly, mustering an innocent expression.

He laughed. "That look, right there. The one that says you're still freaked out by how old I am, but you're trying to pretend you're not."

"I'm not freaked out," I said defensively. It was true, too. Sort of. But he just shook his head, so I left it alone and handed his camera back.

Oliver darted off across the lawn, scouting out vantage points, adjusting the settings on his camera, and snapping pictures. He looked totally immersed in his own artistic process—and more than that, he looked like he was really enjoying himself. I briefly wondered how much of that was for my benefit, but then told myself to stop overthinking it.

At first I just hung back and watched him. But after a few

minutes, he beckoned me farther down the fence. "Stand over there, would you?"

I jogged across the short stretch of grass between us, and leaned against the fence. "Why?"

"Just do it," he said, a mischievous smile crossing his face as he began to back up, camera at the ready.

"Oh, wait a minute," I said, holding my hands in front of my face. "Don't take my picture. I've been at school all day, and I look gross, and my hair's all——"

"Margo," he interrupted firmly. "You do not look gross. You look beautiful, just like you always do. What's more, despite what you're telling me, you very much want me to take your picture right now, because you want to see what kind of special effects I'm going to use on you."

I lowered my hands slightly, peeking over my fingertips at him. His grin was so smug that I could have slapped him. "You're such a cheater," I said. "Fine. Do your worst."

Oliver knelt in the grass to look at me through the viewfinder. On a whim, I struck a pose, with the back of my hand dramatically against my forehead like a Fosse dancer. He laughed. "I like that! Hold it for just——" His camera made a clicking noise. "There we go. Give me another one!"

So I did. I moved from pose to pose, pausing each time to wait for the click. I gave him dramatic poses. I gave him outrageously silly poses. I even climbed the fence for a few of them—until I lost my footing, banged my ankle against the fence, and nearly fell off. After that, I made my way back over to him and demanded to see the pictures. Wordlessly he handed the camera over to me, pointing at the button I could use to scroll through them.

They were stunning.

Somehow he'd captured me entirely in silhouette; against the warm glow of the sunset, my exaggerated poses somehow became attractive. Elegant, even. How could the girl in these pictures possibly be the same person whose form Xavier had taken in the parking lot, not even half an hour ago?

"You like them?" he said, suddenly shy.

"I love them," I said honestly, cradling the camera in both hands. "It's just . . . they don't look anything like me."

He smiled warmly. "They look exactly like you. Come on, let's take some more. Let's see," he mused, looking critically at our surroundings.

"We could go inside," I said, before I even realized I was thinking it. Oliver gave me a look that was more than a little wary, but I just grinned, handed his camera back, and motioned for him to follow me.

I followed the fence around to the side of the center house, almost to the edge of the lawn. There, half hidden by an evergreen bush, was a small hole in the fence. This was how all the junior high kids sneaked in at Halloween, and how all the highschoolers sneaked in whenever there weren't junior high kids around. I'd never gone inside before, but I'd always felt a little bit more worldly for knowing about it. Plus, it was probably one of the few things in life that I knew about and Oliver didn't.

Getting down on my hands and knees, I crawled through the hole, taking care not to catch my clothes on the sharp edges. Once I was through, I jumped lightly to my feet and brushed the dust from my knees. Oliver hung back, an uncertain expression on his face.

"Come on through!" I said. "It's just a fence. It won't bite."

He gave me a pointed look. "I don't do fences," he said. And before I could reply, he disappeared—and reappeared at my side. "My way's much easier."

Giving me a quick peck on the cheek, he ran off toward the house. I ran after him, but as soon as I did, he sped up, calling "Come on, slowpoke!" as he rounded the back corner of the house.

So I ran faster. I rounded the corner mere seconds after he did. Standing a little bit farther away, he snapped a shot. He checked the result on the screen, then looked up just in time to see me about to catch him—and vanished again.

"Up here!" he called. I craned my neck up, following the sound of his voice, only to see him standing right on the edge of what would eventually be the second floor.

"No fair!" I shouted.

"What's no fair?" he said, too innocently. "I thought we were taking pictures." He held his camera up and clicked, this time with the flash. By the time I'd blinked the splotches of color out of my eyes, he was gone again.

I turned where I stood, looking and listening for him—but aside from the faint whistle of the wind through the empty houses and the sound of traffic in the distance, I heard nothing. I waited, willing myself not to get creeped out. Still nothing. I wrapped my arms around myself and tried not to think of Xavier and wished it would stop getting dark so fast—

"Don't blink," whispered a voice right by my ear. I yelped, and the camera flashed again.

"You asshat!" The words came out in a shaky puff of laughter. Whirling around, I moved to punch his arm, but he smiled and disappeared again.

Thrown off balance, I stumbled, and was rewarded by quiet laughter. "You blinked," said Oliver, holding up the camera screen from about ten feet away. I couldn't see the details of it, but I couldn't imagine it was anything good. I shook my head and leaned over, hands on my knees, taking a moment to recover my balance and my breath.

Old leaves crunched as Oliver sauntered toward me. "My memory card's getting full," he said, frowning at his camera. "Do you have a computer I could use? And maybe a USB cord?"

"Probably," I said. "I have a whole bunch of wires, and no idea what they're for. But if you want, you can come over and see if any of them work."

He grinned. "I was hoping you'd say that."

Chapter TWENTY-TWO

About twenty minutes later, we were sitting in my room. As my computer booted up, Oliver rooted through a box I'd labeled "Random Wires and Stuff," which usually lived out of sight under my bed. Both his hoodie and his boots had mysteriously vanished now that we were inside, leaving him in a blue T-shirt and socks with little palm trees on them. Ziggy Stardust had visited us for about ten seconds, before deciding we weren't worth her time. I, however, remained firmly planted on the bed, watching Oliver with fascination.

"Cell phone charger," he muttered. "External mic. Extension cord. Bottle of purple nail polish. Margo, I find it comforting to know there's a part of your life that isn't organized. Even if it's just this one box."

"Shut up," I said, stifling a smile.

"Bottle of *green* nail polish. Phone charger. Bike lock. Ah, USB cord." He pulled out a wire that looked pretty much like all the other wires, then hoisted himself into my swivelly desk chair. Once my computer stopped humming, he clicked the browser icon and navigated to a photo hosting website, where he logged in. Then he plugged the camera into the computer, clicked a few more buttons like it was an old routine, and turned and smiled at me. "This'll take a while. I've taken a lot of pictures since I came here."

"Of the play?"

"Some," he said. "But I already stuck those on a flash drive so I could give them to your director." After a moment, he added, "Mostly they're of people I like."

I smiled at the sly little compliment. "So does that mean you have pictures of all your masters, stashed away somewhere?" I asked, thinking of the closed doors in his empty apartment.

"Yeah, most of them. And no, I'm not telling you where they are."

"What if I ask?" I teased. "Wouldn't you have to tell me?"

He side-eyed me. "I would. But I'm sure you'd never do such a thing."

"Fine," I said, rolling my eyes dramatically. "Can I at least see these, then?"

"Once they download from my camera, they're at your service."

There was a little bar across the screen, slowly measuring the progress of the download in question. I found myself wondering how many pictures he had stored on that site. How many differ-ent lives had he captured on film? How much effort did it take to remember them all? Were there any masters he hadn't taken pictures of?

Did he have pictures of Xavier somewhere?

Oliver must have seen the direction of my thoughts, because when he moved from the chair to the bed, he wore a somber expression. "Now will you tell me what happened today?"

Almost immediately, my eyes dropped to the bedspread. As much as I didn't want to tell him, I couldn't rightfully keep this from him any longer. "It was, um," I faltered. I tucked one knee carefully underneath myself, buying a moment to assemble the right words in my head. "He gave me one day."

"What?" said Oliver, his voice dangerously low.

I looked up at him. "One day. If I don't make my wish by sun-set tomorrow, or if I go after him again, he'll . . . It won't be good."

"Sunset tomorrow," he repeated to himself, nodding slowly. Then something seemed to click, and he narrowed his eyes at me. "Wait. What do you mean, 'go after him again'?"

I shifted uncomfortably, looking down at the small stretch of bedspread between us. "That's sort of why he found me in the first place. I wanted to find his coin, and he sort of . . . he heard me."

"He *what?*" Oliver jumped to his feet, both hands in his hair like he was about to pull it out.

"Calm down, okay?" I whispered. "My parents are right downstairs."

He stilled, eyes darting to the door. After a few hushed moments of nothing happening, he looked back at me, taking care to lower his voice. "Seriously, he heard you? What do you mean? How?"

So I told him what Xavier had said, about the blood exchange. Oliver's face went white as he listened. "I didn't know you could do that," he murmured. "But I should have. God, I'm sorry. I should have known."

"How could you?" I said. "I didn't."

He shook his head. "But you don't know him. I do. And he may be a little . . . well, unhinged . . . but he's never been one for hands-on violence. Magic, yes. Knives, no. I should have known he was up to something."

"Something other than trying to kill you," I added icily.

His eyes were dark as they met mine again. "I asked you to stay away from him. I meant it, Margo, and this just proves it. You have no idea what you're getting yourself into."

"Yeah, Xavier made it very clear that I am young and stupid and mortal and all this stuff is way beyond me. Thanks for the reminder."

"Margo, I didn't mean . . . Look, I already said I don't want you killing him for my sake. Using his vessel as the weapon instead of mine doesn't make it any better."

"I wasn't going to kill him," I said hotly. "Honestly, why is that all you people think about? If you must know, I was going to wish for him to change his mind about killing *you*. You said you didn't have enough power to do that yourself."

"Oh," breathed Oliver, his eyes going wide. "That's actually kind of brilliant."

Sighing, I leaned back on my hands. "Not brilliant enough. He must have heard me wanting to do all that stuff, and that's why he confronted me. Lots of threats, lots of 'Look how powerful I am.' Some illusions." There was an uncomfortable silence. "Also, he told me about the djinn."

His eyebrows shot up, and his mouth twisted. "The djinn?"

"Yeah. You never told me, Oliver."

"Told you what?" He sat carefully back on the bed, watching me closely.

"Everything." I swept one arm around in an expansive gesture. "True magic, and how you . . . you know. Lost it." It didn't sound as impressive when I said it. Apparently Oliver thought so, too, because he just looked at me with the same bemused expression.

Then he burst out laughing.

"Are you serious?" he said, voice suddenly light with mirth. "He's still using that old line? 'Poor us, we used to have all this magic and we don't know where it went, so now I have to kill everyone'? For heaven's sake."

"What?" I said, annoyed. "What's so funny?"

"The djinn!" he said again. I raised an expectant eyebrow, and he rolled his eyes. "I never lost any magic. I knew exactly what I was getting into when I made my fourth wish. The djinn are . . . I don't know. A legend. A fairy tale. Something you can talk yourself into believing, if you want to feel like you came from something bigger than what you are. But they're just the same word in different languages."

"That's what I said," I murmured. "But he told me all that stuff like it happened to him personally."

Oliver smiled. "Here is something you may have noticed about Xavier. He is very, very dramatic." As if to illustrate his point, he stretched his arms out and flopped backward onto my bed. Even with his legs hanging over the end and his feet touching the floor, he could almost reach my headboard with his fingers.

I waited for him to say something else, but it seemed like that was it. I scooted back so I could lean over him, and he grinned up at me. With his arms reaching like that, his shirt had ridden up, leaving a thin stretch of bare stomach between his shirt and his belted jeans. I tried very hard not to stare at it.

"So none of that stuff really happened?" I said.

"Xavier believes it did," said Oliver placidly. "But no, I don't think so."

"Hmm."

He reached over to touch my knee. "You seem disappointed."

"I'm not," I said, distracted by his hand. It wasn't doing anything untoward, just resting on the fabric of my jeans, but between that and the little stretch of bare skin above his belt, I felt my cheeks start to heat up. "I mean, maybe a little? I don't know, it's just the thought of infinite magic. It's so huge. Romantic, almost."

"You think so?" he said, with genuine curiosity. "Seems over-whelming to me. I don't know what I'd do with that much magic."

I smiled down at him. "If I were a genie, I think I'd want infinite magic."

"Yeah, I bet you would," he said with a laugh.

I stretched myself out languidly beside him, looking up at the ceiling fan. "And a house furnished entirely with pillows and candles and drapey things."

"Drapey things," he echoed thoughtfully, his hand rubbing small circles on my leg. "Indeed."

"And a magic carpet."

"Obviously."

"And a handsome young man whose only job is to fan me and feed me grapes."

"A perfectly reasonable request. In fact . . . hmm."

He sat up and pushed himself to his feet. I propped myself up on one elbow, watching curiously as he looked around. It was only a moment before he spied what he was looking for, sitting on my dresser.

When Oliver sat beside me again, he held my fern, now slightly more brittle than when he'd first given it to me. And he started to fan me with it. I laughed and buried my face in a pillow—and when I chanced a peek at him again, he was still waving the fern up and down, looking absolutely solemn.

"Does this please my lady?" he asked, in a fake accent that was probably supposed to be British. He looked at me expectantly, like he was awaiting further orders.

I cleared my throat, schooling my face into an expression as serious as his. "It pleases me greatly, handsome young man. But where are my grapes? I demand grapes."

He tilted his head to the side, considering. "If thou desirest, lady, I could raid thy refrigerator and find grapes for thee."

I grimaced as I pushed myself back up to a sitting position. "Bad idea. Parents. Downstairs."

"Curses! Foiled again."

"How about a kiss instead?"

"Oh?"

"Come now, handsome young man. I command it."

A grin tugged as his lips, but he bowed his head to try and hide it. "As my master commands," he said, "so shall it be."

Setting the fern gently aside, he bent over and kissed me. One hand cradled my neck, fingers burying themselves in my hair and sending tingly prickles of magic shooting down my spine. I stretched into the sensation, leaning closer to him.

But after a short moment, Oliver broke the kiss, pulling away just far enough to give a little flick of his fingers. In an instant, my ordinary bed was gone, leaf-patterned bedspread and all. Instead, Oliver and I were surrounded on every side by silken drapes, all red and purple and gold, hanging languorously down from the framework of a four-poster bed. Soft, richly colored pillows cocooned us. I started at the sight of it.

"Too much?" asked Oliver. "I know you don't like surprises, but you said you wanted drapey things. . . ."

"I did, yeah." Even the sound of my own voice was more intimate, with all this fabric closing us in. "No, not too much. This is a good surprise."

He lifted one of my hands and pressed it to the center of his chest. "And what else does my master command?" he asked. The phrase rolled comfortably from his lips. Too comfortably. I drew in a sharp breath, remembering.

He tilted his head to the side. "Margo? What is it?"

What does my master command? The Oliver illusion had said the same thing, in the same tone, with practically the same inflections, back in the parking lot. Right before he let Xavier kill him.

I grabbed his shirt in my hands and pulled him down toward me. "Kiss me," I whispered. "Hard."

Something flickered in his eyes, but he didn't say anything. He pressed his mouth against mine, so hard it almost hurt, hard enough that it felt real, so real, and then I was pushing myself up against him, threading my fingers through his hair and holding tight and *pulling* and kissing him as hard as I could while his fingers sought out the small of my back, touching the skin just under my shirt, trailing magic everywhere, and before I knew it he was tumbling over onto the pillows and I was pinning him down with the weight of my body, feeling his breath moving his chest up and down beneath me, and my hands were holding his wrists firmly against the bedspread, just inches above his head.

We breathed together, silent. I looked at Oliver. Really looked at him: willingly trapped beneath me, watching me closely. He leaned up a little, as if to try kissing me again, but I pressed his wrists hard against the sheets. "Don't," I said.

He instantly went still. I could barely even feel him breathing. He was tense and coiled beneath me, waiting for my cue.

Want to play? echoed Xavier's voice in my head.

"He said I want you gone," I whispered. "Xavier. He said he saw that in my head—that I want you out of my life."

His features went rigid. He pressed his lips together, and didn't reply.

"Can you see that, too?" I asked.

Eyes still locked on mine, he nodded, very slowly.

My throat went tight. I forced myself to speak anyway. "That was Saturday night, though. I was angry, and I'm sorry. But I swear, I don't want to lose you."

"Sometimes you do, though," he said, still making no move to escape my hold on him. "Sometimes you wish you'd never met me."

I didn't know if it was the words themselves, or the matter-of-fact way he said them, but suddenly I felt on the verge of tears. "Sometimes? As in more than once? How long have you been seeing that in my head?"

He smiled, sort of sadly. "Since the day you found my vessel."

I drew in a sharp breath. "All that time?"

"Yes."

273

"And you still . . . ?"

"Yes," he said again. "I still let myself fall for you. No matter what you think about me when you're sad or angry, there's another part of you that's very happy I'm in your life. And that's the part you've acted on, the entire time I've known you."

"I guess so, but—"

"Listen," he interrupted. "Nobody ever feels just one way about another person, Margo. We're so much more complicated than that. I can see a million things you want from me, just like the million things I want from you. Some of them are wonderful. Some are awful. Some contradict each other, and some don't make any sense at all. But none of those things matter, not really. What matters is what you do about them."

He spoke slowly and evenly, and for a moment I was silent, letting his words settle into the space around us, absolving me.

"You want a million things from me, too?" I asked. He nodded. "Like what?"

"Well, you already know the big ones," he replied with a smile.

That was probably true, at least after our last conversation at Tom's. He wanted acceptance. Love. A girlfriend who didn't abuse her wishes. "The little ones, then," I pressed. "Tell me one."

"Hmm," he said, narrowing his eyes in thought. "Here's one: I'd very much like to take you on a picnic. In summer, so you could wear a pretty sundress."

"A sundress?" I said. I was pretty sure I hadn't owned a sundress since fifth grade.

"So I could ogle your legs," he explained. "And we'd go somewhere with a river, so we could dangle our feet in the water."

"And then, let me guess," I said, grinning at him. "We planned to go swimming but, oops, we forgot our bathing suits, so we have to go skinny-dipping instead?"

"If you like," he said, returning my grin. "Although if you want the X-rated picnic, I can do way better than skinny-dipping."

"Yikes," I said, as a little thrill raced up my spine.

"You asked," he said sweetly. Turning his head to the side, he nodded at one of my hands, which still held his wrists in place. "Now, are you gonna let me up? Or should we bust out the handcuffs?"

I pulled my hands off him like he'd scalded me, and he laughed softly as he sat up. I watched him, thinking about what he'd just said. *Nobody ever feels just one way about another person.* I wondered if that included Xavier, Oliver's friend-turned-assassin. How many things did Oliver feel about him?

Oliver looked up at me, his brow furrowed. "Something about Xavier?" he asked. "What is it?"

"It's just, the way he talked about you. There was something . . ." I frowned at him. "What were you like, back then? When you and he were . . . when you were Ciarán?"

He looked surprised at the question, but didn't hesitate before answering. "Still me. I just looked different."

"Okay, then what did you look like?"

"Shorter," he said, which made me smile. "My face was . . . I mean, just different." He paused. Swallowed. "I could show you. Do you want me to?"

Something fluttered in my chest. Apprehensive but insanely curious, I nodded.

As he stood, he flicked his fingers again, and all the drapes and pillows disappeared, replaced by my familiar room. But then Oliver himself began to change. The air shimmered around him. His face grew tight with concentration, and he began to go blurry . . .

And then, someone new was standing in his place.

"Ta-dah," said Oliver. Ciarán. Holding out his arms, he stepped back so I could get the full picture.

Ciarán was shorter than Oliver, just like he'd said. It was only a difference of an inch or two, but it was enough. He had a similar build, slender and strong—but instead of Oliver's usual jeans-shirt-hoodie combination, Ciarán wore brown pants with a loose-fitting white shirt. The clothes were simple enough, but even with my limited fashion sense, I could tell they hadn't been in style for at least a hundred years. And that wasn't even counting his hat, which made me want to put on a production of *Brigadoon* and cast him in the lead.

His face was different: slightly longer and thinner than Oliver's, with a nose that turned up ever so slightly at the end. A casual scattering of freckles emphasized the incredibly pale skin of his cheeks. His hair was lighter and wavier than Oliver's, but the way it fell into his eyes was pleasantly familiar.

Looking at Ciarán and knowing that he was Oliver wasn't

nearly as jarring as I'd thought it would be. In fact, he looked like he could be Oliver's cousin or something . . . except for the eyes. His eyes were exactly the same. Bright green and shadowed by dark lashes, they shone as they looked at me.

"Ohhh," I said.

"Oh good, or oh bad?" he asked. A thick Irish accent curled comfortably around the words.

"Oh *oh*," I said. "You're more the same than I thought you'd be."

"I am?" He looked down at himself, uncertain.

I frowned, stepping toward him and touching one hand lightly to the front of his shirt. He felt warm underneath, just like before. "I mean, obviously you don't look the same. But there's a certain . . . I don't know. The way you look at *me* is the same."

"That's because it's still me. Like I told you. Just a slightly different version." He leaned down, and I soon discovered that the way he kissed me was the same, too.

A few minutes later, my computer made a little noise, and Oliver, still looking like Ciarán, got up to check on his pictures.

His hand worked the mouse, and his eyes darted to and fro across the computer screen that lit his face. He moved like Oliver did. It relieved me to know that he could look so different, but still be the person I thought he was—not the person Xavier wanted me to believe he was.

And then there was Xavier, who adopted the bodies of living people without thinking twice. Who changed faces on a whim, just to mess with my head. Who wouldn't tell me his real name.

But he'd told me the name of the persona he'd adopted for his current master. Shen. Maybe there was a way to find this Shen and track him back to his master. If only I could do it without Xavier overhearing, before sunset tomorrow. . . .

"Margo," came Oliver's soft voice, cutting into my thoughts. I looked up: Ciarán was gone, and Oliver was slumped in my chair, watching me with tired eyes. "I can hear you. Please, just stop."

"But why?" I said. "Just give me time. I'll think of something."

He took a deep breath. "I already told you, there's nothing—"

"Don't give me that 'nothing I can do' crap. Remember my idea? Making him change his mind? You already said it was brilliant, and I saw the look on your face when you said it. You wanted me to do it."

He pressed his lips into a thin line, but he didn't deny it.

"And if I find his master, I'll be able to. I just need to keep him from overhearing me."

"He can probably overhear you right now, you know."

That shut me up.

"And what's more," Oliver continued, resting his elbows on his knees and leaning forward, "he won't let you anywhere near his master. Whoever it is, he's been protecting them ever since the initial binding."

I frowned. "What do you mean?"

"You think I haven't wondered who his master is?" he said. "I've looked, believe me. Do you remember that day in the park? I told you I felt something, like a call?" I nodded. "Normally, I'd be able to feel it every time Xavier's master called him, or made a wish. But ever since that first call, it's been nothing but radio silence. No calls. No wishes. No anything. I don't know how he's kept his master from using any magic, but as long as this goes on, I could stand face-to-face with Xavier's master and never know it."

"Is that how he found me?" I asked. "By following your magic?"

He hesitated, then nodded. "But it should have taken him a lot longer than it did. The last time he tracked me down, it took him a solid month. Feeling another genie's magic is easy, but following it is quite the opposite. And I've been keeping a pretty low profile. Even when I went to school for Vicky, I was just the kid in the corner that nobody noticed, you know? And now that I've stopped going, I don't see much of anyone except you. I come when you call, and aside from your wishes, that's pretty much it."

"Could he have spotted you at school?"

He shook his head. "Nope. If he were hanging around the school, I'd know it. Even without his master making wishes, he'd need to draw on his magic to create and maintain a human body. And that magic would be visible, at least to me."

"Wait, wait, wait," I said. "Hold on. What if it's his *master* hanging around the school, not him? What if it's a student who helped him track us down?"

He looked as stricken as I felt. "That does make sense," he said slowly.

"It does, doesn't it," I said, feeling my heart begin to race as I began to piece it together. "Someone at school. Someone who isn't using magic, so you'd never know it was them. God. Whoever this guy is, I will find him and I swear I will kill him. I'll kill him right in his stupid face."

"Will you please calm down?" Oliver said. He moved to the floor, sat back on his heels, and rested a hand on my knee. "You're not killing anybody, in the face or otherwise. Look what he did to you on Saturday, Margo. Look what he did to you *today*. If he thinks you're going after him again, he won't hesitate to do even worse next time."

I tensed, but forced myself to hold Oliver's gaze. "Not if I get to him first. *Or,* and let's not forget this one, I could do nothing, and we could live one more day like everything's all kittens and rainbows, until he comes and wishes you free and you *die,* and in case that's not bad enough, I'll have to live knowing that I could have done something about it, but I didn't." Oliver looked down, and I heard him take a ragged breath.

"Come on, Oliver," I said, as gently as I could. I slid to the floor too, positioning myself in front of him so our knees were touching. "You don't want Xavier to decide whether you live or die. You said so yourself. Your magic might be bound by other people's wishes, but your life is your own."

"You're right," he said, a sudden intensity in his eyes as they met mine again. "My life is my own, which means nobody else gets to control it. Not even you. I love you, Margo, and if I have one day left, I want to spend it with you. Not playing spy, or trying to track Xavier's master down, or complaining about how life isn't fair. Just . . . living. With you."

It was a moment before I realized my jaw was hanging slack. "You love me?"

"I thought I'd made it kind of obvious," he replied with a wry little laugh.

I lowered my gaze, feeling suddenly shy, and he reached for my hand. Magic zinged up my arm, but he remained silent, waiting patiently for me.

"One day," I said after a moment. "Okay. What do you want to do? We should make a list. Here, I'll get a notebook, and we can write everything down and make sure we fit it all in before, um . . . before the deadline."

But Oliver squeezed my hand harder, keeping me from going to my desk. "I don't want a list. Let's just see what we feel like doing."

"But—"

"One last day of spontaneity," he said with a grin, "and then you can go back to being your adorable little control-freak self."

"But what if there's something you really want to do, and we forget, and I only remember when it's too late, and then—" I looked at Oliver's face, and stopped myself. Took a breath. "Sure. I can do that."

"Excellent!" he said, clasping his hands together. "How about if you start by skipping school tomorrow? That'd give us more time together, since I'm a dropout and all."

I couldn't skip school. I'd *never* skipped school, except when I was sick. Besides, there was an English essay I needed to turn in, and I was pretty sure we were having a quiz in chemistry, and . . .

And I stopped myself again. I had one day left with Oliver. One day of being spontaneous. Worrying about school would just have to wait.

"Skip school," I said. "No problem. And . . . and you could stay here tonight, if you want. Not like that," I added quickly when his eyebrows shot up. "I didn't mean that. Not that I don't want—I mean it's just so—um, unless *you* want . . . ?"

And if he did want to sleep with me, would I say yes? Apparently I was about to find out. Three cheers for spontaneity!

A touch of color crept into his cheeks. "I do want," he said, "or I *would* want, if it weren't like this. If it weren't because it's our last chance, you know? I don't want to be with you like that when I'd just be thinking about the why of it—about the . . . the deadline. Um. You know what I mean?"

"Oh," I said, halfway between relief and disappointment. "Yeah. I know what you mean."

"But I'd still love to stay," he said, "if you want me to."

Of course I wanted him to. He would sleep over, I would ditch school in the morning, and we would spend the rest of the day doing . . . whatever we wanted. Without a plan. And after that,

I would sink back into the safe, comfortable life that I'd always known. A life without magic, and without Oliver. The thought of it broke my heart.

It also brought me a small, secret measure of relief, though I knew I could never tell Oliver that.

But maybe he already knew.

"Oliver?" I whispered, a little while later.

"Mm-hmm?" he replied.

I wriggled a little, adjusting myself in his arms. "Before, when Xavier found me, he . . . you died. He made me watch you die."

"What do you mean?" His body was still, and his voice was calm. Too calm.

"It was an illusion," I explained, still trying not to replay it in my mind. "An illusion of you, that he created. And I—I mean he, pretending he was me—he had that knife again and, and he used it. He killed you. And you just let him do it."

He swore under his breath, and I closed my eyes against the darkness that surrounded us. "It scared me," I said. "You scared me."

"It wasn't real." He'd lifted his head a little, and his breath tickled my ear as he spoke. "You know that, right?"

"Yeah."

"That wasn't really us." He drew me closer, pressing my back against his chest, curving his body protectively around mine. "This, right here, this is what's real. I'm real."

I smiled into the darkness. "I know."

A few minutes passed in silence. The only light in the room came from the clock on my bedside table. It said 3:26. "Oliver?"

"Mm-hmm?"

"Did you love a lot of people before you met me?"

There was a pause. "A few. I wouldn't say a lot, but a fair few."

"You loved Maeve."

"Very much."

"Did you love Xavier?"

I felt him hold his breath for a couple seconds.

"I did," he said cautiously. "A long time ago. Is that . . . Does that bother you?"

"I don't know," I said. "It might. I just don't know yet."

He hugged me tightly and pressed a kiss to the back of my neck.

Another minute ticked by.

"Oliver?"

"Mm-hmm?"

"You remember when you asked if I was in love with you? And I said no?"

"Yeah."

"I maybe lied a little."

A quiet laugh rumbled against my back.

"I know," he said. "Believe me, I know."

Chapter TWENTY-THREE

After convincing my mom that I felt sick and needed to stay home, I spent the morning hiding in my room with Oliver, listening carefully until I heard both my parents' cars pull out of the driveway. Only when I was certain they were gone did we creep downstairs in search of sustenance.

Mom had left a box of cereal and a bowl of fruit on the counter for me, but Oliver proclaimed her meager offerings unworthy. "Wait here," he told me, and disappeared—only to reappear a few minutes later with an armload of groceries. "Don't worry," he said, before I could ask. "I paid for them."

And then he began making breakfast. Not just breakfast, but *breakfast*. Blueberry pancakes from scratch. Three kinds of eggs. Maple syrup that had been in Canada only ten minutes ago. Fresh bacon. And, of course, waffles.

"This looks amazing," I said as he presented me with a full plate and a glass of orange juice. "I didn't even know you could cook."

"Neither did I, until just now," he said cheerfully. "I just saw that sad little box of cereal, and I thought, why not? And then, poof! Oliver Parish, master chef."

I shook my head. "That's so weird. Not that I'm complaining." I took a bite. "Okay, now I'm *really* not complaining. What the hell did you put in these eggs—nectar of the gods?"

He wiggled his eyebrows. "Nope. Trade secret," he said, and started shoveling monster-size bites of waffle into his mouth.

For a few moments, I just watched him. He looked so happy. And this would probably be one of the last meals he ever ate.

A little while later, when we finally began to slow down, Oliver leveled a curious look at me. "You know," he said, "I never did get to hear you play that opening set."

I quickly swallowed my mouthful of orange juice, so I wouldn't end up spitting it all over the table. "Thank you, Captain Obvious. You may recall that nobody heard my set, on account of how I didn't play it."

He rolled his eyes. "I do recall, as a matter of fact. That's not the point. The point is, I didn't hear it, but I'd really like to. I mean, think about it: you, playing songs that my wish helped you write, on a stage with a bunch of people cheering. I don't know about you, but it seems to me that'd be a pretty great way to spend the day. Or at least six songs' worth of the day."

"Really? That's what you want to do?" He nodded, and I tapped my fork against my lip, thinking. "Well, we could always break into the South Star and hold them hostage until they let me play."

He laughed. "Well, getting arrested wasn't a high priority on my bucket list, but hey, if that's what floats your boat . . ."

"Got a better idea?" I asked, raising an eyebrow as I forked the last bite of blueberry pancake into my mouth. He reached for my plate, but I swatted his hand away. "And no cleaning up. You make food, I clean up. That's how it works. Unless you can do it with magic or something."

He winced slightly, like he was embarrassed. "Er, no. Sorry." I shrugged and began to gather both of our dishes into the sink.

"Better ideas," he mused, following me over to the sink. "Well, I'd be willing to settle for a living room concert at worst, but there has to be a stage somewhere that we can use, right? I mean, what about the one at your school?"

I flicked a few droplets of water at him, making him jump back. "My school? As in, the place I'm specifically avoiding today so I can hang out with you instead? Sure, Oliver. Totally brilliant."

He tilted his head to the side, giving me a too-innocent smile. "As a wise woman once said: Got a better idea?"

Since I couldn't exactly walk through the front door of school when I was supposed to be home sick, we had to settle for using the maintenance stairwell, a musty old thing that led from the boiler room to the teachers' parking lot, then continued up to the theater wings. I'd never known the reason behind that particular aspect of Jackson High's erratic design, but generations of actors had used it to sneak out for intermission smoke breaks.

Today, I was using it to sneak in. Clutching my guitar case in one hand, I felt my way up the stairs with the other.

"Shouldn't we turn on some lights?" hissed Oliver from behind me.

"Not till I'm sure there's nobody else here," I whispered back. "Watch out, there's a tall stair coming up."

"This was a bad idea."

"Says the guy who's following me around in the dark when he could just teleport into the theater."

"Touché," he said wryly, but kept following me.

"And watch those hands, mister. That's my butt."

"Oops. My bad. Completely unintentional."

"Uh-huh."

When I reached the top of the staircase, I tiptoed down the short hallway and peeked into the theater. The wings were dark, but the stage was illuminated with the harsh white glow of work lights. I frowned. This was fourth period, which meant there shouldn't be anyone there. Maybe someone had left the lights on by accident?

But just when I was about to go and find out, I heard footsteps. Very quiet footsteps, which made me think that whoever it was, they didn't have any more right to be here than I did. "Crap," I murmured under my breath.

"What's—"

"Shh!" I hissed, cutting Oliver off. Not because he was being loud, but because I'd heard something else. Voices. There were at least two people here, and they were talking. I strained my ears, trying to hear them better. Oliver remained silent behind me.

I only had to wait a moment before one of the voices rose above a whisper. "Come on, man, just give me one!" someone whined. "Just one!" Something about the voice's cadence sounded familiar. I could hear it, somewhere in my recent memory, protesting a failing grade.

Oliver tugged at my hand, signaling that we should probably leave, but curiosity got the best of me. What did this guy want one of? Was I witnessing a drug sale or something?

A second voice, completely unfamiliar, murmured something just below the range of my hearing, and the first let out a loud noise of frustration. "Not cool, dude. Why the hell'd you tell me to—"

"Shh!" went the second voice, just like I'd done a moment ago. I shrank back against Oliver, and they continued to speak in whispers.

And then, all of a sudden, the first voice called out, "Margo? Is that you?"

As soon as I heard him say my name, I recognized the voice. It was Simon. But a chill jolted through me. Just yesterday I'd thought it was Simon, too, and then Xavier—

Oliver put a hand on my shoulder, silently steadying me.

"Is that him?" I whispered frantically. "Can you tell?"

He squeezed my shoulder. "I can't. Not without seeing him."

But even without Oliver's certainty, I knew it was him. Every single one of my nerves was telling me so. I had to run away, I had to hide—

No, that was just paranoia talking. That was just the darkness of the wings, shrinking around me like it wanted to trap me right where I stood. I took a deep breath, focusing on the calming feeling of Oliver's hand on my shoulder. Focusing on what Xavier had said the day before. I had until sunset to make my final wish, and to say goodbye to Oliver. That was hours away.

But if it was really Simon out there, then how did he know it was me?

I tensed again, and poised myself to run—only to realize that if Xavier was after me, he could just as easily cut me off when I reached the parking lot. Or the boiler room. He could hear my thoughts, which meant he could follow me anywhere. I was trapped, trapped, trapped.

"Margo," Oliver murmured against my ear, in a voice clearly meant to calm me. It didn't.

"Screw him," I said, through gritted teeth. "He said I had until sunset, and I am damn well going to keep you until sunset."

"For heaven's sake, don't—"

"Stay here," I said firmly. "Stay right here until I come back. I'm getting rid of him." Setting my guitar case down with a clunk, I strode out onto the stage. I would have those last few hours with Oliver. I *would*.

With the house lights off and the work lights shining in my face, the theater was a vast cavern, stretching past the limits of my vision and into formless emptiness. All at once I remembered the unnatural sky that Oliver had created for me in his apartment— but this was different. There were no stars here, and no treasure. There was only the overwhelming feeling of being watched, like the seats themselves could see me, even though they didn't yet hold an audience.

No audience, that is, except for the lone figure in the orchestra pit, just at the edge of where the light reached.

Simon crossed the few feet of space between the first row of seats and the stage, smiling at me. "Hey, dude."

I walked right up to the edge of the stage, and crossed my arms. "You gave me till sunset," I said coldly. "I agreed to your terms. So did Oliver, even though you never bothered to ask him. So, if you don't mind, please *do me the honor* of leaving us the hell alone until then. Got it?"

Simon just stared at me, looking completely befuddled. "Huh?"

I stared back, willing him to drop the act. But the seconds ticked by, and he just looked more confused. After a moment, he said tentatively, "Um, Margo? You okay?"

My shoulders slumped. I was an idiot. Not to mention para-noid. "Sorry, Simon. I thought you were someone else."

He laughed uneasily. "Well, I'd hate to be that guy."

But before he'd even finished speaking, the auditorium blinked away into nothingness. No seats, no orchestra pit, no Simon— they all vanished. I whirled around, my heart in my throat. The stage was still there. But it was no longer empty. Standing center stage, a familiar switchblade in his hand, was Oliver. His face was gray and expressionless. A ribbon of red marred the too-pale skin of his neck. Just like yesterday in the parking lot. Just like when I'd watched him die.

He began to lurch toward me, moving way too fast for my liking, and I instinctively stepped back. But my foot landed right on the lip of the stage. I threw my weight forward again, barely managing to keep my balance.

"Illusion," I gasped. "You're not real."

I could see it now: He was hollow. Transparent. A hologram. But he kept coming at me, and I wanted so badly to run, and it was all I could do to stand where I was, to keep from falling—

The blade went through my chest, and the Oliver illusion went through me like a ghost, and then . . . everything was normal again. The auditorium was back. The illusion was gone.

"What's not real?" asked Simon warily, his voice barely cutting through the sound of my heart pounding.

I didn't answer him. Xavier was here, somewhere. He wanted me to make a third wish. Every muscle in my body thrummed with tension, and I tried to look everywhere at once. Whatever illusion he threw at me next, I'd be ready. I wouldn't fall for it again.

"Bring it on, asshat," I muttered. Simon looked like he was about to call the men in the white coats to come get me.

But then something knocked into me, and I was spinning, stumbling, and then my back was pressed against someone's body.

An arm was squeezed against my throat. I tried to cry out, but there was too much pressure. Definitely not an illusion this time.

"If you insist, Miss McKenna," said a pleasant, unfamiliar voice, right into my ear.

Simon blinked fast, like he wasn't sure what he was seeing. "What the hell, Shen? Chill out. This is the chick from the gig. She's cool."

Shen. Xavier had said that name in the parking lot yesterday. Shen was one of his alter egos—the one he was using for his current master.

Simon.

Simon had seen me with Oliver in the parking lot, on the night I'd first kissed him. Just a few days before that, he'd asked if Vicky and Oliver were dating, and I'd been stupid enough to think it was Vicky he was curious about. . . .

"Xavier, let her go," came Oliver's voice from somewhere behind me. In a flash, he appeared in the pit, right beside Simon, who jerked away from him.

"Let me think," said Xavier. "Sure, I will—if she gives me your vessel."

Simon gaped at Oliver, then at Xavier. "Wait, that's why you told me to meet you here? So you could choke Margo to death? Lame sauce, man. Let her go."

I saw understanding dawn on Oliver's face—and for the span of that moment, I was certain that Oliver would strangle Simon with his bare hands. But then he took a long, heavy breath, and turned his anger toward the person behind me. "Xavier," he said, his voice carefully controlled. "Niall. You promised."

The arm squeezed harder, and I clawed and pried at it, but that only made it worse. My vision blurred as the pressure on my windpipe increased, and I gasped for breath.

"Don't talk to me about promises, Ciarán," Xavier seethed. "You really think I wanted to spend the next eight hours listening to *this*?" He jerked me up onto my toes and twisted his voice into a high-pitched mockery of mine. "I want Oliver to kiss me all over! I want Oliver to *touch* me and *love* me and *f*—"

"That's enough," said Oliver. Cheeks burning, I sent him a quick mental thank-you.

Xavier laughed. "I swear, I will never understand why everyone thinks teenaged girls are so innocent. This one's even worse than Simon. And that's saying something."

Simon held his palms up defensively. He looked scared out of his mind. "Whoa, man, what are you—"

"Mr. Lee," Xavier interrupted smoothly, "please wish for this room to be secure."

Simon frowned. "But you said the first two wishes could be whatever I wanted."

"And now I'm saying something different," said Xavier sweetly. "We have at least four open doors here. Make the wish."

"But—"

All at once, the pressure disappeared from my neck, and I stumbled back, gasping.

A pair of sturdy arms caught me. Oliver. But before I could catch my breath long enough to ask him what the hell we were supposed to do now, I looked down and saw a familiar blade glinting against Simon's clavicle. I barely caught a glimpse of Shen before he shimmered back into Xavier, holding the switchblade steady the whole time.

"How'd you," sputtered Simon, backing away. His shins hit one of the seats in the front row, and his eyes widened. "Dude, okay, fine, whatever you want. Just put the knife down, okay?"

Xavier lowered the blade by an inch, if that, and Simon dug his hand into his pocket. He pulled out a small, dull coin. Xavier's vessel. It was *right there*. Only Oliver's hand on my arm kept me from lunging for it.

"I wish for this room to be—what'd you say?—to be secure." Simon scrunched his face up as he looked at Xavier. "But why—"

"Hush," said Xavier, and held up his hands.

Everything, from my heart right down to the dust motes dancing in the work lights, seemed to go still. I heard a door slam. Then another. Xavier nodded. "As it should be. Nobody leaves this theater until I do."

"But you said—"

"I said *hush*," snarled Xavier, pressing the switchblade to Simon's throat again. Simon whimpered: a sound I'd never have expected to hear from him.

I felt Oliver move behind me, and within a split second he appeared behind Xavier, took him by the shoulders, and pulled.

Xavier stumbled, but recovered quickly. Too quickly for Oliver. The blade flashed, and then embedded itself in Oliver's shoulder, just below the bone. Oliver cried out—and Xavier took hold of the handle and shoved it deeper.

And all I could do was stand there.

I couldn't move. I could barely breathe. I just stood there, useless, on numb legs that were growing increasingly unsteady, and watched as Oliver squeezed his eyes shut. As blood began to stain his shirt. As Xavier pulled the blade out, and Oliver hunched over in silent pain. This time, it wasn't an illusion.

Xavier rested a hand almost casually on the back of Oliver's neck, and turned an amiable smile up toward me. "Now, Miss McKenna," he said in a chillingly reasonable tone, "let's chat, shall we?"

"Oliver," I said hoarsely.

I still couldn't move, but I was infinitely relieved when he raised his head and met my gaze. His eyes were clouded with pain, but he managed a smile. "I'm okay," he said. "Shapeshifter, remember? I'm already good as new. See?"

But all I saw was the blood glistening on the front of his shirt, and the paleness of his face, and why wasn't he moving? Why didn't he just disappear, and why was his shirt still bloody? Had it really cost him that much to heal himself?

Without warning, Xavier brought the blade down again, slicing it across Oliver's back. My hands flew to cover my mouth, and Oliver made a horrible, almost inhuman noise. He sank down to one knee. Xavier chuckled, watching. And then he turned his attention back toward me.

He took one step toward the stage. Two. Three. I still couldn't make myself move.

And then came Simon's voice, cutting through the fear and the smell of blood and Xavier's horrible smile. "I wish for—uh, wait, um—okay, Shen, or whoever you are, I wish you couldn't hurt anyone who's on that stage!"

Xavier stopped dead in his tracks, his expression growing murderous. But he couldn't undo the wish that Simon had just made, and he knew it. He lifted his hands again, and lowered them, and just like that, I was safe.

For now.

"Simon," I said, forcing my voice to stay steady. "You have one wish left, right? Wish for him to stop chasing us. Do it. Now."

Simon was already edging toward the stage, but Xavier was at his throat again before he could get very far. "Mr. Lee," he said, just loudly enough for me to hear. "If you move from this spot, or if you utter one more word without my permission, I will end you right here, right now."

"Come on, Simon," I pleaded. "Make the wish. Or throw me the coin, and I'll do it. *Please.*"

The blade dug into his skin, and I saw him tense up. He looked from me to Xavier, and back again. Slowly, he shook his head, mouthing the word *sorry*.

But while Xavier had been busy threatening Simon, he'd failed to see Oliver beside him, screwing his face up in concentration, drawing in breath after deep breath, until finally he shut his eyes and disappeared. He reappeared beside me, stumbling but safe, and I caught him. Unable to support his weight, I lowered him to the floor, where he sat pale and panting, his head in his hands.

Dark red soaked both his hoodie and the T-shirt underneath. On his back, just below his neck, a large pool of it had seeped through both layers and trickled downward. I pressed my fingers tentatively against the bloody spot on his back, but the skin beneath felt whole, and he didn't flinch. "You're okay," I whispered to him, kissing his cheek and his hair and his lips. "You're gonna be fine."

But exhaustion was written all over his face. How much magic had he used to heal himself from the injuries that Xavier had inflicted? And then the jump to the stage—even I could see the effort that had taken.

I brushed a lock of hair off his forehead, and he opened his eyes. They were surprisingly bright. "I'm not fine," he said softly, like the admission pained him. "I can't . . ."

"You can't what?" I asked, touching a hand to his cheek.

"Everything," he said, screwing his eyes shut again. "All of this. I can't live like this anymore, Margo. I can't."

It had been painful to watch Oliver shrug off Xavier's attempts on his life like they were no big deal—but that was nothing compared to seeing his calm façade crumble before my eyes. There was nothing I could say. I just hugged him tighter.

"You don't have to, Ciarán," said Xavier, just past the edge of the stage. His voice was gentler than I'd ever heard it. "I'm here to help you. You can be free of all this. Our magic is calling us home. Our true magic, not these games of master-and-slave. You would never have to be bound to anyone again."

"True magic," echoed Oliver derisively, still leaning into me.

I narrowed my eyes at Xavier. "And what's in it for you? Kill everyone else so you can be the last one standing?"

"No, that's not it," said Oliver, before Xavier could reply. "He doesn't want to be the last. He wants to die, too. Don't you, Niall." They regarded each other keenly, but Xavier made no move to deny it.

"You used to love this life," Oliver said wistfully. "You told me so, back when we first met. What happened to you, when you were gone all those years?"

Something shifted in Xavier's face. "The First Battle of Manassas," he said shortly. "Up here you'd call it Bull Run. A major victory for the South. That was my doing."

"Your doing," Oliver said faintly. "What do you mean?"

Xavier smiled mirthlessly. "Never been bound to a soldier, have you, Ciarán? Well, I was. First wish: to get out of that war alive. Second wish: a victory for his brothers-in-arms. He kept hold of my vessel through the entire battle. I couldn't leave his side. Do you know how many times a genie can heal himself after being pierced with bullets?" He paused, looking from Oliver to me and back again. "As many as his master desires."

Oliver tensed, and my hand moved to rest again on his blood-stained shirt.

"He took another three years to make his final wish," Xavier continued, eyes fixed on Oliver. "When it was over, I tried to find you again, hoping you'd managed to stay clear of the war. And you had. But you were caught in the middle of a smaller war, a whole ocean away. I was there when your master made his third wish. I watched you kill that boy with your bare hands, on his orders. The look on your face . . ."

He shook his head. "Ciarán, after our magic was lost, I promised my maker that I would give help to those who needed it. Not just her. Everyone. And you needed my help."

Oliver nodded slowly, his face drawn tight against the memory. "That was it, then. You made me, and then your maker told you to kill us all?"

"No," said Xavier slowly. "I wished Dunya free almost three hundred years ago. Long before I met you."

The words hung thickly in the air, and it was a moment before I realized their full implication. Oliver exhaled sharply, and I knew he understood, too. He heaved himself to his feet, and when he finally spoke, his tone was low and dangerous. "You mean you let me have a fourth wish *after* you began killing us? You made me into what I am, when you knew you'd turn around and kill me one day?"

"It wasn't like that." For the first time, I heard a note of panic in Xavier's voice. "You were the first one created after we lost our magic. The only one. I thought it would be different for you, because you didn't know what it was like before. But it wasn't different at all. Living through the war, and then seeing you turn killer . . . those things just proved the truth of my maker's words. There's no hope left for any of us. We don't belong here anymore. Not after what we lost."

"Will you shut up about lost magic?" Even though he was still pale and unsteady, Oliver seethed with anger. "You knew. You knew you would end up killing me."

Xavier paused. Shrugged. "Believe what you will. I only wish you could see how wrong you are."

"Why did you do it?" Oliver asked. All the menace had seeped out of his voice, leaving him sounding sixteen again. I stood up beside him and took hold of his hand. "Out of all the people you could have talked into making that fourth wish . . . why me?"

Without even hesitating, Xavier said, "Because you were good. Because you loved making people happy. And because of Maeve." He said her name with a tenderness that surprised me. "But I was wrong to do it, and I'm sorry, and now I need to make it right. First for you—and then for me."

He spread his hands expressively, making it impossible to miss his meaning. When he'd wished all the others free, he could force someone—probably Simon, probably at the point of a knife—to wish him free, too. It was like Oliver had said: He actually wanted to die.

And I want to help him do it, I thought fiercely. They both looked sharply at me. Oliver opened his mouth as if to protest—but closed it again, and remained silent.

Xavier's face grew hard. "Come now. You and your teenaged bodyguard can't stay on that stage forever."

I clenched my hands into fists. Every plan I'd come up with was dead in the water, and now we were being robbed of our one last day together. I didn't know what to do, and I hated myself for it. But I still hated Xavier more.

I want you to let me wish him free, I thought at Oliver. *I want you to be okay with it.*

"But I," he began, frightened and uncertain. He looked down at me, and out at Xavier, and couldn't finish.

Xavier grinned. "What'll it be, Ciarán? We all know you like taking orders, but this one's up to you." He paused, and turned slowly to look at Simon. "Or maybe it isn't."

Simon had been still as a statue ever since Xavier had threatened him, like maybe if he didn't move, this would all turn out to be a bad dream. But now that Xavier's focus was back on him, he looked like he was about to be sick.

Xavier took a single step toward him, and he held the coin up like a shield—like he'd been preparing for this moment. "I wish you couldn't touch me!" he said.

Xavier held up his hands just long enough that I knew the wish had been granted—and when he was finished, he sauntered slowly toward Simon, still grinning, switchblade in hand.

"Funny thing about wishes," he said. "You really have to be careful about how you phrase them. For example, I have a feeling that you and I have very different definitions of the word *touch*."

I realized what he was about to do. So did Simon—I could see it on his face.

"Oliver," I whispered.

"Do it, Margo," came a hoarse voice from beside me. When I looked up, Oliver's face was tight, and his eyes shone with sorrow. But he didn't change his mind. "Wish him free. Now."

Relief flooded me. I could actually end this. Just one quick moment, and it would finally be over.

"I wish," I began—but the ring was still in my pocket. I found it quickly, but my fingers fumbled, thick with adrenaline and fear, and it took me a second too long to get a grip on it. Only a second. As I uttered the words "I wish" again, I heard a cry of pain. Dread coiled in my gut, and I stopped speaking. I was too late.

I looked up just in time to watch Simon double over, clutching his side. He'd made a break for the stage, where it was safe, but Xavier's blade had caught him first. The coin flew out of his hand and rolled under the stage. I listened, helpless, as it clinked into a dusty wasteland of stored set-pieces and trapdoor machinery. Out of my reach. All because I'd fumbled the ring.

Behind me, Oliver made a choked noise. He dashed across the stage and leaped into the pit, reaching Simon just in time to support him as he crumpled to the ground.

His blade glistening with Simon's blood, Xavier watched the scene dispassionately. Then he flicked his gaze up to me, his lips curving into a perfectly serene smile. "Aren't you going to wish me free?" he asked, as easily as he might ask if it was raining. Then he held up a finger, like a brilliant idea had just occurred to him. "Or, I know! You could wish your little Simon safe, before that wound in his gut kills him. It won't be long. A few minutes, if he's lucky."

Simon cried as Oliver held his head, and somewhere in my memory, my finger went *snap* all over again. "Make it stop," he sobbed. I felt dizzy. "Oh god oh god oh god it hurts so much make it stop."

Oliver moved him just enough to check his wounds, then looked up at me. "Margo," he said. Then he mouthed the word *please,* so that only I could see it. He looked pointedly down at Simon, and I knew what he wanted me to do.

Two people to save. One wish left. This was all my fault. If I'd only been a second faster . . . but that ship had sailed. My throat felt tight and hot. I had to think. I had to choose. But how could I, when both choices were wrong?

Xavier watched me, oozing patience, just waiting for me to heal Simon and unbind Oliver. And Oliver watched me, waiting for the same thing. There was no way I could choose Oliver. If I let Simon die to save him, he'd never forgive me for it.

My fault.

Holding the ring tightly, I forced the words out: "I wish for Simon to be healed. And safe."

Chapter TWENTY-FOUR

Oliver was ready. He pressed his hands to Simon's wound, and in the blink of an eye, they both vanished. When they reappeared at my feet, safe within the protective boundary of the stage, Simon looked stunned. Oliver helped him to his feet, and he ran a hand over his side, gasping out a little sob when he found his body intact. Even his shirt was clean.

"Holy eff," he breathed, looking at me in disbelief—like he couldn't believe what I'd done. I didn't blame him. I couldn't believe it either.

Oliver reached out to touch my arm, but I shied away from him. I'd failed him. Why had I ever thought I could handle this? Any of this? Why hadn't I given the ring back when I had the chance?

"The ring, Miss McKenna," came Xavier's voice from the pit. He held his hand out, palm up.

I stared at him, numb, uncomprehending. I'd just forfeited Oliver's life. How could Xavier sound so patient about it?

Utterly defeated, I turned back to Oliver. "I don't have any wishes left," I said, even though we both knew it already. "What do I do? I can't just let him . . . I can't. . . ."

As he folded me into his arms and held me close, I thought fiercely, *I want to save you*. But he didn't reply, verbally or otherwise. He couldn't hear my thoughts anymore. The realization made me want to cry.

Over his shoulder, I could see Xavier watching us, waiting calmly for me to make the next move—to follow the script that he'd written for me when he'd stabbed Simon.

Simon, who was right beside me, alive and whole.

He narrowed his eyes at me when he saw me looking at him. "You need another wish, right?" he asked uncertainly, and held out his hand. "I'll do it for you. Just tell me what to wish for, and I'll do it."

My hold on Oliver grew slack as I stared at Simon's outstretched palm. *Of course*. Simon could take Oliver's ring and wish Xavier free, and this would all be over. Xavier would be gone, and I would be safe again, and I could still have Oliver.

"Do it," said Oliver, realizing what Simon was talking about. "Give him my vessel."

"Don't you dare," warned Xavier.

It would be so easy. So neat and clean and perfect.

Perfect, except that I'd used up all my wishes—which meant that Oliver would disappear soon, unless he found a new master. And then another new master, and another, and another, while I stayed safely within the comfortable, predictable bubble of a life that I'd always known. How long would it be before I grew tired of his erratic lifestyle, just like Maeve had before me? How long before I gave up on him, just like she had?

If I took the easy way out of this, could I still be the sort of person who was capable of loving someone like Oliver?

I wanted so badly to be that person. But I also wanted Simon to make that wish.

I clutched the ring harder. I did not give it to Simon.

Taking hold of Oliver's hand, I silently wove the fingers of my left hand through those of his right. His eyes widened—but even as I held the ring up between us, he didn't say anything. He just nodded.

"Oliver," I said, my voice surprisingly steady, "I wish Xavier free."

Xavier's shoulders sagged, and his eyes closed. The wish was made, and he knew as well as I did that there was no taking it back. He moved back from the edge of the stage, and sank into one of the seats in the front row.

When he looked up again, I braced myself for the accusing stare that I was sure he'd level at me. But he looked only at Oliver. "Ciarán," was all he said. There was depth to that word, and I couldn't begin to guess at all the things that lay hidden inside it. But I wasn't supposed to. The name wasn't meant for me.

The ring began to grow hot between my fingers, and Oliver jumped down from of the stage and knelt smoothly in front of Xavier. Something shimmered, and Oliver's shape changed. I recognized him immediately, and so did Xavier. Oliver was going to grant my fourth wish as Ciarán.

Xavier reached out and grasped Oliver's forearm. His grip looked desperate and painful, but instead of flinching, Oliver just gave him a sad smile—a reminder that they'd been close once, a long time ago. The thought made me want to turn away, but I couldn't. This was my doing, for better or for worse, and I needed to witness it.

"Do it," said Xavier. His voice was shaking.

Slowly, Oliver reached out and placed one hand on Xavier's chest, fingers splayed right over his heart.

At first it happened slowly: a deep, warm glow between Oliver and Xavier, so subtle that I almost mistook it for a quirk of the stage lights. But it grew, faster and faster, until the strange light encompassed Xavier's whole body, roiling and churning and shining like beacons out of his fingertips.

Then a huge flame engulfed him, knocking Oliver backward. I stumbled backward, too, thinking in a moment of panic that the whole theater—the whole school—would burn down. But of course I shouldn't have worried. This wasn't an ordinary fire. It didn't care about anything but Xavier.

Blurred by a sheen of flame, Xavier's face twisted into a grimace—but just as quickly, he relaxed. He actually smiled, almost peacefully, as he locked eyes with Oliver again.

"I hope you find your magic," said Oliver softly, from where he knelt on the floor.

Xavier threw his head back and let out a loud laugh, underscored by the crackling of the fire. "You don't believe I will," he said. "But you'll see. One day you'll follow me, and you'll see."

And all at once, the fire glowed white-hot, and he was gone.

The fire disappeared as quickly as it came, and the only thing left of Xavier was a little shimmer in the air. I watched, my throat tight, as it dissipated into nothing. Xavier was right. In a strange way, it was beautiful.

"What the eff was that?" said Simon as he ran over to join me. "Dude, that was *insane*. . . ."

Oliver and I looked at each other, the air between us heavy with what had just happened, and what was about to happen. In one smooth movement, he heaved himself onto the stage again.

"Just remember to breathe," he said, looking calmly at me as he shimmered into Oliver again. "You're fine."

"Oliver," I said, worried, and tried to move toward him. But I was stuck. My muscles had gone rigid, and I felt a weird, warm glow in my chest. It tingled, like Oliver's magic. I could feel it spreading outward, into my limbs, into my head, touching each finger and toe, making my eyes and mouth shiver. "Oh god," I whispered. What had I done? What would happen? Would there be fire for me, too?

The tingling grew stronger and stronger, growing into a pins-

and-needles sensation that covered my whole body. Like part of me had fallen asleep, and was being shaken rudely awake. I was vaguely aware of Simon saying a lot of things, many of which were frantic repetitions of my name and the word *dude*. I was vaguely aware of Oliver, who wasn't moving to help me. But eclipsing everything else was the light. It wasn't fire, but it shone just as brightly, and it was growing, in and around me. Oppressive and gentle at the same time, it lifted me, filled me, and made me feel like I could fly.

Something tore. I felt the kind of fast, uncontrollable falling that you only get in the seconds just before you wake up. I felt myself crumple to the ground, felt the heavy weight of limbs and clothes and hair landing in a messy pile. And then—then I felt fine.

And I was still standing.

When I looked down, something shimmered at my feet—something shaped like a female body. Then the shape dissolved, leaving only a gleam of light that drifted upward and, somehow, inward. I felt light. I felt happy. I felt—

"Margo!" yelled Simon, my name tearing at his throat until I winced in sympathy. "Parish, what the goddamn hell did you do to her?"

"She's fine," said Oliver.

"Yeah, I'm right here," I added, somewhat surprised and utterly confused.

But the words sounded hollow, even to my own ears, like an

echo of an echo. Simon, looking frantically around the stage, didn't seem to hear me. Or see me. He fixed his eyes on Oliver one last time, and shook his head. Sparing a moment to cross himself, he jumped down from the stage and ran up the aisle. Light burst into the auditorium as he threw the door open and fled into the hallway.

I made myself look down again. I was the same as I'd always been—and at the same time, I wasn't. There was something insubstantial about what I was seeing, like my body was just as hollow as my voice. I was there, but I wasn't . . . *there*. I had no weight. I couldn't feel the stage beneath my feet. I couldn't even feel the rhythm of my heartbeat in my chest.

I wasn't there.

Panic seized me, and I sucked in breath after shallow breath— but I couldn't feel my lungs working, and I couldn't feel the air. I touched my own arm. I could feel the contact, but my skin didn't feel like skin anymore. It felt like pure magic: shivering, shifting, and waiting impatiently to become something else. Something solid.

I wanted to cry, but I didn't dare. I didn't want to discover one more thing that I couldn't feel.

But suddenly, a warm presence was in front of me, hugging me against his chest. He was Oliver again, and he felt totally, completely real. I pressed myself against him, infinitely grateful that he could actually feel me.

The embrace only lasted a moment, before he pulled away

and held me at arm's length. "My ring," he said, calm and quiet.

Looking down, I realized that I was still clutching the ring in my hand. It felt oddly solid. "But if I give it back to you," I said slowly, "won't you disappear?"

He curved his lips into a sly smile. "If anyone else were here, then yes. To their eyes, I'd disappear. But not to yours. Not anymore." He touched my cheek again, and a thrill rushed through me. "Trust me," he said, holding out his hand.

And I did. I trusted him completely.

When I placed the ring in his palm, he drew in a deep, full breath, and let it out again, like a great weight had been lifted from him. As I watched, he seemed to blur around the edges, becoming as insubstantial as . . . well, me. But he was right: I could still see him.

With a smile that made his green eyes shine, he looked around us, above us, and below us, seeming to see right through the theater walls that held us in. Then he looked back at me. "Come with me," he said, his voice teeming with secrets.

I took his hand, and we went.

Acknowledgments

First and foremost, the biggest thank-you *ever* to my family, who have supported my writing ever since it took the form of stapled-together construction-paper "books" about the adventures of my cats. Dad, thank you for demanding to know what happens next. Megan, thank you for being patient while I ramble on and on about my characters as though they were real people. Mom, thank you for the ring, and for saying hello to Oliver every time you hang up the phone. (He says hi back!) I love you guys so much.

Another immense thank-you to Nina Lourie, the best friend and beta-reader in history. Thanks for not being afraid to tell me when my ideas are dumb, for giving me countless brilliant brainstorming sessions, and for rocking the Boat with me. And, of course, for knowing that there's only one thing that X can ever stand for.

Thanks to Andrea Robinson, for helping me sort out countless plot holes, and for calming me down every time I'm sure I will never be calm again. To Meg Deans, for your incredibly nuanced character notes. To Amy Spalding, for constantly reminding me that the real stuff is just as important as the magic stuff. To Diana Fox, for your high standards of sexiness, and for the best blackmail experience ever. To Diana Rowland, for being convinced that Oliver was secretly evil and forcing me to think outside the box. To Blake Charlton, for dying of cute and for giving me my first title.

Thanks to Larry O'Keefe and Nell Benjamin, for helping me figure out how genies work, and for your constant inspiration and friendship. Special blame-thanks to Larry for that one Incredibly Frustrating Comment, which instantly turned this story from a stand-alone into a trilogy.

Thanks to my many wonderful friends for their feedback, criticism, and encouragement along the way—especially Tim Federle, Liz Kies, Chris Lough, Megan Messinger, Miriam Newman, Navah Wolfe, Ellen Wright, Jen Linnan, Soumeya Bendimerad, Courtney Miller-Callihan, and Rachael Dillon-Fried. If there's anyone whose name belongs on this list but isn't there, I apologize profusely, and I promise to buy you a cookie when next I see you.

Thanks to everyone who ever beta-read for me, and let me beta-read in return, back in the days of FAP, circa OotP. (I'm especially looking at you, Beth Comer!) You guys taught me so much about how collaborative writing can be, and I'm incredibly grateful for it.

My most peculiar thank-you goes to all the musical artists who unknowingly inspired me during this process, especially Coyote Grace, Great Big Sea, the Indigo Girls, Suzanne Vega, Butch Walker, and, of course, Neko Case. And a special thanks to Carbon Leaf, whose songs have book-ended this story from the moment I started writing it.

Thanks to everyone at Sanford J. Greenburger Associates—coworkers and clients alike—for cheering me on. Thank you, especially, to Matt Bialer, who constantly asks me whether or not he is the best boss ever. Yes, Matt. Yes, you are.

Finally, my infinite thanks to the two most amazing people in this entire business, for taking this story of mine and holy crap turning it into a *book*....

Brenda Bowen, agent extraordinaire! Thanks for your guidance, your badassery (yup, I said it), and for letting me bang my head against the wall of your office more times than I can count. Sometimes literally. You are the actual best.

Kathy Dawson, editor of editors! Thanks for your patience with me, for pushing this book further than I ever thought it could go (and then pushing even harder), and for helping me figure out who Margo was meant to be. Having you on my side makes me the luckiest author ever.